BASQUE MOON

This Large Print Book carries the
Seal of Approval of N.A.V.H.

A NELLIE BURNS AND MOONSHINE MYSTERY

BASQUE MOON

JULIE WESTON

THORNDIKE PRESS
A part of Gale, a Cengage Company

Farmington Hills, Mich • San Francisco • New York • Waterville, Maine
Meriden, Conn • Mason, Ohio • Chicago

Copyright © 2016 by Julie Weston.
Thorndike Press, a part of Gale, a Cengage Company.

Thorndike Press® Large Print Clean Reads.
The text of this Large Print edition is unabridged.
Other aspects of the book may vary from the original edition.
Set in 16 pt. Plantin.

LIBRARY OF CONGRESS CIP DATA ON FILE.
CATALOGUING IN PUBLICATION FOR THIS BOOK
IS AVAILABLE FROM THE LIBRARY OF CONGRESS

ISBN-13: 978-1-4328-5061-6 (hardcover)

Published in 2018 by arrangement with Julie Weston

Printed in Mexico
1 2 3 4 5 6 7 22 21 20 19 18

For Melanie and David

ACKNOWLEDGMENTS

Beginning in the early 1950s, my family drove from northern Idaho through the Stanley Basin in central Idaho every year on our way to Sun Valley. The Sawtooth Mountains startled this girl from an Idaho mining town where the mountains were rounded and shorn of trees. The rocky heights, the snow chutes, the saw teeth seeming to rip into the blue sky were nothing like I'd ever seen. The Salmon River tumbled between green verges and cattle appeared painted on the foreground. Wildflowers bloomed and sometimes we saw sandhill cranes, their awkward gait and chuckling sounds reminding us of creatures out of time.

Since then, my husband and I have spent many days and nights exploring the whole Basin and we have visited several of the lakes. We have traveled the Fourth of July Road and hiked up to the Fourth of July Lake. These settings struck me as perfect territory for a photographer — as it is for Gerry — and another Nellie and Moonshine story took form.

Both the Basin and the Wood River Valley have been known for the masses of sheep that graze in the meadows, hills, and mountains of the area. In the early years, Basque men were lured to the western United States by the discoveries of gold and silver. They transitioned into sheepherding and they and their descendants and others from the French–Spanish border became valuable employees of the mostly Scottish sheep ranchers. Although a lonely occupation, Basque herders were once synonymous with sheep tending. All summer, they would travel the back country of Idaho, grazing their sheep along canyons, mountainsides, and byways until fall. They bunked in canvas- or tin-covered wagons drawn by horses and referred to as sheep camps. We feel fortunate to have Basque friends who have assisted with knowledge about traditions, food, dogs, and language.

Both writers and readers helped me with the events in *Basque Moon.* Mary Murfin Bayley, Charlene Finn, Belinda Anderson, and Alice Calvert read and critiqued this manuscript. Without their assistance and advice, I may never have found an ending to the story.

Again, I thank Five Star Publishing and Tiffany Schofield for believing in the fiction of the West. Hazel Rumney continues to be a star editor with an appreciation of Idaho and its environs as well as a sharp eye and comprehensive knowledge, not only of writing, but of the characters in this book. The Regional History Department of the Community Library in Ketchum, Idaho, is my primary source for newspapers in the 1920s in the Wood River Valley and an extensive collection of historical books and photographs, including books about the Basque language and traditions in Idaho.

This past year, my son-in-law David Andersen, also a photographer, gave me his Premo camera, the exact camera that Nellie used in her photographic work in Idaho. His description of this camera when I worked on *Basque Moon* near the beginning helped me to visualize how Nellie would do her work. My photography expert and husband, Gerry Morrison, once again helped me with the mechanics and details of taking photographs with a large-format camera. Any errors in technique and translation, however, are mine. I also value Gerry's willingness to read the manuscript in its many permutations, as well as his sup-

9

port in this endeavor to place Nellie and Moonshine in a world we both know and love.

CHAPTER 1

Lulu spent half her time directing tourists in the mechanics of driving their automobiles backward over Galena Pass. The steep road, dirt and gravel in summer, hugged the curves of the mountainside, and the drop-off to the valley hundreds of feet below frightened more than one brave man and myriads of women who were unused to riding in a horseless carriage on anything other than a flat city street. Convincing the men that most autos wouldn't make it over the pass facing front was a difficult sell, until she had to send someone up with water and a tow back to her store at the base of the pass for a hefty price. Whatever the market would bear, her shopkeeper father had advised before he disappeared into a snowstorm in the winter of '18 in the Stanley Basin of Idaho. That was the fifth winter Lulu had spent with him at the Galena Store, a lonely, Spartan existence without the summer travelers and the miners who once peopled the town of Galena.

The women drivers accepted the advice more readily, confirming Lulu's opinion of the basic difference between the sexes: Women were smarter.

Not everyone drove. Basque sheepherders rode horses or walked with their dogs and bands of sheep. In exchange for corral space for a few days in bad weather, the Basque agreed to stay far enough back in the woods and meadows to keep down the dust and smell and noise on their spring trip up and fall trip back. Lulu didn't hold with the local cattlemen, that sheep were "maggots of the range." Cattle were a sight smellier than sheep, and those big cowpies drew flies and poisoned the creeks. There was room enough for all in the Boulder, White Cloud, and Sawtooth ranges and the big spaces in between.

Every summer brought something new. One year a Model T drove right off the edge of the road and made two grooves all the way to the bottom, just as if the driver had steered his way down. And maybe he had. He lived.

Another summer, it snowed up until the tenth of July, stopped, then started up again around the twelfth of the same month. Business was really bad that year. The road never dried out and even her team of horses had trouble pulling autos from the gumbo that mired tires to the top of the wheel wells. The Basque lost sheep right and left to the coyotes; same with the cowboys and their cattle. Summer grazing in the highlands never took hold.

In the summer of 1923, several events took place that were a shade out of the ordinary. It wasn't until the summer was over that Lulu began to think of them grouped under the heading of the summer of the Basque moon. A gunfight wasn't all that usual anymore, but it wasn't unusual either. Same for a grudge-match between the cowboys and Basque sheepmen. More tourists than usual embarked on campouts in the mountains and Lulu's business soared. She sold more sugar, beans, coffee, smoked bacon, flour, and tourist trinkets than two summers' worth, and travelers filled the beds in the lodge almost every night.

Several packers made Galena their headquarters for the dudes who wanted to ride horses and experience life in the open, "just like real cowboys" one of them said. She couldn't remember which group ran into real trouble, whether it was Rob's or Luke's

13

or Joe's, but no one could forget Sheriff Charlie Azgo's disgust with the whole thing. He almost up and quit at the end when the perpetrator got off Scot-free — well, almost — and Charlie probably would have thrown that star of his at the county fathers, the few of them that were left, if he wasn't responsible for helping to raise two boys in the fall and needed the job. Even so, the camping "experience" gave Lulu the idea to think about a dude ranch of her own.

What stuck in her mind was the appearance of Nellie Burns, the woman photographer from Ketchum, along with her dog, Moonshine, and that camera of hers. The summer would have been boring without them, Lulu supposed, but sometimes boring was better.

"I'm Nellie Burns." This announcement came from a young woman standing at the counter in front of Lulu. She was pretty in a town sort of way, wore pants, which most women didn't, even when they intended to camp alongside the road, and she stood as straight as any soldier who had come through Idaho during the Great War. Her high cheekbones and widow's peak would help her age well, and her rounded jawline gave her a soft look.

"Howdy, Nellie Burns. I'm Lulu. I own this place."

A wide smile showed good teeth. "I know. I thought you might have a message for me. I'm supposed to meet Gwynn Campbell here. Has he come yet?"

"Ole man Campbell? Can he still get around? I heard he almost died of pneumonia last winter. Thought he'd give up his sheep outfit."

"No, he recovered, and he assured me that I could spend several weeks with one of his sheepherders in the summer range. I plan to take photographs of life in a sheep camp. I'm on assignment." The photographer might have been announcing the awarding of a grand prize at the state fair. "I'm supposed to meet him here and then he'll take me across Galena and up Fourth of July Creek."

Lulu craned her neck to look outside. "Where's your gear?"

"It's out with my dog. He's guarding it for me." Nellie pointed to the door. "Not that I think anyone would steal it. I don't want anyone to touch it, is all."

A growl and a series of barks confirmed Nellie's statement. She strode out of the store and Lulu followed.

"Moonshine. What is it?"

15

A man in a new Stetson, completely out of place above his grizzled face and worn clothes, stood beside a Model T drawn up next to her battered Oldsmobile. The black Labrador dog stood in front of a wood case, three bags, and a folded-up tripod, his feet braced, his teeth bared. "You ought to teach your dog some manners, Miss."

Nellie blushed. "You ought to mind your own business and stay away from my things."

"Ha, ha, ha!" The man took off his hat, revealing a greasy flap of hair, dirty blond in color. "Feisty, ain't ya?" He took a long step onto the porch of the store. "Hiya, Lulu. I need some stores to take back to the Basin with me."

"Sure thing, Dick. Round 'em up on the counter there. I'll take cash this time." She stepped down to stand next to Nellie, ignoring the scowl the man directed at her.

"That your auto, Nellie?" She tipped her head in the direction of the Oldsmobile.

"In a manner of speaking. It belongs to Rosy Kipling. He's back East and said I could use it, at least until it falls apart, which it may do any day now."

"What do you plan on doing with the auto if you're going up into the mountains?"

"Gwynn said he'd see it got back to

16

town," Nellie said, "unless you'll let me leave it parked here somewhere." She looked around for an out-of-the-way place, but the store and lodge had been built before automobiles appeared. The hitching post would have held a dozen animals, and maybe a wagon or two, but only a few automobiles. Out-buildings crowded close around the store. A barn, a tool shed, what might have been or still was an outhouse, a corral that was empty at the moment. "Could I leave it there in the corral?"

"Sure, if you don't mind sheep piling up and over it and dogs makin' themselves comfortable on that cloth top there. Might come out smellin' a mite ripe." Lulu stepped back onto the porch. "Got a customer I need to watch. Wait 'til Gwynn gets here and we'll talk about what accommodation I could make. I'd have to figure out what to charge."

Nellie's expression fell. "I couldn't afford much. Maybe it would be best if the auto went back to town. It's just — I might want to leave — there's no place —"

Lulu disappeared into the store.

"Well, Moonshine, here we are. Do you suppose I'll really get paid for this 'assignment?' I must have sounded like a . . . a man. 'Pride goeth before a fall' as they

17

say." She stooped to put her arms around the dog, who rested his muzzle on her shoulder. It was then she noticed a woman passenger in the Model T. Nellie waved and said hello. The woman didn't respond except to turn her face the other way. The auto windows were grimy, as if they'd gone through a dust-bath, so Nellie didn't get a good look at the woman other than to note pale hair and a profile that could have been carved on a Greek statue, so classic were its lines.

Moonshine left his guard post and smelled the tires of the Model T. A dog, who must have been asleep in the back of the auto, started up a ruckus, barking, snarling, and pawing at the windows. The woman shouted, "Shut your mouth, Cowpie." Her voice carried a southern drawl.

"Moonie. Come back here." The dog barked at the auto and returned to Nellie's side.

A pickup truck rattled up to the Galena Store. Gwynn, looking older than God, or maybe like God himself, sat in the driver's seat, his arm gesticulating out the window. A darker-skinned man occupied the seat next to Gwynn, crouching low, his hands in front of his face to ward off what he probably thought was going to be a crash into the store's porch. Nellie thought so, too, and jumped aside, dragging her camera pack with her. The tripod could be replaced. Amidst a screech of brakes, a hurricane of dust, and a "Goldurnit, you —" the truck stopped a few inches shy of Nellie's baggage. The tripod escaped harm. Spryer than Nellie would have expected, the old sheep rancher jumped down from the running board and beamed at her.

"Lassie. You made it! I like a woman who arrives on time." When he pulled off his hat, greased around the headband and mottled with years of handling sheep, his white hair sprang up. "If you're all ready, we'll pile your gear into the back and get you up and over the Pass. There's been bad doings up there, and the sooner I get there, the sooner it'll stop." Gwynn's Scottish brogue was deep and strong, in spite of the fact that he had lived in Idaho for forty of his sixty-odd years.

"What kind of bad doings? Sheep rustlers?"

"Lulu already tell you? Those blasted cowmen think they own the high country. There ain't no fences and I'll be darned if I'll kowtow to 'em." A roar of laughter softened his leathery face. "*Kow*-towed. Get it?"

Nellie smiled. Last winter, Gwynn had

given her and a fellow photographer in Twin Falls, Jacob Levine, a bad time and then nearly died of pneumonia. The old man had his faults, one of which had been to try and control a strong-minded daughter, but he had paid dearly — losing his daughter and nearly losing his two grandsons for good. Ever since Nellie had helped arrange the future return of the boys to Ketchum, Gwynn had taken her under his wing, trying to stay on her good side.

"I'm ready, but my camera goes inside on my lap, not in the back. And where are Moonshine and I going to sit? You've got a passenger."

"That's just Alphonso. He can ride in the rear or hang onto the running board. I'm takin' him up to the camp to replace Domingo, who's gone 'round the bend, accordin' to the supply man."

" 'Around the bend?' Died?"

"Nope. Just lost his bearings. Too much loneliness. Occupational hazard." Gwynn picked up Nellie's bags and placed them in the truck bed, sandwiched between boxes and two bags of flour. A strong medicinal smell hovered over one of the boxes.

Nellie called for her dog to climb in the front and she followed, settling herself on the seat shyly vacated by Alphonso, who

20

dipped his head as he swept his hat off, letting his long black hair fall over his eyes. The same sour odor penetrated the sheepskin covers. It was enough to make her stomach turn, so she breathed through her mouth, hoping she'd get used to it. Moonie sat between her legs on the floor, his head resting on her knee.

Lulu came out on the porch. "Hey, Gwynn. You goin' up to set them cattlemen straight?"

"Straight, no. Crooked yes. I'll bend 'em around some of them lodgepole pines up there, those thieving, sons of —"

"Watch your language, Gwynn. You got a lady next to you and one here on the porch. I won't tolerate all that swearin' and cussin' around here. Tourists don't like it."

Nellie would not have thought it possible, but the sheepman blushed. "Sorry, Lulu. I forgot you been tryin' to turn the Wild West into a sissy picnic." He pointed to the Oldsmobile. "I'll get that rattle-trap outta here when I come back with Domingo. He can drive it to town and leave it at Bock's Boardinghouse for our famous photographer here."

Lulu spoke to Nellie. "You can leave it here for a while, if you want. Most of the sheep have already come through. Then if

21

you change your mind. . . ." She let the sentence drift and walked up to the open door of the truck. "But, I'll need the key, honey. Can't leave it out there in front like that."

Nellie dug it out of her pants pocket and handed it over. She wanted to caution Lulu not to let a strange man drive it, but decided to say nothing.

"Gwynn, you better back up over the Pass like the rest of 'em. This here truck don't look like it'll make the first switchback," Lulu said, then took two steps toward the porch.

A roar was her response. "I'll be —. I'll be a horse's behind before I look like one of them tourists takin' the namby-pamby way up that mountain road, Lulu. And you can kiss it if I don't make it up frontways."

Lulu grinned and her laugh came up from her belly. "Knew you'd say that. I'll charge double if I have to tow you over to the other side." She winked at Nellie. "You might want to get out and walk when the truck gives up. His language will turn everything in that there cab to a brilliant blue."

The other customer came out from the store, scowl still in place. "What's a maggot wagon doin' in this country?" His question wasn't directed to any one person.

Nellie remembered the Model T. She glanced over and saw the door open and a long, slim leg touch the ground.

"Dick Goodlight, if you had a ounce of sense in you, I'd say you were worth savin'," Lulu said. "But you don't and if Gwynn wants to shoot you right here, he has my permission." She stepped back into the store.

"Get back in there, Pearl." He used the same tone of voice she had used on the dog. "You ain't goin' nowhere but home with me." The leg disappeared back into the auto.

Gwynn started up his pickup, looked at Nellie, winked, and turned the truck so that its rear faced the store. Then he stomped on the gas and dust and rocks spun out behind, raising a curtain of dust in front of Goodlight that settled on him. Nellie glanced around as they pulled onto the roadway and saw him dancing up and down, swatting his hat against his legs. His mouth worked, but she couldn't hear a word.

"Ha, ha, ha! That'll teach the son of a gun!" Gwynn shifted gears and concentrated on the road.

Nellie turned to wave to Alphonso in the back of the truck. He held on to each side of the bed, and he laughed, too. His black

23

hair was parted by the wind and blowing almost straight out.

The pickup coughed and jerked every time Gwynn changed a gear, but it didn't stop. The old sheepman kept up a stream of low mumbles interspersed with a few words Nellie understood, mostly references to a "gol-blamed, woolly, son of a. . . ." Like an incantation, whatever he said seemed to pull them up the narrow, switch-backed road and over the top. One more turn and she gasped at the open vista far below.

Jagged blue teeth tore at the sky — the Sawtooth Mountains. Most of the high peaks wore snow patches leading down to rocky chutes that ended in deep green forests, which in turn gave out onto a basin of lush grasses and a river, winding like a silver thread the length of the valley. Sagebrush, dusty green and purple, covered the southern slopes of the foothills facing the pass. "Oh, stop, Mr. Campbell! I must see this!"

"Wouldn't hurt to put a little more water in the radiator, I guess." He pulled to the side of the road and Nellie and Moonshine both jumped down and ran across to the drop-off.

"What river is that? It is so beautiful and so remote!"

24

"Salmon River. River of No Return, it's called. Begins back there," he said, pointing to an unseen source at the southern end of the Basin, "and makes its way north. In the fall, it's filled to overflow with sockeye salmon returning from the ocean. A sight to see." He returned to the auto, pulled the hood up, and fussed under it. "Alphonso, get me some water and let's cool this thing down."

Nellie let the breeze coming up the mountainside blow her hair and sweep around her body. The smell of pine pitch and dust warmed by sun filled her nostrils. She breathed deeply, thinking she could stand and watch this scene forever. White clouds billowed and fluffed around the mountain peaks, casting moving shadows, permitting highlights to change and gather, making her fingers ache for her camera.

"I want to photograph this panorama. Will you wait while I get set?"

Her answer was a mumble from under the hood. She took it for assent and eased her pack out of the pickup, set up her tripod, and began assembling the large-format camera that accompanied her everywhere. Her "assignment," as she had so boldly declared to Lulu, was from the Oregon Short Line Railroad. The railroad wanted scenic pictures to lure tourists to the West, according to the railroad man she had met riding back and forth from Ketchum to Twin Falls. She took portraits of townspeople and visitors in Ketchum. Then she traveled to Twin where she processed the photographs at the studio belonging to Jacob Levine. If the railroad man really bought the photos, she might have enough to establish a small darkroom in Ketchum and wouldn't have to travel to the larger town so often. She wouldn't see Jacob as often, either. But, he was engaged to that silly woman, so she really shouldn't care.

As she threw her black cloth over her head to get the focus of the scene without interfering light, Gwynn called: "Get back in, Lassie. We're heading out!"

"Wait a minute, please." She gritted her teeth. Gwynn and she were never traveling the same paths, no matter how much she tried to accommodate his gruff needs. Once in a great while, she wondered what it would have been like to have him for a father instead of her drunken one. Not much better, she decided. The old sheepman would have been around more than hers was, but his natural arrogance would have driven her and her mother crazy. Look what he had done to his own daughter! Dragged her

26

away from her intended husband, disowned her for years at a time, and then blamed her death on a Chinese herbal doctor rather than on the cancer that took her. No, Nellie would rather have been what she was — fatherless.

The composition was good — two aromatic pines framed the series of craggy mountaintops, an array of clouds behind them, brilliant sunlight on two of the snow patches, and a beam of light focused on the tallest. She removed the cloth and the dark slide, picked up the shutter release, and pushed the plunger.

"Hurry up, gal. I can't wait all day for you to fuss with that contraption."

Nellie removed the film holder and placed it in her film carrier. She folded up the camera and tripod, placed the tripod in the pickup bed, and climbed with the camera back into the cab. "I'm ready to go." The pickup jerked forward. "Wait! Moonie is still out there!"

For a second, Nellie thought Gwynn might not stop, and then he stomped on the brake, throwing Alphonso against the back window. Nellie opened the door and called for Moonshine. From a patch of huckleberry bushes on the hillside, he came dashing, his black coat shining in the sunlight. "Were

27

you after a rabbit, you sweetie?" Nellie made room for him, and then slammed the door. "Thank you." Off they drove down the mountainside.

"Did you notice the woman in the Model T at Galena Store?" she asked her companion. "She was with that Goodlight man. And a dog, too."

"Nope. Only saw you and Lulu. I don't pay no attention to moonshiners and cowboys. They're the varmints of this place. Ought to string 'em all up."

"I think she was a pretty woman, but not someone I've seen in Ketchum."

"Probably Pearl, Goodlight's wife, some say. She runs off regular and he brings her back to the Basin. Can't say as I blame her, but she's no prize, either. Hangs around the saloon in Stanley, making eyes at cowboys."

For someone who didn't pay attention, Gwynn knew a lot of gossip. "Which is he — a moonshiner or a cowboy?"

"Depends on the weather."

Nellie didn't want to ask what that meant. She watched the mountains, letting her spirits soar with them. Would living among such gorgeous scenery jade one to all else?

At Smiley Creek, Gwynn stopped for news and gasoline. A substantial mining settlement had once occupied the bend in the road, but many structures stood derelict. A broken wagon half blocked a road headed back into the scrub pine. The general store looked well used, but much less inviting than the Galena Store. A few men lounged around the porch, their cowboy heels run down, their clothes seedy and unwashed. One man even wore a gun stuck into his belt, as if he thought he were a cowboy of Zane Grey fame. Alphonso stayed in the pickup, slumped down almost out of sight. One of the men said something and the others laughed, glancing toward the truck.

Nellie waited for Gwynn without getting out. She didn't want to hold him up and she didn't want to get into an argument, something she might do if she were close enough to hear actual words. She felt sorry for Alphonso. Staying with a sheepherder in the mountains had sounded romantic when she first proposed it to Gwynn. Now she was less certain. Everyone had heard of the fierce range wars in Wyoming and Arizona between cowmen and sheepmen. Was she heading into trouble again? She didn't know how to use a gun and wondered if that was a skill she should learn. In town, guns hadn't seemed necessary, but out here, maybe some of the stories about gunfights were true. Good heavens! She was beginning to believe the fables published in the eastern press.

To prove to herself that those stories were fabrications, she opened the door and stepped down. Moonie jumped from the cab, sniffed and looked around, then trotted toward a mangy mutt scrounging alongside the store's foundation.

"Moonshine! Here, boy."

Her dog turned his head toward her and the mutt leaped at him, growling low. Moonie yelped, side-stepped, and counterattacked.

Dust, fur, growls, barks turned the lazy scene into a maelstrom.

Nellie hurried to the writhing, furry twosome, but couldn't grab Moonie as they rolled, their teeth clenched into each other's hides. She was afraid her hand would get bitten. The men stood and watched.

"Kill the maggot dog, Cowpie!" The cowboys laughed.

Moonshine shook himself hard and Cowpie loosened his hold long enough for Moonie to grasp the mutt's neck in large white teeth. They rolled again. This time one of the men brought out a gun. Nellie dove toward the fighting animals, no longer afraid. She knew her dog was the target. Only her pants prevented her legs from being scraped by tooth or claw. Her hands weren't so lucky as she fell amidst the dogs.

Gwynn ran out of the store, grabbed a bucket under a sign that read "Fire," and threw the contents on the dogs. It wasn't water. It was sand. The spray stung Nellie, but the dogs separated long enough for her to scramble back with the scruff of Moonshine's neck in her hand. Gwynn jerked her up and they both dragged the dog to the pickup where Gwynn tossed him into the back with Alphonso. "Hold him while we get out of here." He turned to Nellie. "Get back in. Now."

The truck jerked and they left the scene behind. Nellie's heart beat fast. She perched on her knees and peered through the back window to see if Moonie was hurt. Alphonso had his arms around the dog and talked to him. He calmed down and soon lay on the truck bed, his head on the man's knee. He shook. His hair was ruffled and he wriggled around to lick his shoulder.

"If that dog of yours is gonna attack other dogs, we got ourselves a problem, Lassie. Them sheepdogs'll kill him soon as look at him. I'll take him back with me when I go. Goldie'll look after him." Goldie Bock owned the boarding house where Nellie lived.

31

"That was the Model T dog. He tried to attack Moonie at Lulu's." Her hands stung, but she held them clasped together so Gwynn wouldn't notice the scrapes of blood on them. "They must have passed us when we stopped. He's a mean dog. Moonshine isn't, and I need him."

The sheep man snorted. "If he so much as looks sideways at one of my dogs, back he goes. Same thing if my dogs don't like his looks. They're not friendly. They fight off coyotes and keep the sheep in line." His face settled into stubborn lines, an immovable stone. "I got enough trouble without your blamed dog causin' more."

"Goldie doesn't like him and she won't watch out for him."

"She likes anythin' that used to belong to that miner, Rosy. How else did my daughter marry the four-flusher?" The lines on Gwynn's face settled deeper.

"Rosy was no four-flusher. He married Lily because they loved each other, and he took care of those boys, even though one of them —" Nellie bit her lip. No sense in bringing up old hurts. "Moonie's never ever attacked another thing. I don't understand what happened back there. He won't do it again," she said, crossing her fingers.

Gwynn switched gears to slow down as

32

the pickup neared a turn-off from the main road. He swung right, barely making the sharply angled corner. The side road was hardly more than a trail through grass and sagebrush. Nellie held on to her seat, hoping her teeth wouldn't shake loose. A cloud of dust spilled out behind them. She looked back again and saw that Alphonso held on to each side of the truck bed rails, jouncing back and forth with a bored expression. Moonie stood, then was shaken back down, where he stayed.

At first, the road headed straight across the flat Basin, then began to climb and wind through sagebrush hills until it reached a line of trees, both aspen and fir, where the road aimed at the sky. This was much steeper than Galena Pass, but didn't last as long. When the truck leveled out, Nellie's hands were cramped from squeezing onto her seat or the armrest in the door. They traveled through a meadow-like area with long grasses and trees, rounded a bend, and came abruptly upon a sheep wagon — what looked like a small Conestoga with a horse hobbled and grazing nearby. When she stepped out of the pickup, Nellie saw the half-cylinder, dirty white top was made of canvas.

"Domingo! Where are you, blast your

hide!" Gwynn shouted and walked up the trail a ways. No sheep were in evidence. No dogs, either. Alphonso joined Gwynn and called out something in a foreign language. He turned to Gwynn and spoke several words, none of which were understandable to Nell.

"He shoulda been expectin' us. I told the supply man to tell him we was comin' up in four days to get him. Where are the gol-durned sheep?" Gwynn stepped up the short ladder to the back of the wagon and peered in, then opened the door, hunched over, and entered. Moonie sniffed around the four corners of the wagon, found one to his liking, lifted his leg, and urinated.

"What the —" A roar came out the door.

Nellie and Alphonso ran over. Gwynn peered out, covering his face with a hand-kerchief. "He's dead. Has been for a day or two." He stepped down and motioned for Alphonso to go in and bring out the body.

"You wait by the pickup, Lassie. This ain't no sight for a woman."

Nell stood her ground, even though she was beginning to catch the smell from inside the camp. Nausea filled her mouth with saliva. She swallowed, hoping she wouldn't throw up or faint. She backed toward the pickup. "Here, Moonshine." The dog was

34

unaffected by the smell and still wandered around, his nose to the grass, sniffing. He lifted his head when she called and came over reluctantly. She patted his head, then crouched by him and put her arms around his shoulders to hold him.

The sheep camp. She should photograph it, begin her assignment now. That would keep her hands and mind busy and maybe the sick feeling would go away. From the pickup, she drew out her camera pack and retrieved the tripod, busying herself finding the right perspective. She took one photo of the camp and horse nearby. But she could not ignore the limp body Alphonso carried out and laid on the ground, so she moved closer without the camera. A camp with a body was hardly what the railroad would want. She managed to take two photos of the sheep camp. Maybe the sheriff of this county would want a photograph, too, so she moved her tripod and camera close to Domingo.

"Can't see anything wrong so far. Maybe out here in the light," Gwynn said. "Ain't much blood in there. I'll check around the area, Al. We'll have to find the sheep. Them dogs wouldn't let 'em get too scattered, unless . . ." His voice stopped and his face calculated. "Blast it! Those good for nothin' cowhands probably drove 'em off. They're all over hell's half acre, scared outta their wits. I hope to god my dogs aren't shot up."

Nellie winced. She appreciated Gwynn's feeling for his dogs, but he seemed more concerned for them than for the dead man lying on the ground.

"All right, Lassie. You got that camera there. If you're so brave, take a picture of Domingo here. May as well have it for the sheriff, 'cause I gotta bury the poor sod. He stinks to high heaven."

It wasn't as if Nellie had never seen a dead body before. Last winter, she'd had more than her share and photographed two of them. This one seemed more dead and the summer's early heat didn't help how he looked. Corpses in winter were like the embalmed bodies in funeral parlors she had once photographed in Chicago as part of the portrait business. This one still held the sense of once being alive. His skin was mottled and sunken around the skull. She didn't want to touch him, but thought a full face would be better than a profile. His hands curled like claws with long dirty fingernails, and his clothes — they were almost in tatters, so much so that scraped skin showed through at his knees and elbows. Small burrs stuck to the material and they were stained with grass, almost as if he had crawled or been dragged through grasses and rocks. Gingerly, she half-turned the body and his hair, so dark and oily that it looked wet, fell to one side. A hole in his temple looked empty and black.

Nellie pulled her hand back as if she had been burned. "Gwynn, he's been shot!"

CHAPTER 2

The sheep man hurried back to Nell. He studied the hole without touching it, and then stepped up into the sheep camp. Nell heard him rummaging around but she stayed outside, once again setting up her camera, keeping her hands and mind busy so she wouldn't think about the smell or the body. Soon enough, Gwynn returned, shaking his head. "Still don't find no blood. He mighta killed himself. Txomin said last trip back that Domingo was in a bad way. I can't find a revolver, though, and if he had been shot up close, there would be more of a mess. I think all Domingo had was his Winchester for shootin' at varmints."

"I'll take a couple of photos of his head and the wound. I won't be able to develop them until I get back to Ketchum."

"There ain't no sheriff these days up here in Custer County. Your friend Azgo'll probably be the one to investigate up here. I want nothin' to do with him. I'll tell him about the body and he can come up or not as he pleases. In the meantime, Al and I'll get him buried and see where the sheep went off to. This place'll need airin' out. I'll get a tent set up for you so you can have some privacy. You'll be pretty lonely up here, Lassie. Al ain't used to having women around and he's got sheep to watch. Sure you want to stay now that you seen some of the trouble?"

Nellie's visions of rambles in the high country, watching and listening to sheep, getting friendly with the talented dogs, maybe conversing in broken English and Spanish with the Basque sheepherders now seemed like something out of a book or a column in an eastern newspaper. The railroad man wanted scenic landscapes, romantic shots of a calm, western occupation, interesting and time-worn visages of cowboys and, if possible, noble savages. These were what tourists wanted to see when they came out West. Maybe this was what Nellie herself had expected. She wasn't immune to the vivid descriptions Zane Grey included in his romantic western stories nor the heroic cowboy characters he wrote about. Never mind that most of his novels took place before the turn of the century into modern times.

"I'll stay," she said, and pulled the black cloth over her head and her camera. She focused for a second picture of the body, this time taking the whole man, not just his head and the grim hole.

"Thought you would. Never seen a woman so determined as you to act like a man. Just remember, you ain't one." His legs and feet moved back to the camp. "Al and I got to bury Domingo here, then see about roundin' up the sheep."

Nellie abruptly pulled out from under the cloth. "Can I help? I can scramble up these hills more easily than you can."

"Shore you can. But I'm gonna take the horse. You can follow Al around if you like. Your dog might be some help, if he don't run into a mutt again. Or a coyote."

Nellie released the shutter and called toward the sheep tender coming down the trail toward them. "Alphonso, I'll come with you."

The Basque looked from Gwynn to Nell, his face impassive. She hadn't really studied him before. He bore a surface resemblance to Sheriff Asteguigoiri, his name shortened by most people to Azgo, also a Basque. Neither was truly handsome nor as noble-looking as Indians were often pictured, but both had a centuries-old air about them, embodied in high cheekbones, dark eyes that seemed to reflect little or no emotion, arms almost too long for their builds but that seemed capable of great strength. Summers alone in the mountains might account for a certain stillness about them, although Alphonso had less of that mysterious air that emanated from the sheriff. The sheepherder was younger, too. His dark skin, the color of burnished bronze from the sun, had few lines.

"Do you mind?" she asked Alphonso. "Maybe Moonshine can find the sheep or dogs faster than we can."

"He don't speak much English, but he can understand some of what you say. Keep it simple," Gwynn said. "And he'll mind or not, whatever I tell him. You know any Spanish?"

"*Por favor* and *gracias.* That about does it. Maybe I can learn while I'm here."

"Mostly he speaks Euskara — Basque. You won't never learn that. Only God's devils can understand it, and the Basque. Language all their own even if most of 'em do come from Spain. Best sheepherders there is." Gwynn's face became almost as impassive as Alphonso's. "Domingo — well, he went through a lot up here with the cattle-

men. A good man. I'm sorry to lose him."
He motioned to Alphonso and the two of
them carried Domingo away from the camp
into an area shaded by a rock outcropping.
They took turns with a single shovel until a
shallow grave was finished. Alphonso laid
the dead man carefully into it. He motioned
to Gwynn to wait and walked back to the
camp, apparently looking for something on
the ground or in the bushes off the trail.

"What do you need, Alphonso?" Nell
walked over to him.

He looked at her and she saw that tears
had sprung into his eyes. "Wool." He continued to pace around the area.

"Wool?" Near the stream on a crooked
branch of a small tree, Nell saw what she
had assumed was white fuzz from blossoms,
seed pods. She stepped closer and felt it.
Wool from a sheep. "Like this?" She held it
up.

The sheepherder took it from her and
bowed slightly. *"Gracias."* He hurried back
to the grave site where Gwynn had begun
shoveling dirt and rocks over the dead man.
Alphonso knelt, picked up Domingo's hand,
curled his fingers around the wool, and laid
the hand on the chest. He said some words
in his strange language, stood, and took the
shovel from Gwynn to finish the burial. Nell

42

helped pile stones on top of the mound, hoping the grave was deep enough and the rock pile high enough to keep animals from rooting up the dead body.

Moonshine trotted across the meadow toward them, making small yips. He nosed the mound, didn't mark it to Nell's relief, and sat down by her, waiting for instructions. His brown eyes looked mournful, as if he knew what had just taken place. "All right, Moonie. We're going out to find sheep."

Nell pulled her bags out of the pickup and opened one. She scrounged around inside and found a red bandana to wrap around her hair. She already wore pants, but tied a jacket around her waist for later. She had learned how cold the air was when the sun dropped behind the mountains. Her boots she had purchased in the winter and they were sturdy leather, already scuffed from use, but comfortable. "I'm ready." She didn't want to miss her chance to search for sheep. Even if it was a dangerous situation — after all, a man was dead — she had learned in the winter that she was braver than she ever thought she could be.

Sheepherder and sheep rancher looked at her and then at each other. Both smiled. Gwynn mounted the horse, struggling to throw his old leg up and over, settling into the saddle, groaning to let them know he wasn't a young man anymore but could still do what needed to be done. "Better fix a rope around that dog so he don't get into it if you come across the sheepdogs. With luck, they'll have the band rounded up some-where, waiting for Domingo. I'll head up the way." He gestured with his head, turned the horse, and began a slow climb to dis-appear around the bend.

Alphonso studied Nell. She didn't know what to say, so just waited. He nodded his head, found a length of thin rope inside the camp, left the door open, and motioned to Nell to follow him. They scrambled around the hill in the opposite direction Gwynn had taken, Alphonso studying the ground as they walked, the rope over his shoulders. Nell found herself having to watch what she was doing. The sagebrush branches and roots tripped and scratched her until she figured that she could not take a straight line. She wove around and through the brush, smelling the fragrance as she went, avoiding ground squirrel holes, stepping high where necessary. Moonie kept apace.

If Domingo had killed himself, Gwynn would have found a gun. Therefore, some-one must have shot him. Who would do

44

that? And where? Gwynn said no blood was evident inside the camp. She was glad she'd have a tent to sleep in and wouldn't have to enter the enclosed wagon. The state of the man's clothes and the scratches on his body were troublesome, as if he had been ill-used. Her talent for composing a good picture accompanied her ability to imagine herself in someone else's shoes, and she found herself trembling from the rage he might have felt if someone beat on him or worse, dragged him in this rough scrub brush and rocky scape.

During her musings, she lost sight of Alphonso and Moonshine. She stopped and turned around. Ridge lines met in a complex pattern. Sage and rabbit brush, just beginning to bud into what would be yellow clumps, turned the slopes gray-green. Looking south, she saw stands of dark fir on the north slopes of a series of small mountainsides, broken by chutes where tree trunks lay scattered like gray toothpicks from winter avalanches. Above and beyond her, white rock peaks lined up as far as she could see — the White Cloud Mountains, Gwynn had identified for her. Snow, unmelted by late spring or early summer sun, marked a slope several ridges from where she stood.

As Nell watched, it began to move, lackadaisically, as if melting before her eyes. "The sheep! I see the sheep!" But no one was around to hear her. She began to hustle toward them, then tripped and fell on her face, breaking her fall with her hands. "Owww!"

Carefully, she sat up and examined her left hand, the same one she'd scraped at Smiley Creek. A small stone was lodged in the pad of skin below her thumb. Tears sprang to her eyes. She heard a bark and then Moonshine trotted over the ridge behind her and wound his way to her. "Oh, Moonie. Ouch. See my hand?" She held it up and he licked it. There was nothing for her to do but try and pressure the rock loose. The dog watched as she pulled her skin apart with her other hand, then tried squeezing from below, and it dislodged. A thin line of blood trailed to her wrist. She wiped it on her trousers and stood up. "I saw the sheep over there," she said, pointing. The patch was marginally closer, and she saw the tiny figure of a dog herding them. "Let's go." This time she watched her step, stopping from time to time to call for Alphonso and Gwynn.

When she and Moonshine came within a hundred yards of the band, Nell stopped and held Moonshine close to her. She didn't want another dogfight. The sheep dog, a black and white animal with one blue eye and one brown eye, eased over to her. The two dogs sniffed at each other, but neither growled or took a fighting stance. "Hey, sheep dog. Are you bringing your charges back? Why are they way out here?" Its eyes seemed to roll in its head and she laughed.

The dog ignored her and ran to herd a stray back into the band, then circled to the rear, continuing to move the band along. If Nell didn't step to one side, she'd be in the middle of it, swallowing dust, so she, too, turned in the direction she'd come, feeling herded right along with the sheep. She noticed a number of black sheep and counted. Gwynn had said each black sheep was a marker for one hundred white sheep. This band was at least fifteen hundred sheep, based on the number of dark wooly backs. It didn't seem that large, but the white backs moved like a small sea of dirty waves rolling up and over sagebrush, streaming around rocky outcrops. Bells on the lead sheep tinkled and a murmuring of "baaas" soon surrounded Nellie. She wasn't moving fast enough, so she took the bandana from her hair and covered her nose and mouth with it. Their butting heads and thick bodies jostled her as if she were in a sheep stampede, and staying upright challenged her. Moonshine was smart enough to stay in front of the band and soon she saw him disappear over the next ridge.

Before long, her dog appeared again, barking. This time, a man followed and Nell saw that it was Alphonso. He waved and jog-trotted toward her, avoiding the kind of roots she had tripped over. He whistled to the sheep dog, made two hand motions as he neared, and the dog circled around to the front of the band, stopping their progress. Nell clambered through the knots of wool to the sheepherder.

She removed her kerchief to speak. "Are these the Campbell sheep? I'm so glad you're here. They were going to pass me up soon."

"Campbell sheep," Alphonso repeated after her. "Dog?" He held up one finger.

"That's all I saw. Should there be more?"

A look of concern crossed the young man's face, the first one Nell had seen. He turned to point to Moonshine. "Dogs fight?"

"No fight." She shook her head. She hated talking as if he were a dunce, so added, "It seemed to accept Moonie."

"*Señora.*" He pointed to the dog at the side of the band. "*Señors vamoose.*"

48

"The missing dogs are male?" She turned around where she stood, scanning the countryside. Nothing else moved, except a hawk soaring high. It was so wild, and its markings, beige and white stripes on the underside of its wings, so beautiful, she hugged herself. A loud call pierced the blue. Was it calling to a mate, or had it found a victim in the scrub below?

Alphonso said something more, but Nell couldn't understand. She shook her head. He motioned for her to continue back to the camp with the band and with Moonshine. He, apparently, was going to look for the other dogs.

"But where do I go?"

The sheepherder pointed with one hand to the sun lowering toward the west. Then he stood with his other hand pointed at a right angle. "South." He touched his chest. "Find dogs." He touched her shoulder. "South." He jabbed his hand again in that direction.

"All right. But come back soon. I might get lost."

He nodded. Whether he understood her was questionable.

Nell rewrapped the kerchief around her face, called Moonshine, and headed in the direction Alphonso had pointed. If she kept the sun on her right side, she should be all right. The sheep dog was much clearer about where to herd its charges, and soon, she was once again in the middle of the band and then behind them, choking from the dust and lanolin smell. It would be hard to lose her way from the rear. Small, dark round pellets marked everything. Not unlike Hansel and Gretel, she thought.

Familiar landmarks appeared. Aspen and cottonwoods marked the path of the creek and a rocky pinnacle and talus slide showed up across the water. Gold and green grass. The sheep camp hove into view, a welcome sight. The horse was tethered to the back of the camp, but Nell didn't see Gwynn anywhere. Maybe he was inside the wagon, looking for the gun or blood. Then she saw that the pickup truck was nowhere to be seen. He must have driven back down that rough road and was returning to Galena Store and points south. A strong sense of abandonment filled Nell. Her elation over the photo assignment and her excited anticipation of a lark in the summer sheep range popped like big balloons.

The dog once again circled the band and then lay down, her tongue lolling. She rolled in the grass. Moonie followed suit, then trotted over to the creek for water. The sheep, too, settled in groups. Nell rested on a log near a fire round, discouraged, tired, and dirty. A couple of weeks? She'd be lucky to last until the next supply manager arrived a week hence. On the other hand, walking down that wagon trail, for surely that was what it was, and then trying to hitchhike back to Galena held little appeal, especially carrying her camera pack and at least one suitcase. Those awful men at Smiley Creek.

Where were her things? She stood up. The ground was empty of baggage. Gwynn must have left everything in the sheep wagon. Nell strode over to it, but hesitated. The door was closed. Concern for her camera overcame any fastidiousness about entering into someone else's home without permission. She climbed one step, peered through the small square window, and could see nothing. A squirrel scolded from a tree branch. As she reached for the handle, a rock rattled behind her. When she turned, she saw one fall to the ground from the rocky outcrop. "Who's there?" A hush surrounded her and she thought she heard several more rocks fall, but somewhere up and beyond her sight. "Alphonso?" No answer.

On the trail leading from below into the

camping area, she saw a horse and rider, and behind the first, several more. Out of the corner of her eye, she noticed the sheep dog stand up, holding steady to guard her charges. Nellie stepped down from the camp wagon and into the path of the rider.

"Whoa, Star." The rider's horse stopped a few yards in front of Nell. "Who are you, little lady? The sheep tender?" The cowboy laughed and turned in his saddle. "Whoa," he called to the string of riders behind him. "We got an obstruction ahead."

Nell stepped back. She didn't consider herself an obstruction. "Who are you?"

"I'm Luke, head cowboy for this crew of tenderfoots. We're on our way up Fourth of July Creek here to a camp thataway — by the lake." He took off his hat, motioned beyond Nell, wiped dust off his forehead with a kerchief, and replaced the hat, shading the light blue eyes she'd caught a glimpse of. Well-worn chaps covered his legs. His flannel shirt bore signs of dirt and sweat. All he needed to complete his get-up was a six-shooter around his waist.

"Did you meet up with Gwynn Campbell in a pickup on your way here?"

"Driving like crazy down this godforsaken wagon track. Near run into me." The cowboy's drawl was slow and southern. Nell

52

couldn't decide if it were fake or not. "Didn't bother to stop. Said to tell someone named Al that he'd be back 'fore dark if he could."

Relieved with at least this little bit of news, Nell smiled. "I'm Nellie Burns. I'm not the sheep tender. I'm a photographer. Alphonso is on his way." She glanced at the rocky outcrop, wondering why the sheepherder hadn't appeared yet.

"We can't stop to chew the fat, Miss Burns. Gotta get this passel of riders to camp, get 'em unloaded, and stir up some chow." He tipped his hat. "Nice to meet ya. It ain't often I get to see a pretty girl out here in the sagebrush. 'Specially not in the middle of those gol-durned sheep." He turned in the saddle and called out. "Get 'em goin'." He rode past. Six others on horseback followed, people clearly not used to riding horses as they gripped the saddle horn as well as the reins and looked to be in various stages of discomfort. Four men and two women, all dressed like a Chicagoan's idea of what a cowboy looked like — ten gallon hats, sheepskin vests, shiny tooled cowboy boots, Levi's without a scratch on the men and divided denim skirts on the women. Nell thought those looked like a good idea. At the tail end was the cowboy she'd met at Galena, Dick something. Goodlight. What a name for such a sour-faced person.

"Hello, again," Nellie said, feeling as if she should acknowledge meeting him, even if his dog was a scoundrel. After Gwynn's scolding, she thought Moonie might have had something to do with the attack, but she would not apologize. Certainly this man would not. Moonshine returned to her side, barked once, and sat by her feet.

The man removed his clean Stetson, not from any polite feeling she was sure, nodded his head, and wiped his neck and forehead. He stared at her as he continued on, leading two pack animals fully laden. Not a peep from him, but Nell's hackles rose as if he had threatened her.

The riders followed the track between the creek and the mountainside, which grew steeper before they turned a corner and left her view. This must be the dude ranch group Lulu mentioned. Nell wondered that Gwynn hadn't told her about a ranch up ahead. On second thought, she doubted there was a ranch. These people were probably on an overnight cookout, the kind of thing the railroad man said attracted tourists from the East.

The sheep quieted as they settled and the

dog did not bark at all. A hush spread over the meadow. Where was Alphonso? She looked back at the camp. "What do you think, Moonie? Should I go in? I don't know what I'm afraid of. The dead man has been buried. Surely, if there were anything else to worry about, Gwynn would have said so." Not necessarily. He'd been worried about his sheep and his dogs, not Nell. A chill ran down her back. "Come on, Moonshine. I've got to see if my camera is in there."

Once again, Nell approached the door. This time, she heard a rustling sound inside. She reached out, turned the knob, and pulled the door toward her, ready to jump back. Inside, all was dark. Her eyes began to adjust and she saw a pile on the floor, almost as if Domingo were still there instead of buried out on the hillside. Moonshine brushed past her, growling. He sniffed at the pile, growled, then sat down in the tiny space at the other end.

"What is it?" Nell knelt, still in the doorway, and touched a blanket. Her eyes adjusted to the darkness. A blanket was wrapped around something. She lifted it and found a dog underneath. Either he was a very sound sleeper or he was unconscious or dead. His fur felt warm and she could feel his chest rise and fall in a half-panting motion. Not dead, yet. His leg shifted, then jerked forward and back as if he were running. That was the sound she had heard. Two *señors,* she recalled Alphonso saying. Here was one, and in bad shape. Dried blood marked the scruff of his neck. He lifted his head. Moonshine licked the other dog's face, but the animal only lay his head down again as if exhausted. Maybe Gwynn went to get help, but why not take the dog with him? A soft groan accompanied each breath.

Nellie could at least get water, and looked around for a container to carry it from the creek. The camp wagon was like a little house with a wood stove, a table that let down for meals, a bunk at the end, drawers under the bunk, pans hanging on a wood structure along the side wall. On the bunk were her camera and tripod. Thank heavens!

A pan with a handle would work. She grabbed one, stepped back outside and went to the creek for water. As she hurried back, she saw a figure up on the rocks. "Alphonso! Come down!" She waved her arm and returned to the prone animal, placing the water on the floor, moistening her hand and dribbling water around his mouth. She eased his head up so he could reach the water himself, stroking him while he lapped with his tongue in a half-hearted way. What was wrong with him? Moonshine had not moved.

The clomp of boots on rocks preceded Alphonso's arrival. His figure darkened the doorway above where she sat. "He's hurt. There's blood here." She touched the animal's neck and it flinched. "Ah, there. I'm trying to give him water, but I don't know what else to do." Her voice cracked.

Alphonso said something in his incomprehensible language.

"I can't understand you. I think Gwynn went to town for help. He's gone, but my camera is here. He left in a hurry, I'm sure. Only the tent was unloaded. Nothing else."

There wasn't room for Alphonso, Nell, and Moonshine in the wagon, so she motioned for the sheepherder to move and she would leave, giving him room to examine the dog. "Moonshine, come with me. This dog might not like someone else in his home." This dog might be beyond caring at any moment.

In the doorway, Nell watched as Alphonso opened the drawer under the bunk, rummaged around, and brought out a wide, short tin. He moved his hands rapidly over the animal, feeling along his legs, his haunches, and then his neck. Again, the dog flinched and whimpered. Moonie made a noise in response and butted up against Nell. "Shhh, Moonie. There's not room for us." Alphonso opened the container and the smell, a combination of Mentholatum and something like rotten fish, instantly permeated the inside of the camp. "We'll wait outside," Nellie said, trying not to gag.

Dust and the smell of lanolin still crowded the outside air, but it smelled fresh in comparison. The sun had disappeared behind the mountains in the west, but the dusk was a long time turning into dark.

Nell decided to erect the tent near the creek and behind the wagon. Twice, it collapsed on her until she figured out how the poles worked. As she finished and stood in front of it, proud of her handiwork, she heard two cracks of branches across the creek. The horse tied to the camp whinnied and side-stepped. She peered into the darkening woods and thought she saw a shadow move under the trees, reminding her of the rock falling earlier. Someone was hanging around, spying on her and the camp. Moonie had become bored with her struggles and ambled back to sit by a fire kindled by the sheepherder. Even with her dog and Alphonso close by, Nell shivered. Don't be foolish, she told herself, but, rather than carry her bag into the canvas shelter, she hurried over to the fire, sensing eyes in the night aimed at the back of her head.

Alphonso motioned for Nell to sit by the fire in the rock surround. "*Hotz,* cold." Indeed, she had already discovered the cool air in the shadows where sunlight had been filtered by the trees. The wrap she had tied around her waist helped allay the chill, but the fire would help more. Not only was she chilly and wary, she was hungry. So was Moonshine. He nosed her lap, wandered around sniffing, then settled down next to her. The crackling of the fire cheered Nell.

Alphonso had started a fire in the stove inside the camp, too. He opened several tins of beans that he had retrieved from the drawer under the bunk, poured them into an iron pot, then stirred together flour, water, lard, and salt and dropped biscuits on the beans as they simmered on the stove. From a sack tied inside the door, he brought out dried meat, tossing several pieces to Moonshine and taking more out to the dog with the sheep. Nell thought she could eat some, too, even if it looked older than dirt, as Rosy used to say.

Nell wanted her camera near her, but didn't want to disturb Alphonso at his chores. It was safe inside and too dark outside to take any photographs. Except for the hurt animal and wondering when the rest of her baggage would return, she was content to watch Alphonso, listen to the rustle of the sheep, pet her dog, and be warmed by the fire.

This was a far cry from her life in Chicago before she came to Idaho. In the middle of winter, she had stepped off the train in Ketchum, a small used-to-be mining town in the south-central part of the state. Stories of the mountains and beauty of the area had brought her there. She had lost her job as a portrait photographer. After many hours at the library, she decided landscape would separate her from other photographers. She searched for an area of the country no one else had claimed, with the hope that she could build a reputation and support herself selling photographs. Then, too, she had wanted to strike out on her own, get away from the presumption that she was an old maid and therefore destined for unhappiness, although it meant leaving her mother alone.

In the West, she didn't feel like an old maid, even though she was almost twenty-six. She felt alive and vital with purpose. Although some of the people she met had questioned her traveling alone and seeking a career in something so outlandish as "taking pictures," notably Sheriff Azgo whom she had come to like even though he thought along the same lines as her mother — she should settle down, get married, and have children — others accepted her as she was. Who her parents were, where she had come from, what her education was, even the fact that she was female — all these things didn't matter so much in Idaho.

Her musings were interrupted by Alphonso bringing a plate filled with beans and biscuits to her. He sat beside her with his own food, and they both ate with relish. The beans had a thick, smoky flavor, and the biscuits tasted as good as the ones Mrs. Bock made at the boarding house. The fire crackled; a piece of wood fell and rolled. Nell stopped it with her foot, set her plate down, and retrieved several more pieces from the pile near the camp, then settled herself again beside Moonie. She noticed he had licked a few beans off the plate, but she finished what was left. Sometime between when Alphonso brought the plate to her and she replenished the fire, night had descended. Stars carpeted the sky, something she never tired of studying. The winter had been difficult, and she still didn't know if some of the photographs she had taken under a full moon in a snowy field would be accepted at a gallery in San Francisco, along with a photo of Mrs. Bock baking pies and another of Rosy. Still, she didn't regret for a moment leaving the city and coming to Idaho. She might yet, though. So far, her introduction to the high country hadn't been auspicious. The smell of the ointment drifted from the sheep camp. Nell wrinkled her nose.

A light bounced up and down the trees and rocks around the camp. Startled, Nell and Alphonso both set down their plates and stood. Then the sound of grinding gears told them an auto approached. Before long, the pickup pulled up by the fire, and Gwynn stepped out.

"Glad you found your way to camp. Did you get the sheep? Yeah, I see you did." The animals had bedded down for the night up the hillside and path from where he stopped his truck. His headlights rested on several bunches, looking like spools of yarn. "Blasted vultures been after us, Alphonso. Find the dog inside? He was bad, but the other one was worse. Didn't have time to unload the pickup and fit both of 'em in."

"The dog you left is better," Nell volunteered. It had limped toward the band a while ago.

Gwynn nodded. "I took the other one to the vet in Stanley, not that he knows anything or gives a —" he glanced at Nell. "— a hoot about my sheep dogs. He'll live, unless that son of a — horse doctor fouls it up."

"I'm glad you're back." Nell was ready to regret her words when the old man smiled at her.

"Get me some grub, Al."

Alphonso hurried into the wagon and brought out a plate of beans and biscuits for Gwynn. The sheep rancher took it and sat down on the log where Nellie shifted to make room. He shoveled in the food. "Sure needed this. Could use a swig of whiskey too. Got any?"

The Basque stepped back inside, pulled out the drawer, and brought a bottle to Gwynn. Nell wondered what else was in the drawer. It was like a never-ending supply source. The bottle was dark green and about half full. "Wine," Alphonso said, his teeth white in a grin. Gwynn took it, popped the cork out, and up-ended the bottle for a long swig. "Aaaah. That's better." He held the bottle to Nell. "Want some?"

She did, but wasn't sure she wanted to gulp from the bottle. Her face must have shown something, as Gwynn said to Alphonso. "Bring a cup. The lady'll take a swig too."

"What was wrong with the other dog? This one seemed to have a wound on the neck," Nellie asked.

Gwynn shook his head. "Looked like this one got into a fight with a bear maybe. Or mountain lion. But that wasn't what hurt the dog I took down."

Nell wondered if what she had heard and seen was a bear or a lion skulking around the camp. "Here, do you think?" She tried to sound nonchalant, but such an animal was more acceptable than the two-legged variety. There had been no sign of a scuffle.

"Nope. Up yonder." Gwynn motioned with his fork. He poured two inches of wine in a cup for Nellie and handed it to her. "Drink up. Good for what ails you. Basque wine."

The wine warmed Nell's throat and all the way down her insides. It was tart and heavy at the same time.

The rancher took another swig himself and the lines etched in his face relaxed. "I was fooling you. No animal did these things to my dog. Or maybe one of 'em." Again he pointed with his fork, but this time to the camp. "Other one is a different story." He paused for another swallow and his shoulders sagged. "Bullet wound in the haunches."

CHAPTER 3

In the clearing where Nellie fell off her horse was a half-built log structure. By the time she recovered herself, groaning and rubbing her hip where she had landed, the horse had moved down the slope a hundred yards but seemed happy munching on grass, browsing his way toward the creek. The possibility that Gwynn had deliberately given her a stubborn animal crossed her mind, but she decided she was being uncharitable. She wished she could have driven up into the mountains. Her temperament was more suited to controlling a machine than steering an animal.

Moonshine came back from whatever spoor he had been following and nosed her. He liked the mountains just fine. So did Nellie, but it was taking some getting used to. The beautiful vistas belied the mundane and often rough aspects of living in them.

"Who began this log house and left it?"

Nellie asked the dog. "Maybe they'll come back and help me mount my horse." Assuming she could catch the animal before it sauntered along to camp, taking her camera equipment with it.

Under the warm sun, the meadow grasses were already turning gold, but in the shade, the mountain chill always lingered. Stands of aspen showed a pure green against the darker fir trees on the north side of the mountain near her. A few cottonwoods lined the creek — she was already pronouncing it "crick" like the other westerners — and the smell of sun on pine pitch mixed pleasantly with the chuckling of water over rock. Behind the log half-house, the white trunks of aspens standing straight and tall guarded the scree slope of a rock mountain, tumbling in on itself. Sagebrush dotted the south slopes of the mountains.

"C'mon, Moonie. If we have to walk back, we'd better catch the horse now and get started. I'm not sure how far we came, but it must have been several miles. I still haven't seen a clear vista back to the Sawtooths, and, oh, how I wanted to photograph them in the morning sun." Noon had passed and her stomach grumbled. The lunch she packed included sourdough bread and two thick slices of mutton smelling of garlic, intended for a picnic after she finished photographing. If she couldn't catch Blade, she might go hungry.

"Nice horse. Nice Blade." Nellie clambered down the slope in her boots, tripping on rocks and sliding on grass. The sheepherders wore boots, too, but they moved with more grace and ease. The horse glanced at her, and then stepped closer to the creek, lowering its head to drink. Moonshine trotted to the downward side of the slope and barked. Blade halted its sidestepping and Nellie managed to grab a rein and hold the horse while she searched for a tall rock or a fallen log to stand on in order to mount. Nothing was high enough and the logs of the structure were too high.

"Walk we must," she told Moonie. The dog didn't care. While Nell led the horse down the slope and along the rough track she had ridden up in the morning, he ran up and down, back and forth, stopping once to roll in a patch of scarlet gilia. She rounded a bend and there in the west was the scene she'd been looking for all morning. Three mountains of the Sawtooth range cut the horizon like the lower half of a giant bear's jaw, framed by a sagebrush slope on one side and alpine fir on the other. A dark pewter anvil of a thunderhead billowed up behind the peaks. She'd forgotten her rule of turning around from time to time to see what was behind her. The sun was high in the sky but white puffs were growing and extending like a line of laundry to the north. Soon, their shadows would mottle the light and Nellie might have just what she hoped for. This time, she remembered to tie the horse to a tree limb while she unloaded her gear.

Nothing was easy about setting up her large-format camera on a rocky hillside. The tripod's legs extended easily enough, but finding firm footing and then leveling the camera always took time, once she had found a suitable foreground. A plain photo of mountains in the distance wasn't enough. Good composition required interesting foreground as well. She calculated the black and white zones with her meter and then the time she would expose her film. On such a bright day, the actual photograph would take the barest fraction of a second — .125 with the fstop set at 22. For the long distance, she set the focus at infinity. Even as she worked, the clouds swelled, the light dimmed, the air cooled. She studied the scene through the lens while protected with the black cloth over her head and the camera. If the sun disappeared behind clouds, the whole scene would look gray. She needed the contrast of bright light in some places, shade in others, and preferred that at least one peak stand out.

By the time Nellie finished and repacked her gear, raindrops were sprinkling and Moonie had begun warning her to hurry with a combination of whimpers and barks. Distant thunder rumbled around the Basin, echoing off the rock faces of the Sawtooths. A zag of lightning was clear warning.

"Darn, now I won't be able to eat." She eyed with regret the pack on the horse where the lunch lay hidden. Again, she looked for a place to stand so she could mount. Being short didn't usually bother her; today it was a real difficulty. "Let's keep walking, Moonie. Maybe we'll find a place." After a short debate with herself, she took the camera pack from the horse and donned it herself, the straps around her shoulder. She didn't want to lose the camera if the horse bolted from lightning or thunder.

The drops thickened and fell faster. She stopped the horse, tied the rein to another tree limb, and retrieved a canvas poncho and hat. With those items placed over the camera pack on her back, it wouldn't matter how hard it rained. The lightning was still a concern. The trees around her were tall, Douglas fir instead of alpine or lodge-pole, and if she moved up the slope, she'd stand out like a lightning rod in the sage-brush. Don't stop, she warned herself, and hoped she wasn't near the tallest tree.

Another group of "dudes" had walked their horses through the sheep camp the night before. Nell wondered how they liked the rain. About as much as she did, she suspected. The clouds had settled in and she could see nothing ahead of her. She kept her head lowered, her eye on the trail, her hand on a rein. Her first week was almost finished. She missed Gwynn, who had left the next morning after taking the dog down, but had returned with a horse tied to the rear of the pickup, possible because the road was so rutted, the pickup could only go as fast as a horse could walk. "This here is yours to use while you're up here. You ride, don't you?"

"Yes, somewhat."

" 'Somewhat?' What does that mean? Either you ride or you don't."

Whenever the old man did something thoughtful, he nearly always added some teeth to it. Nell wanted to think she was growing fond of him, that in some ways he was replacing her father, but it was all sentimental slop. He was a hard man, caring more for sheep and dogs than for people, except perhaps his sheepherders, and he definitely felt those men belonged to him.

"I learned to ride in Chicago, in a park, on an English saddle." She decided not to add that her lessons all took place when she was ten years old, while her grandparents were still alive and wanted her to have some treats.

Gwynn snorted. "Guess you'll have to relearn with the western saddle. Anyway, here it is. Alphonso can help you get on." He turned to the Basque who watched the scene, his face impassive as always. "She's gonna take pictures of you, the sheep, the bee-eautiful landscape. Your first responsibility is the sheep and dogs, but help her out if she needs it." And then he had left them alone.

Nell spoke to Alphonso in English. She never knew for certain when he understood her and when he didn't. He spoke to her from time to time in a combination of Spanish and English words, when he spoke at all. Maybe it was Gwynn's English that she missed. It was almost like being alone in the mountains to be with Alphonso.

The sheepherder went about his business and Nell followed him or not, as she chose.

72

The first few days, she did what he did: arose early, before dawn, to see that the sheep didn't scatter as they began to graze at first light. He stayed with the herd as they ambled along to find grass, using the dogs to keep them from scattering widely. Sometimes he rode his horse, sometimes not. At midmorning, the sheep lay down in whatever shade they could find, chewing their cuds and looking like big-nosed preachers about to deliver sermons, and both Alphonso and Nell ate a sandwich and drank from a leather bag filled with water.

Around midafternoon, the sheep stood, rising in clumps like wool bundles, to graze again. Alphonso or one of the dogs moved the lead sheep back in the direction of camp, and slowly the mass of yarn followed. After feeding the dogs, including Moonshine, Alphonso fixed supper, usually beans and biscuits, often with chorizo sausage, one night mutton chops, and another time, a large ham that he and Nell ate for several days.

While Nellie wandered nearby seeking good photographic material, Alphonso sometimes rode off on his horse. She didn't know what he did while he was gone, but twice he brought back unusual-looking rocks and once a spear head. His explorations seemed more fruitful than hers. He allowed her to photograph him in several different poses: on his horse, standing in front of the camp, working at the stove, resting with his arms behind his head on a grassy slope, and calling the sheep for salt. "Brrrrr, brrrrr." It was a pleasant sound and the wooly animals clearly knew what it meant for they moved more quickly than usual to crowd around a salt lick, a block of salt, their tongues rasping, reminding her of a bee's nest that had been disturbed.

The aspen grove near where they camped gave Nellie a place to sit and plan her photographs while she basked in the sunshine, breathing in the smell of green leaves and sage. The continuous rattle of aspen leaves sometimes lulled her to sleep. Then she discovered the carvings in the white bark: names and dates and on one tree, two sheep. Alphonso identified them as the markings of earlier sheepherders, and then pointed out one carved by Domingo. She insisted on a photograph of Alphonso carving his own name.

Moonshine stuck by Nellie and steered clear of the sheep dogs. The wounded animal had been up and around quickly and, although the two males had circled one another, a few words from Alphonso had settled whatever challenge they were thinking about. Occasionally, her black dog wandered close to the sheep and one of the sheep dogs would herd him away from its charges. Moonie didn't seem to mind. Mostly, he ran the hills, looking for ground squirrels to chase or trees to mark. Often, he lay beside Nell as she once again set up her tripod, fastened her camera, leveled it, peered through the lens, studied scene, animal, or man from under her black cloth, and shot photographs.

Nell's boot slipped in the muddy track she was following and she was jolted out of her reverie. The rain had stopped, but fog and clouds still hovered around her. Moonie wasn't by her side. She turned backward to be certain the horse was still at the end of the rein she held in her hand. How far she had walked was a question she couldn't answer, but judging by the state of her boots, at least a mile, perhaps two. She estimated she was at least two miles from camp, a warm fire, and the cozy sheep camp, which Alphonso shared with her during dinner and in the evening, until she stepped down to her tent for the night.

The fog hugged the hillsides around her and she felt swathed in gauze, a suffocating feeling. "Moonshine!" Her voice was tinny and traveled no farther than the ghostly sagebrush and rabbit brush she could see. Her horse clopped to a stop behind her and wouldn't move when she tugged on the rein. "Come on, Blade. Giddy up." Still, he stood, nodding his head at her. A chill crept along her arms up to her neck.

Nell turned in a circle, forgetting which way she was traveling, the fog was so disorienting. Then she heard what the horse must have heard, a lowing and bawling, accompanied by a vibration in the ground. Which direction and how far away, she couldn't tell. "Blade, I've got to get on you." A quick glance around confirmed there were still no rocks, nothing to stand on, to mount the horse. She pulled on the rein and began to walk as quickly as the mud allowed. Even a steep-sided slant to the hillside would help. "Moonshine!" The track turned sharply and the sounds and vibrations surrounded her.

With her hands on the reins and the saddle horn, Nell talked to the horse while she placed her foot in the stirrup. "Hold still. Stop. Whoa!" For once, the animal cooperated, although his eyes showed more white than color. He was frightened too, not good for her. She managed to get herself up to his side, and just as she was swinging her other leg over the top, he began to side-step again. "Whoa!" Panic almost made her lose her hold on the saddle horn. The pack on her back was an unbalancing factor and she could feel herself begin to slide off. Then Moonie showed up and barked. He acted like a sheep dog, herding the horse back on the track, then stopping the horse. Nell's right leg swung over and she was on.

Before she could properly settle herself, a half dozen steer loomed close, coming out of the fog directly in front. They moved around her, walking and jogging in turns, like water eddying around a log in a stream as they continued up the track, followed by a herd strung out behind. The stench as they passed made her pinch her nose. Two riders clad in canvas ponchos and Stetsons brought up the rear.

"Hello," she called, not certain what range courtesies might be called for, if anything.

"Hallo yourself," answered one of the riders. "Rainy day to be out and about alone in the wilderness, ain't it? You wandered off from one of them dude campouts?"

"I'm not alone. I'm with a sheep camp down the way."

The rider came alongside. "Oh, you're that picture lady I heard about." The man's voice was singular, deep and with the timbre

77

of a singer.

"How do you know that?" Nell took in the man's lean face, grizzled chin and cheeks, and his eyes. They were like one of the sheep dog's — one was brown and the other blue. She tried not to stare at such a strange sight and glanced over his shoulder to the other rider, who sat hunched and looking miserable in the damp.

"We nattered awhile with the Basque," the cowboy said, motioning with his head in the direction from which they'd come. "Phew, those sheep smell." He shook his head, reached up under his poncho, and brought out a cigarette, which he stuck in his mouth while he fumbled with a wood match, striking it against something on his saddle horn, and then cupped his hand around the flame while he lit up. The expelled smoke hid his face a moment and Nell breathed in the burning tobacco odor, wishing she could do similarly. Smoking had become such an inconvenience, she'd given it up in the spring. It had been more for effect anyway.

"Not as much as those cattle," she said. "Theirs is a constant dung smell. And the cowpies. How do you stand it?" She hadn't meant to be so defensive about the sheep, but she was used to their lanolin odor, which wasn't nearly as strong as the cattle.

"Guess it's all a matter of what you get used to, ain't it?" When he dragged on the cigarette, it quivered in his lips, which were a deep pink in color and shaped like a cupid's bow. Then he took the cigarette from his mouth and smiled at Nell, before turning back to his companion. "You know this girl?" Then back, "What's your name?"

"I'm Nell Burns." The cowboy's wide smile had confused her. He was one of the handsomest men she'd ever seen in her life, unshaven face and mismatched eyes not-withstanding. Before she could ask his name, the other rider came forward. It was Goodlight, the man she'd seen at Galena Store and again with the dudes the first day she arrived. He did get around. His surly face was unchanged.

"Yeah, we met."

"Hello, Mr. Goodlight. We seem to cross paths often."

"Ned, we've got a long ways to go. Let's keep movin'." Goodlight nodded to Nell. He'd not yet been courteous enough to greet her with a word, but he didn't seem so threatening this time.

"Maybe we ought to see Miss Burns gets back to her camp. She's wandered a bit off course, I'd say."

Moonshine chose to bark.

"That mutt'll get her back, or the horse will." Goodlight pulled his horse's head to the side. "All she has to do is follow the cowpies." Then he gave his horse a small kick and continued up the trail.

Nellie and the unnamed cowboy looked at each other. "I can find my own way back. Thank you. Your friend is right. Moonie or the horse will get me there if I can't." She smiled, wishing she'd sounded more independent. "What's your name?" The fog was making her addle-brained and forward.

"Ned Tanner. I'm a cowboy for the Rocking O outfit." Again, he motioned with his head back down the trail. "Out of Stanley." He finished his cigarette and flicked the butt into the surrounding fog. "Take care now, Nell Burns. When you get down off this rise here, take the fork to the left and that'll get you back to your sheep." He lifted his hat briefly, winked the blue eye at her, and rode past.

The fog lifted as Nellie rode down to the sheep camp. By the time she arrived, late-afternoon sunshine broke through the clouds in several places, aiming streams of light at the camp and the aspens. The beauty of scenes in these mountains filled her with happiness. Then she realized something was amiss. Alphonso and the sheep should have been nearby, but they weren't. No smoke came from the crooked chimney on top of the roof; the door was open and pots and pans were scattered about. Two of the wood boxes that held food supplies were broken into pieces near the fire and flour and sugar were spilled on the ground like lumps of paste.

Moonshine barked, dashed up the steps and looked inside the camp, returned, and barked again, circling around the area. Nell sat her horse, not certain what to do — wait or try to find Alphonso. If he'd been inside, hurt, Moonshine would have entered. Besides, his horse was gone.

"Let's go, Moonie. This morning, he headed north. Grazing is getting a little skimpy nearby. He said we'd move in a day or two." Her rump was sore from riding a good portion of the day, but maybe she could help Alphonso. He must be in trouble somewhere.

After crossing only two ridges, she came upon the sheepherder. He and his dogs were rounding up sheep ranged far and wide. Only a small band clumped together where one ridge met another. One dog urged another small group toward the band. As soon as they arrived, he circled and headed back over a ridge. A long whistle sounded and another dog appeared on the horizon, herding another bunch, followed by Alphonso on his horse. He stopped short and waved to Nell. She waved back, but stayed where she was. There was nothing she knew how to do to help. The words "Come by, come by," a command to one of the dogs, floated toward her.

"Come along Moonie. We can go back and clean up, maybe get the fire started at least. I've never seen the sheep so scattered." She turned her horse, glad to think of something to do. "Alphonso will be in a hurry to herd the sheep back near camp. Out here, we're just in the way." She waved once and the sheepherder disappeared behind the ridge she traveled down.

Nell salvaged all the flour she could, but the boxes were beyond her. "May as well use them for firewood," she muttered. Most of the sugar had melted in the rain, but half a bag was usable, although already hardening. Several of the tins were squished open, their contents spewed on the ground, as if pounded or maybe stepped on. "The cattle. Did they come through here?" The ground was hard, but when she began looking, Nell saw the tracks of horses if not cattle. She didn't remember that the ground had been churned up the same way it was on most of her trip back. At the fork the cowboy had mentioned, the churned ground had extended to the other fork where she turned. His offer to help her back had indeed been specious. She could hardly miss the trail of the steers.

Someone had done this damage on purpose. Her first thought had been that lightning had struck the sheep wagon, causing so much damage, but it wasn't burned. The bunk was torn apart, but not so badly she couldn't put things together again. No one had touched her tent, maybe because it was back in the trees and not clearly visible from the camp. "Those cowboys did this. I know they did. They 'nattered with the Basque' he said." She stomped up and down the stairs, cleaning up, putting things back in their places. " 'Nattered' my foot." Moonshine followed her every step, responding occasionally with a drawn-out groan, as if he understood her.

By dark, the baaing of the sheep told her they were mostly together and Alphonso was close. The fire in the stove had heated the camp and she had a pot of mutton stew simmering. The meat had to be used and, after she'd cleaned off dirt and leaves and fir needles, was none the worse for wear. She'd rolled it in some of the damaged flour, browned it in the bottom of an iron pot on the stove, added wine and water and garlic, just as she'd seen Alphonso do, then cut up some of the potatoes after cutting off sprouts, and carrots she'd scraped of the hair they grew in the dark boxes. Wild greens grew along the creek, which served as a salad with a touch of vinegar. Nellie had no idea whether they were poisonous or not, but they tasted of nuts, so she figured they were edible. Alphonso would know.

While she waited, Nellie curled up on the bunk, making notes of the photos she had taken during the day before she forgot what she had done. One heavy step was followed by the door opening and Alphonso's welcome face, even if he looked tired and drawn. A bruise welled up on one cheek, and dried blood marked where his lip had been split.

"Alphonso!" Nellie leaped up. "You're hurt."

He waved her off, lifted the lid of the pot, and sniffed. "Good. Hungry." His face was almost blank, but she detected a movement of one corner of his mouth.

"What happened?" Nellie motioned for Alphonso to sit on the bunk while she served up her stew. First, she brought down from a shelf the bottle of wine she'd opened for the stew and poured him a cupful. She had already been sipping on her own cup of wine.

He took the wine, sat, then lifted the cup in a half-toast. "Sheep back. Not all." Such a look of sadness crossed his face, Nellie thought he would cry. "*Vaqueros.*" He mimicked riding a horse, then uttered several *baaa*s and moved his hands in circles, almost spilling his wine. He stopped and drank.

"The cowboys did this, didn't they? Hurt you and scattered the sheep and tried to destroy the camp." She pulled down the tabletop that was latched to the side of the wagon's cover, spooned a huge serving of stew into a metal bowl that served as a plate, and plunked it down, along with a fork and spoon. Then she served herself. "I met them on the trail. Goodlight was one of them, and a man named Ned Tanner. I'm surprised he told me his name. He knew I would come back to camp and find this." She had been taken in by his good looks. That wouldn't happen again.

"*Como va?*"

"I went up there," she said, motioning with her hand. "South I think. I got caught in the rain. That must have been when they came in here. Who hurt you?" She pointed to her own cheek and mouth. "Why were you here?"

Alphonso shook his head, drank again from his cup, and began eating from his plate. Both of them ate as though starved. Nellie knew she was.

In her tent that night, she couldn't sleep. She'd heard of the difficulties between cow and sheep men, but what was happening with Gwynn's sheep and the Basque sheepherders who worked for him was more than just a "difficulty." One man was dead, Alphonso had been hurt, the camp turned out like so much trash. This country was so big, so empty, why couldn't they leave each other alone? Although grass was not growing everywhere as it seemed to in the Basin floor along the Salmon River, a few bands of sheep and a few herd of cattle ought to be able to graze in widely separated locations without coming to blows over the presence of each other.

Men seemed determined to treat each other like vermin. The stories in the Chicago newspapers about how men and even women were treated in the slaughterhouses and rending plants were horrific. She had hoped for better conditions and more free-spirited people in the West who could honor each other's humanity. How naive she was. She thought she'd found big-hearted men and women in the small towns of Ketchum and Hailey, even in Twin Falls, along with the less generous. Finding herself in the middle of a range war was unsettling at best, but the photographs she had taken so far would satisfy the railroad man, even if they weren't all that she had intended when she began this excursion.

Her tent was generally watertight, both because she had erected it in a stand of fir trees that protected the ground and because lanolin had been used on the seams. Still, the water dripping from branches pattered aimlessly, keeping her awake even after she had come to a decision. She would go down with the camp tender when he arrived in a day or two. When she picked up her auto at the Galena Store, she might spend a night there, taking photos. Lulu had seemed capable and Nell was interested in her story. So far, some of the strongest, most competent people she had met in the West were women. That, at least, was gratifying and accorded with what she had hoped when she left the city. Nevertheless, thoughts of Lulu, Mrs. Bock her landlady, and Mrs. Ah Kee, the Chinese widow in Hailey who withstood discrimination every day of her life, made Nellie feel slightly ashamed that she couldn't stick it out for another week or two in the high country. Would any one of those women leave this situation? She didn't know.

In the morning, Nell felt as if she had not slept a wink. When she heard Alphonso stirring before dawn, she dressed herself in the tight quarters of her tent and joined him in the camp.

"Alphonso, I think I'll leave when the camp tender returns. I have the photos I need, and someone should tell Gwynn about what is going on up here."

The sheepherder watched her as she talked. He was so quiet and his face so still, she had no idea whether he understood, cared or not, wanted her to go or stay. They had seemed companionable in the hours they spent together, but Alphonso never seemed to mind when Nellie wandered off with her horse and dog and camera equipment. Only his dark eyes exhibited anything like emotion. Sometimes they twinkled with reflection of light; other times, they shaded into black holes.

Nell searched for some Spanish words to convey what she intended doing. Pointing to herself, she said, "*Vamos a la* Galena Store." She mimicked taking a photograph by holding air in front of her and saying "click click." "Photographs finished, un, *finito*." Then and there she resolved to learn more Spanish when she returned to town. Learning Basque was probably out of the question.

While she waited for the camp tender, Nell resolved to stay close to Alphonso. If the cowboys returned, she didn't think they would try any tricks in her presence. Knights of the range was what Zane Grey had called them. So far, they failed to live up to that billing.

As dawn rose in shades of pink and purple, Nell and Alphonso walked with the sheep. The bells on the lead ewes tinkled softly and Nell felt as if she could be anywhere in time, perhaps centuries back, tending animals as herders had done since the days of the earliest Indians in the West. A slight breeze ruffled the meadow flowers, loosening their delicate scent. The wings of two hawks flapped with a brushing sound as they passed over and a meadowlark's burbling song announced it would be another clear, warm day.

The two kept a sharp eye out for coyotes, as sunrise was as dangerous a time as sundown. Nell hoped Moonshine's presence was a deterrent. He didn't run at the sheep or interfere with the sheepdogs who kept pace at the outer fringes of the band, but he did scamper back and forth behind them as they stepped slowly through the sagebrush and grass. Nell carried her camera pack.

The morning passed quickly as Nell set up her tripod in several different locations, trying to capture the way sheep flowed like water around a bend or through a gully. By midmorning, she returned her camera to its case because the sun was getting too high. All the interesting shadows had disappeared. She and Alphonso sat down on a large flat rock to watch the sheep bed themselves down for the midday cud-chewing session. The heat of the rock and the warmth of the sun conspired to send Nell to sleep.

"Yah-hooooo!" The wild yell startled Nell awake. She was alone on the rock.

"Alphonso! Where are you?" Moonshine, who had been sleeping next to her, leaped up and toward the yell. The sheep had all risen and some were beginning to move. A lead ewe, her bell tinkling madly, dashed and stumbled around the sagebrush.

A horseman came up over the ridge, swinging a lariat. While Nellie watched, he threw the circle around the head of the ewe with the bells and stopped his horse, tugging the loop tight. Then he backed up, dragging the ewe through the roots and branches of the sage. The clumps of sheep scattered in every direction.

"Stop it!" Nell screamed. "Stop!" Moonshine raced toward the horse and rider as they dragged the sheep, its head at an angle that told Nellie it was dead. "Murderer!" She scrambled off the rock and began running after Moonshine. "Get him, Moonie. Sic'em!"

The cowboy looked in her direction. From the distance, she saw his mouth form an "O." He reined his horse in, unwrapped the rope from his saddle horn, did something to loosen the sheep from the noose.

"Sic'em," Nell called again, with as much force and anger as she could.

Moonie reached the horse and rider and leaped toward the man with a ferocious growl. The cowboy grabbed a rifle from the scabbard tied to his saddle and raised it to club the dog, but not in time. Moonie knocked him off and the gun dropped as the man fell to the ground and rolled. He scrambled to his knees, hatless, and was upright before the dog recovered from his own tumble.

"Blasted dog. I'll kill you." The man searched hurriedly for his gun, but Nellie was faster. She reached the melee and grabbed the rifle as she stumbled into the brush, then righted herself, standing.

"Stop right there! You . . ." She didn't know a word loathsome enough. "Moonshine. Come." The dog hesitated. His quarry was grounded. When Nellie repeated the command, he walked to her side, a low guttural sound still rumbling in his throat. "I should put that rope around your neck and drag you. See how you like it." She had little idea how to use the rifle, but the cowboy didn't know that. Then she realized who he was — the man with two different eyes, Ned Tanner.

"You! How could you . . . ?" She motioned with the barrel of the gun. "Get back on your horse and get out of here. I'm reporting you to the sheriff."

He tried a smile. "This ain't what it looks like, Nell Burns."

"It looks like the murder of a sheep. What would you call it?"

"Protecting our range is what I call it. You're grazing on cattle allotment."

"And were you 'protecting the range' when you trashed our camp and beat up Alphonso yesterday?" Her voice shook. It was anger, not fright, but this man wouldn't know. She raised the rifle a little higher, her finger on the trigger.

"What are you talkin' about? We didn't do nothin' to that sheepherder." His gaze passed Nellie and he said, "That one there?"

Nell turned and the cowboy grabbed the gun. Alphonso was coming over the ridge toward them. The man moved the lever and raised the rifle.

CHAPTER 4

"If you do anything, I'll sic Moonie on you and he'll kill you." She didn't know if her dog would do any such thing, but it was the most she could threaten.

The rifle barrel lowered. Ned Tanner studied Nellie. "I wouldn't kill a man."

"No? You'd kill a sheep. How much more would it take to murder a man?"

The cowboy caught his horse, mounted, and replaced the rifle in its scabbard. "I'll take my leave now, little lady. If that dog gets near me again, I'll kill it, that's for sure." His hat was dusty from his fall and he slapped it on his knee and replaced it on his head. As he wound his rope, Alphonso neared them. "Get these maggot sheep to their own allotment, or worse will happen." He rode off.

By the time Alphonso reached Nell, she was crying in relief that the gun hadn't been fired, either by her or by the cowboy, and in sorrow over the dead ewe.

"I'm sorry, Alphonso. I didn't protect them at all."

The sheepherder whistled a command to the sheepdogs, and then mounted the horse he was leading. He looked down at her. "Hurt?"

Nellie shook her head and wiped her eyes. Her hands were grimy and her shirt torn at one shoulder.

With one hand, Alphonso made a circle. He would round up the sheep. She nodded. He leaned down and patted her head, the only time he had ever touched her. "Cowman pay. Wait." That was as much English as he'd ever spoken to her. The pair, horse and rider, rode back over the ridge and Nellie was alone with her dog, who eyed her anxiously. He stood, took a few steps after the sheepherder, then came back to nudge Nellie.

"What are we doing here, Moonshine? This is the twentieth century and we're lost in a western moving picture show." She knelt and wrapped her arms around the dog's neck, nuzzling him. Talking to him had become a habit, partly so she could hear English words spoken. Tears wouldn't get her anywhere, so she stood and headed back to camp. "How does he know what allotment we're in? There are no fences. How can you divide the West like that?" As she walked, a new determination came over her. Getting her photos back to the railroad man would bring more people to the West, people who would civilize the place, bring manners and understandable rules. Men wouldn't be able to run around killing sheep and men. Law officers would make sure crimes were solved and the perpetrators brought to justice. Even if the first people to come were only tourists wanting a "true West" experience, some of those people would settle in Idaho. This county didn't even have a law officer if what Gwynn said was true.

The walk back settled Nellie. The open spaces calmed her; the distant bleating of the sheep floated on the breeze and she knew Alphonso had found most of the sheep and was settling them down, too. Off to her left, the rolling voices of grouse called to each other. Moonie dashed toward them, but only succeeded in flushing a covey into the air. He barked and ran in circles and returned to Nellie when the birds disappeared again into the sagebrush.

At the second ridge, Nellie looked down again into the camp to discover an auto with a man leaning against the front fender. Both man and machine seemed familiar, but it wasn't a camp tender or Gwynn Campbell. Although he wore a Stetson, he wasn't a cowboy. She could see that much. As she drew closer, she recognized Sheriff Azgo, Charlie, from his square-shaped torso, balanced by long legs and arms. Her step quickened and her spirits lifted. Moonie ran down the slope, barking, and trotted up to the man, who leaned over to rub the dog's neck. The two knew each other from other times.

"Sheriff!" She scrambled down the slope, for once not tripping and falling, and walked into camp. "I'm so glad to see you!" Then she flushed. She must sound like a . . . she didn't know what. Still, she thrust out her hand to shake his vigorously. The sure, rough feel of his hand warmed her.

"Glad I am to see you also," he said, his own wide smile mirroring hers. "I thought this camp might be deserted and I had the wrong place."

"You came to find me?" Nellie let go the sheriff's hand and automatically reached to her hair to straighten it, then remembered it was cut in a short bob like the pictures she'd seen in *Ladies Home Journal.* Unlike the long hair she used to tie back with a ribbon, the short hair always sprang around her head like it had been electrified. Mere patting wouldn't tame it.

"Gwynn sent word to me that you had trouble up here. I called the state police and received permission to come and check it out, there being no one else available."

"Oh. Yes, of course. Gwynn." Nellie patted Moonshine's head. "Is he all right? Where is he?"

"Mad as a coyote in a hornets' nest. He's up in Stanley, finding out what he can find out." He looked around. "Where's the sheepherder? And where's the dead one? Or are you the only one here? Gwynn wasn't too clear on the telephone. He didn't leave you here alone, did he?"

"Alphonso is bringing in the sheep." Nell turned to go to the camp. "We've been attacked this morning. A cowboy — Ned Tanner is his name — killed one of our sheep and almost shot Alphonso. If it hadn't been for Moonshine . . ." Her voice rose with anger. "I'm forgetting my manners. I'll start a fire and heat some coffee for you. Then I'll tell you everything that happened."

While she was in the wagon, Alphonso rode up. The banked fire didn't take long to rekindle nor the coffee to warm up. It was full of grounds, but then camp coffee always

98

was. Nellie eyed the wine bottle. She'd prefer to drink some of that. Maybe Charlie would arrest Tanner, take him to jail. When she stepped down with two cups of coffee for the men, they were deep in conversation, one conducted in Euskara. What was it Gwynn had said? This language was spoken only in a small area of Spain and France and was thought to be one of the first spoken by man, long before Latin or Greek or any of the Romance languages. At the moment, all she cared about was being left out.

"What are you saying?" She wanted her own coffee and hurriedly retrieved it.

"Alphonso explained what you found here. Said Domingo was dead and buried over there." He gestured toward the grave. "He said you found a bullet hole in his head." He looked up at her. His face had regained the serious, thoughtful expression Nellie associated with him. "I am sorry that you see the bad side of life in Idaho." Then his gaze lifted to the surrounding hills. "The sagebrush is like the sea, moving with the wind."

A non sequitur if Nellie had ever heard one. "Maybe Idaho only has a bad side." How would he know about the sea? Even she had only seen Lake Michigan and neither ocean.

"No. The land is neither good nor bad. It is there. People are bad. Or good." He finished his coffee. "Did you take photos of Domingo?" He couldn't keep the distaste from his voice. She knew what he thought of her profession as photographer. Like most people she'd met, he thought she should not wander the West seeking to do something only men should do.

"Yes, of course. We had to bury him and we wanted you to know what he looked like. No one else was equipped to do this job." Maybe she would throw together something to eat after all. She was tired of this ongoing argument. She turned, but Alphonso was already bringing out bread, sliced ham, cheese, and wine. Her stomach rumbled.

"Hungry, are you?" The sheriff laughed. "Now you tell me what happened. Alphonso did not see all of it."

Nellie wanted to walk away. She had been brave and now the sheriff, and probably Alphonso too, laughed at her. "You'd be hungry too if you chased after a man on horseback, attacked him, took his rifle, and saved a sheepherder." She sat on one of the cut-off logs by the dead campfire and helped herself to a slab of ham and slapped it between two slices of bread. "My work," she said as she chewed, "will bring people out West. They'll tame this place, obviously something you men haven't been able to do."

The sheriff ruminated on his own sandwich. "The wild in men, no one will tame. And it will be sorry for all of us if the animals and wild spaces be tamed."

Alphonso sat between them, looking from one to the other. He and the sheriff shared the square body build, but otherwise, they appeared worlds apart. Charlie's features already had taken on town proportions and his dress was modern — khaki pants tucked into polished black boots, a short brown leather jacket over a collared shirt. The sheepherder's worn Levi's and scuffed boots, the poncho affair he wore as a shirt and that exposed the sides of his chest, his brush of black hair standing almost on end, and his skin, darkened already by the sun, made him seem part of the land and the wild spaces.

"What did Tanner say?"

"That we were on the cattle allotment, but I haven't seen any fences. He lassoed the lead sheep and dragged it, breaking its neck, I think. Moonie jumped him and when they both fell to the ground, I grabbed the rifle. He tricked me, took it, and pointed

101

it at Alphonso." Nellie wished there were a more heroic way of describing what had happened. "He said he wouldn't kill a man. Someone beat up Alphonso yesterday. I accused him, but he said not."

When Nellie stopped talking, the sheriff nodded his head. "Rough bunch of cowboys." He stood and walked over to the grave. "I'll need to dig the body up. Why don't you go watch sheep or take a walk."

"Why don't you go after those cowboys?"

"I'm not here to find sheep killers. And Alphonso said the sheep had been scattered into the cattle allotment. Tanner may be a good-for-nothing cowpoke, but I doubt he's a killer, or would beat up on a sheepherder. Killing a ewe is more his style." He motioned to Alphonso, saying something in their mutual language. Alphonso took a shovel from his wagon and began to unearth the dead Basque sheepherder.

Nellie felt trapped. She didn't want to see the dead body again, but she also didn't want to appear squeamish. She clutched her cup and began walking up the track in the direction of the sheep, then turned. "But where is the cattle allotment? Why didn't I see it?"

The sheriff had been watching her. "See any stone piles? Marks on trees or rocks?"

"There are stone piles everywhere." She shook her head and began walking again, aware of his eyes, studying her. But when she chanced a glance back to the camp, he and Alphonso both worked over the grave.

Sheep, unlike cattle, flock together. Moonshine had remained with the men, but she found one of the sheep dogs resting in the shade of several aspen trees, keeping his eye on his charges. She joined him and rested her back against a tall rock. She felt wrenched with the emotions of the last few days: fear, anger, scorn. Life in Chicago, working at the portrait studio, had contained nothing like this. A tedious schedule, day after day, with hours spent posing people and pretending to be happy and smiling, had ground her down. Only the time in the darkroom seemed worthwhile. When the head of the studio accused her of taking credit for one of his photos — a photo that *she* had taken — he had fired her. Her mother and one or two friends tried their best to marry her off. She would have none of it. The tedium of the studio would only be replaced by the tedium of cooking and keeping house. Her talents lay elsewhere, and she'd make the effort or die trying, she had sworn to herself.

Her daydreams of wandering the west, an

itinerant photographer, taking photos of the stark and beautiful landscape, being acclaimed as a female Alfred Stieglitz, soon shattered on reality. She was not a man. Unlike Edward Curtis, she did not know how to fund expeditions into Indian territory. She knew no other photographers with whom she could work or anyone who would support her ambitions. She was alone and never had she felt it so keenly. Her small portrait studio in Ketchum was successful enough to pay for her board and room, film and chemicals. Her work for Jacob Levine in Twin Falls added a few extra dollars a month. But unless her photographs garnered a favorable reaction from the group in San Francisco, she was still no further ahead with her dreams than if she had stayed in Chicago. And now she was once again mixed up in Idaho mayhem. So far, the only photos people really wanted from her were those of murdered men. Nell Burns, Crime Photographer. This time, she'd send the sheriff a bill.

As if the thought conjured the man, a shadow moved across Nellie, and Charlie Azgo stood above her, Moonshine by his side. How long had he been there? She looked at him. Whatever he was thinking, she could not tell.

"I'm going down to Stanley. Do you want to come with me?"

Nellie scrambled to her feet. "What would I do there?"

"What you do everywhere else. Take photographs."

"Of what?" What a stupid question.

"You are the expert. Not I. If you want landscape, you will have the whole reach of the Sawtooths. But you might also want to photograph a small western town for your railroad. Western sunsets. Cowboys at a bar." His tone was even, but Nellie thought he might be making fun of her once again.

"We met some of your cowboys at Smiley Creek. They looked more like criminals on the run. Them and their stupid dog. He would have killed Moonshine if Gwynn hadn't broken up a fight."

"You named it. Moonshine. The boys at Smiley Creek were more likely moonshiners than cowboys. Tough hombres. They have stills up in these mountains and supply all the towns along the Wood River." He took her arm as if to help her walk back to camp.

Nellie stepped away from Charlie. She didn't need guiding. "Why don't you catch them?"

"I did. Then they moved out of my jurisdiction. Federal marshals will get here one of these days, now that Prohibition is a federal crime. These stills have been in operation one place or another for several years, ever since Idaho went dry. They are well hidden and efficient."

"I should stay here and help Alphonso."

Charlie's deep laugh stung Nellie. "He's been herding sheep many more years than you've been acting like a man. I think he'll get along without you."

"But someone might attack him again." She had felt needed in the sheep camp.

"Then better you are out of the way. I don't think the cowboys will be back. Their point is made. Alphonso will stay in the sheep grazing area. He and I talked."

She wanted to add that Alphonso had promised to make the cowboy pay, and she wanted to be there when he did. This was not something the sheriff would understand, she was sure. "Can I come back?"

"Gwynn must make that decision. It is his sheep outfit."

"When will we go?"

"Tomorrow at first light. Alphonso is cooking up the ewe and we will have a big dinner tonight. He wanted to thank you for your help and company."

Somewhat gratified, Nellie agreed to accompany the sheriff to Stanley, but first she negotiated a return to Galena for her own automobile. She was curious to see what he had described. Back at camp, though, she waited for Alphonso to return from the sheep. She had something to say to him.

While Alphonso cooked, the sheriff loaded Domingo into his auto, in back. Nellie entered the camp. "Can I help you?" The sheepherder grinned at her and shook his head. She lowered her voice.

" 'Cowman pay' you said. When? I want to go with you." She touched her chest and then touched Alphonso. " 'Cowman pay.' We go?"

Alphonso craned his neck around Nellie to see what the sheriff was doing. He was not paying them any attention. Then he touched his own chest and then Nellie's shoulder. "Cowman pay." He motioned eating, pointed up the draw toward where the sheep were, and said, "Two horses. You. Alphonso."

Satisfied that he had a plan in mind, Nellie nodded. "After dinner, you and I will take our horses to the sheep. Then the cowman will pay." She stuck out her hand. Alphonso took it. "Deal," she said, not knowing how they would do this without the sheriff coming with them. But then, he had shown no interest in the sheep at all,

107

and there was no extra horse.

After a fine meal of stewed mutton with garlic, sage, wild onions, and bread and wine, Alphonso said something to Charlie and retrieved his horse and Nellie's from a grassy patch near the creek. He motioned to Nellie to accompany him.

"We're going to check on the sheep," Nellie said. "A last look around for me. Would you keep Moonshine here? He bothers the sheep dogs." Her words were unnecessary and made the sheriff look up. "I'll pack up my gear when we get back." Button your lip, she told herself, but failed. "Don't worry. We won't be long." He said nothing in return, just waved slightly as they passed him.

Nellie mounted from a log Alphonso had dragged near the camp for that purpose, and the two of them rode slowly up the track and around the bend. The sheepherder grinned at her, his teeth even whiter in the evening light. It was at least another hour before dusk would deepen to darkness. He picked up the pace and Nellie's horse followed. The sheep grazed in a dell above an aspen stand. Both dogs patrolled the edge of the flock. Soon the sheep were behind and the two horses climbed a ridge, trotted up a gully, and then climbed two more hills.

Before they crested, Alphonso stopped, motioned for Nellie to be quiet, dismounted, and crept to the ridge to look down the other side. In the evening hush, she could hear the faint lowing of cattle.

"What did you see?" she asked in a whisper. She never knew how much of what she said he understood. "What are we going to do?"

"Cattle. Cowmans." He held up two fingers. He pointed to himself and motioned with his hand that he would go up the crest and down again. He pointed to Nellie and motioned for her to dismount, follow him going up, but then held his hand up. Clearly, she was not to do whatever he did when he went down the other side.

"What are you going to do? Maybe we should return. The sheriff . . ." But Alphonso was already leading his horse toward the crest. If Nellie dismounted, she knew now she could remount by herself, not easily but she could do it. If she stayed astride, she would be clearly outlined against the sky. She didn't want to spoil Alphonso's plan or endanger him. Neither did she intend to miss anything. She dismounted. She'd do whatever Alphonso did.

Their movements were not quiet. The horses' shoes clomped and struck rocks.

Nellie tripped once and swore, but she was certain the cattle on the other side of the hill would cover up any noises the two of them made. At the crest, Alphonso moved quickly, over and down. She followed his example, hoping the two cowboys had not seen them on the skyline. The sheep herder motioned for her to stop. He remounted and headed away from her.

In a wide flat gully, a herd of cattle moved leisurely with two riders, one on either side. The twilight was much deeper where they were and Nell could not identify either man, although one's head was almost on his chest. Coyotes were less of a menace to cattle because of their size. Here and there, she could pick out smaller animals, calves or heifers, that might be vulnerable. Nowhere could she see a stack of rocks either as markers to grazing allotment or as help for remounting. She held the reins on the saddle horn, placed her foot in the stirrup, and, with a giant heave, swung herself up and into the saddle. Without a camera on her back, it was easy.

"Ai-ee-ee-ea-aa-aa!" The ear-splitting war cry made her jump. Clearly, it came from Alphonso. He called again, as he slapped his horse's rear. "Ai-ee-ee-ee-ea-aa-aa!"

The cry reverberated inside Nell and

chilled her blood. The one cowboy's head snapped up. The heads of the steers moved up and around, their eyes white. Then they began to move. Her own horse skittered sideways, but she had a firm hold on the reins. "It's all right," she mouthed.

"Ai-ee-ea-aa-aa!" Alphonso cantered toward the herd, his horse sure-footed, his cry continuing. The cattle gathered speed. Their hooves began to pound and Nellie felt the vibration through her horse. She wanted to join in; instead, she watched, her heart racing with the sheepherder until the cattle flowed around a bend in the gully. A last scream echoed in the sky, sharp and keen as a hawk's cry.

Nellie waited, fearing for Alphonso, but knowing they had their revenge. The cows would run for miles, losing weight. By the time she heard a rider, darkness surrounded her. Just as he reached her, a full moon began to ascend behind him. "You were wonderful, Alphonso."

"*Irrintzi,*" he said, then, in a muted voice, called "Aa-ee-ea-aa" again. "*Irrintzi!*" He was as pleased with himself as she was with him.

Together they rode back to the sheep. With a short whistle, Alphonso commanded the dogs to herd the band back down the draw.

When they arrived at the camp, the sheriff

sat by a small fire. All the sheep camp's gear had disappeared. "Ah, success, I see."

By the moonlight and firelight, Nellie saw him grin. He knew what they had done.

"Now, I'm ready to leave," she announced. "Unless Alphonso is in danger."

"No sleep tonight," the sheriff said by way of an answer. "We pack up and help him move camp. Take down your tent, pack your gear in the auto, and we'll hitch the horses to the wagon."

Nellie was not particularly fast at taking down her tent, but she finally had it rolled with the stakes inside into a decent-sized mound of canvas. Her camera gear took little time. Cramming everything into the auto was more difficult. By the time she finished, the two men were ready to move. "Now what?"

"Ready for walking?"

She wasn't, but didn't say so. "What about the . . . Domingo?" She gestured toward where the sheepherder had been buried.

"I took the body to Stanley while you and Alphonso were chasing cattle." His teeth gleamed in a smile. "We're following Alphonso for a while. We've got to bring down that horse Gwynn borrowed for you. The auto will go a little farther, but not much. You start out with Alphonso. I'll finish up

112

around here and catch up."

The night stretched out until Nellie wondered if it would ever end. When the moon set, she was so tired she thought she could fall asleep walking, until she stumbled and fell three times in half an hour. Charlie insisted she climb into the wagon and sleep. She refused, but she made Moonshine climb in to sleep. With the sheriff's going and coming, he must be as tired as she, and if the men could do it, so could she. At last, Charlie called to Alphonso. They talked a few minutes and then released the horses from the hitch. The saddles had been strapped to the back of the wagon, but the sheriff made no move to retrieve one. With a small motion, he mounted the horse Nellie had been using. Then he reached his arm down to her. "Climb up behind me. We'll ride back to the old camp and head out from there."

Nellie had never ridden bareback on a horse. She called for Moonshine, and with Alphonso's help, her leg slipped easily over the haunch and all of her slid into the sheriff from behind. Her arms felt like useless appendages, ones she was reluctant to use. She waved them helplessly and finally settled on holding on to Charlie's coat on either side, like handles. "Wrap them around me, or you'll fall. We will move faster than a gentlemanly walk." He kicked the horse, and indeed, if she hadn't wrapped her hands around his waist, she would have slid off.

"Goodbye, Alphonso." Her legs swung loosely until she gripped the horse lightly, hoping the horse wouldn't take that as a signal to go faster. Moonshine trotted along with them. "What does *irrintzi* mean?" All through the night, none of the three had spoken of Alphonso's and Nell's errand.

"War cry."

She waited for the sheriff to say something more, but he concentrated on finding their way back down the mountain. The motion of the horse felt different, so close to her skin. She finally relaxed and let her body sway with it, and with her head rested on the rider's broad back, she fell asleep.

CHAPTER 5

While Lulu waited on a group of tourists who had appeared in three cars in the late morning, she noticed Sheriff Azgo's auto drive up to the lodge. He wasn't alone, but she was surprised to see that photographer woman, Nell Burns, climb out on the right side, which reminded her of the Oldsmobile parked in the corral behind the store. Where had she put the key? The two saw Lulu was busy, and sat down in the willow chairs along the front. Lulu waved and called, "Be right with you."

Two of the men tourists left with ten-gallon hats on their heads, along with the fixings for a large picnic. The women, in dresses and fancy hats, looked as if they wouldn't be able to walk ten feet off a sidewalk in their town shoes with heels. Her sales patter about cowboy boots hadn't been successful with them, but the third man had bitten. Lulu figured by the time they all returned from their trip over Galena Pass and a picnic near one of the lakes, one or two others would be ready to buy. Their autos were the latest models and should have little trouble climbing over the Pass. Nevertheless, she had warned them to back the cars to the top. They decided to leave one auto with her and pack all six people into two.

"Good morning, Miss Burns. You look all done up. Can I get you something? Maybe a seltzer to drink?"

Nellie thanked Lulu and then asked about her Oldsmobile. "Moonie and I are going to take it back to Stanley with me, so I can leave when I want. Sheriff Azgo and I are meeting up with Gwynn Campbell. We had trouble in the sheep camp." She looked at the sheriff who had made a small motion with one hand.

"I already heard," Lulu said. "Word gets around. One of the cowboys with the dudes said a man was killed — Domingo. I was sorry to hear that. Domingo didn't deserve that kind of end, even if he was a drinker and not so reliable."

Sheriff Azgo leaned forward. "What else did you hear, Lulu? You know more about what happens in the Basin than most of the people there."

"Not much else. I think the Wild West dude stuff might calm the other rowls down. No one wants to scare off tourists, except maybe the moonshiners. And they're not so smart. The more visitors, the more liquor they'll sell. I'll get you two something to drink." Lulu went into the store and came out with two seltzers. The sheriff refused one and so she drank from it herself and sat down on the porch railing. "Those dudes had a wet couple of nights up there. Came back early looking like drowned rats. I don't think they'll be back. That second bunch that went up with Joe had a better time of it after they went through Smiley Creek. Them moonshiners are gonna scare off the trade, I'm thinking. Mean bunch."

"Their dog almost killed Moonshine," Nellie said. "Omigosh. Poor dog. I better let him out. He's been cooped up too long." She dashed off the porch and opened the rear door of the sheriff's automobile. Moonshine jumped out, sniffed the ground, and headed for the corral area.

Lulu asked the sheriff what he was doing there.

"Gwynn Campbell telephoned from Stanley, asked if I could investigate. There's no law officer in Custer County these days, not since the last one disappeared in the winter.

He thinks one of the cowboys killed Domingo, trying to scare sheep outfitters from their grazing territory."

"What do you think?"

Nellie joined them again on the porch. "About what?"

"About cowboys cutting up rough in the grazing areas."

Nellie glanced again at the sheriff. "I think a cowboy named Ned Tanner did all the dirty work up there. I saw him lasso and kill a sheep. He threatened me and Alphonso." She sat down, as if her legs wouldn't hold her up, and took a long drink from the seltzer bottle. "The sheriff disagrees with me."

"I wouldn't think Tanner had it in him to do something like that," Lulu said. She knew the cowboy. He was a handsome devil, but curious-looking, too, with those mismatched eyes. "And the rest of the cowboys, they're not mean, just ornery when it comes to sheep." She stood up. "I'll get your key, Miss Burns."

"What do I owe you?" The worried look on her face told Lulu that the young woman hoped not much.

"Nothing. I didn't need the space for anything else." Nellie's look of relief confirmed Lulu's suspicion. "Do you need

118

anything to take back with you to Stanley? That may be a town in some people's opinion, but I call it a bunch of log lean-tos around a saloon. One that ain't supposed to be serving whiskey, but does." She turned to the sheriff. "How come nobody enforces the law up that way?"

"I told you — no lawman."

"No, it's because those moonshiners done away with the lawman, and the saloons down in Ketchum and Hailey still need their supply of liquor. You better be careful up there, Charlie. You might disappear, too. There ain't nothing quite so powerful as a moonshiner with some money behind him somewhere. Arrogant sons of guns too." She turned back to Nell. "And I'd not stop at Smiley Creek again. They got no respect for a woman there at all. It might be better at Stanley, but you should stick with Charlie here, or Gwynn. Won't nobody bother you with them along. But alone? Don't think I'd do it, and I'm no shrinking violet."

Inside the store, Nellie whispered to Lulu. "Do you have a gun I could buy?"

"Do you know how to shoot one?" Something more must have happened in the high country than Lulu had heard. "If you have one and ain't willing to use it, or don't know how, you're in more danger than if you don't have one."

"I'd be willing to use it." The hesitancy in the other woman's voice told Lulu all she needed to know.

"No guns here. You'd have to go back to Ketchum to Jack Lane's." Lulu opened the drawer in the counter and felt around for the key. She'd remembered while she was sitting on the porch. "Here you go. Do you need gasoline? I'll fill you up. You better back up the Pass too. That's an old rig there, although I think Rosy took pretty good care of it until he began drinking again." She shook her head. "He used to drive up here just to shoot the breeze with me. He was lonely after Lily died." Two lonely souls, Lulu thought to herself, wondering, not for the first time, if she could have done something about Rosy's drinking. Likely not.

While she filled up the gasoline tank on the Oldsmobile and checked the level of oil, she watched Nellie and Sheriff Azgo. They argued over something next to his auto. Even so, she thought there was an understanding of some sort between them, even if they didn't know it themselves. Sheriff Azgo was a courteous man, but his attention to Nellie went beyond courtesy. Lulu had never known him to work other than alone, and taking a young, good-looking woman

120

with him on an investigation was unheard of. Still, this woman was determined. Lulu had seen that from the beginning, although she wasn't sure just where that determination was headed.

"Your car's ready," Lulu called.

Nellie's face was red. "He doesn't think I can back it up the road, so I'm going to drive his auto to the top and he'll follow with mine." She leaned close to Lulu. "He's probably right. I just learned to drive this past winter and I've not had to back up often. Just once, though, I'd like to prove him wrong."

Lulu reached out to take Nellie's hand. "Don't let him rile you, Miss Burns. He's an old hand around here and you aren't." She squeezed. "But I know what you mean. Most men think women are helpless, scared of mice, and just want someone strong to carry them off. I ain't that way, and I can see you ain't, either."

After Nellie drove off in the sheriff's auto, Lulu stopped Charlie as he was climbing into the Oldsmobile. "Don't you treat her as if she was some pussyfootin' easterner. That girl has heart." She smiled. "Or do you know that already?"

"Courage is what she has, but also she is foolhardy. The Basin is not a safe place these days. You are close to civilization here," he said, nodding to the store. "There, telling the difference between coyotes and men is not always easy. Miss Burns does not have enough practice." Lulu swore the sheriff blushed when he said Nellie Burns's name, but his skin was dark and she could have been mistaken.

At the pull-out on the other side of Galena Pass, Nellie stopped and climbed out to take in the panorama again. The sun sloped down to the Sawtooth ridge and its light reflected off the headwaters of the Salmon River below. She knew talking the sheriff into helping her retrieve her auto had angered him, but she wanted her freedom in the Basin. Also, she worried her presence might hamper him. And his might get in her way. He was so . . . so nursemaid-y around her. Below the edge of the road, she heard a meadowlark in the grass. Its warbling was joyful, and Nellie felt her own breast swell with the sound and the summer day's warmth.

A paneled truck held together with wire and rope pulled off the road and stopped next to her and the driver leaned out his window. "Trouble?" He was unshaven, and his one-word question was surrounded by the odor of alcohol. His dog sat on the seat beside him.

"No, I'm fine, thank you. I was just enjoying the beauty of the mountains."

The dog growled and Nellie looked more closely. It lunged across the man and tried to leap from the cab.

"Shut up, you hound dog! This here's a lady." The man jerked the dog back hard enough to make it yelp. "Say, ain't I seen you before?"

His breath was so intoxicating, Nellie stepped back. Had he been one of the men at Smiley Creek? "Perhaps . . . at Smiley Creek a week or so ago." She wished she'd said no.

"Oh yeah. That black cur of yours attacked Cowpie, my friend's dog. Bled for two days." A scowl darkened the man's face. "You oughta keep him tied up better."

"I!" Nellie wanted to spit in his face. "That dog attacked mine!"

"You alone up here?" His voice changed abruptly from accusing to leering. He winked, or blinked, she wasn't sure which. "No place for a little lady. Never know who might come along." He stepped out of his truck. The automobile door groaned as it opened. "Some men might take advantage —"

Nellie stepped back again, her eye on the dog. She could handle the man. That animal was another thing. Its light blue eyes looked part wolf. It made to follow its master and her stomach squeezed.

"Don't be scared now. All I want is a little smooch." The man grabbed her shoulder and pulled Nellie toward him. He smelled of dirty clothes and old tobacco along with the liquor, and as he moved in close, she saw white spittle in the corners of his mouth. Still, the teeth of the dog as it snarled scared her more.

"Let me go!" Nellie lifted her boot and stomped on the man's foot. At the same time, she shoved on his face, feeling the whiskers with her fingers and the sweat on his neck as her hand slid across his throat.

"Owww! You little witch!" He'd fallen back two steps but lunged for her, his arms stretched out, his hands grasping for her neck. His dog jumped from the cab and headed straight for Nellie, the growl in its throat as wild as anything she'd ever heard.

Before she could swing her leg to kick at the dog, he'd tangled himself in his master's legs and they both tumbled to the ground. Nellie opened the door of the sheriff's auto and jumped in on the passenger side, slamming it behind her. The wild dog was on its feet again and smashed against the auto, barking and clawing as if it would force its way in after her. She was sorry she had left Moonie in her Oldsmobile, but maybe not. This dog would kill hers.

Charlie must have a gun! She searched the box in the dashboard. Nothing but two papers. She turned around and glanced across the back bench seat. His coat and a leather satchel rested at one end. She grabbed the coat, felt for some kind of weapon, found nothing, pulled the satchel toward her, and a revolver with a brown handle and blue-black in color slid out and onto the floor.

The wolf-dog scraped at the window and the man had recovered his feet. Anger reddened his features and his snarl was as wide-mouthed as the animal's. The only difference was his teeth weren't pointed. They were rotten. He grabbed at the door handle, twisted, and pulled. At the same time the door opened, Nellie brought the revolver around and pointed it.

"Get away from me! And take that wolf with you." Her voice sounded as panicked as she felt. But she knew one thing. She would use the gun. She lowered the muzzle until it aimed right at his genitals. "And I'll shoot this right where it's pointing if you put one hand on me."

The man had been about to grab at the gun but stopped short. "Now, now. You don't want to do that." He backed up. His dog growled low and crouched, ready to spring at Nellie.

"If that wolf so much as moves a whisker in my direction, I'll still shoot you." The gun didn't waver in her hand.

"C'mon, Wolf. Down." The last word was an order and the dog turned to his master as if to verify something it couldn't believe. "Down." The man backed up again. "Now, lady, I didn't mean nothin'. Just a little tomfoolery." He bumped against his truck and opened the door. A short, sharp whistle called his dog to him. They both climbed in and the man pulled the door shut. He leaned out toward Nellie. "Next time, witch." His engine coughed, and he drove away.

Nellie trembled as she slipped the gun back in the satchel and returned it and the coat to the bench seat. The wild honk of a horn brought her attention back to the road up which she'd come. She stepped out of the auto again and went to the edge of the turn-out. Her own Oldsmobile put-putted around the bend and into sight, tail end first.

"Blasted drunk," Charlie muttered as he jumped from the driver's side.

Nellie had never heard him swear before. She laughed, realized she sounded half-hysterical, and forced herself to stop. "If you'd enforce the liquor laws, then maybe the roads wouldn't be dangerous with drunken drivers."

"Did he trouble you? He looked like a bull who had tangled with a red flag."

"Just call me Red," Nellie said, speaking as lightly as she could. Her insides still squished around like gelatin, and she had an urgent need to relieve herself.

Charlie stopped short. "He did trouble you. That man is a moonshiner. Wolfman Pitts, because of the animal he keeps — part wolf, part hound. You do not want a run-in with him."

"Indeed, I didn't. But I managed." She dusted off her pants. "Um, I need to visit a bush. Could you wait here for a moment?" Without waiting for him to answer, Nellie crossed the road and climbed up the short bluff. Any other time, she would have been too embarrassed to acknowledge she had any bodily need at all, let alone needing to urinate. She found a place, took several deep breaths, made certain she was out of sight, and squatted, being careful to keep her pants out of the way. By the time she returned, the sheriff was sitting in his car, its motor turned on. She wondered if he were embarrassed. He leaned out his window. "I plan to stop at Smiley Creek, ask a few questions. Just continue on this road and it will lead you to Stanley. I should be there an hour or so after you arrive. Gwynn will be at the main store. It used to be a saloon. You can't miss it."

Moonshine waited in the Oldsmobile for Nellie. "I'm not getting separated from you again." She climbed in and waited for the sheriff to lead the way. The dog clambered over the seat and sat upright beside her. Without him, she had been vulnerable, but he might have been killed by the wolf dog.

The town of Stanley fit Lulu's description to a tee: a row of log lean-tos and ramshackle out-buildings. The only structure that looked habitable was the saloon. Even the sign painted in large, uneven red letters remained, in defiance of all authority. The entire scene composed the kind of Wild West photograph she thought the railroad man would love.

The day was three-quarters spent with coming down from the camp, driving to Galena Store and back, but a second wind and the fresh mountain air energized Nellie. With relief, she saw Gwynn's pickup at the end of a line of Model Ts. The sun was at the right angle, the time of afternoon in the summer when ridges backed one another like glass in an art deco lamp. Her news for the sheep man could wait. It was all bad, anyway.

While Nellie again assembled her gear, a woman strolled onto the porch of the saloon, glass in hand. It was the same woman in the auto at Lulu's. Her profile would lend elegance to a picture, although her clothes might not. Her shirtwaist and skirt were rumpled but still looked too modern, too short, for an old-fashioned photo. Then she sat on the rail and a slit in the skirt bared her leg to the middle of her thigh, showing pale skin. A dance hall girl, Nellie thought.

"Do you mind if I photograph you, Miss — ?"

The sullen cast on the woman's face brightened. "Pearl. That's my name. Do I get a copy?" She stood up and walked closer. Her voice was almost as deep as a man's, but she minced, as if unused to the high heels on her shoes.

"No, stay where you were. And yes, you'll get a copy." Nellie adjusted the camera on

129

the tripod. "I'm Nellie Burns. My studio is in Ketchum."

When Pearl sat, it was with more modesty, her hands, like two small birds resting, holding her skirt together. "Like this?" She smiled wide, showing small, crowded teeth. The expression was as unnatural as a painted doll's face.

"The way you were before was better. More like a true western scene. Maybe you should look up that way, as if you were waiting for your cowboy to ride home." Nellie pointed toward the saw teeth of the mountains, catching her breath at the rugged beauty. She ducked under her black cloth to focus the lens.

Pearl did as requested, letting the split of her skirt open to reveal her leg again, tilting her head up and turning it to the western sky. She held her hand against her heart, as if it ached, and closed her lips over her teeth. "Like this?"

"Perfect. Hold it." Nellie held her breath and took the photo. "One more?"

"Sure. This is fun. I feel like a movie actress."

If it weren't for her teeth, Pearl could have passed for a movie star. She didn't look as innocent as Mary Pickford nor as seductive as Clara Bow, but her profile could have walked onto an Egyptian set and been right at home with sphinxes and pyramids and Valentino. Nellie replaced the first dark slide and turned the film carrier over, then removed the second dark slide. For the second photo, Pearl leaned forward across the porch railing with her arm outstretched as if she were waving goodbye. Nellie released the shutter. The saloon door opened and a man with coffee-ground stubble on his face, a handlebar mustache, and wearing a dirty apron wrapped around what looked like a sack of rocks stepped out.

"Get in here, Pearl. Customers are thirsty." He turned to Nellie. "Who are you? Pearl works for me. You want pictures of her — do it when she ain't busy." He stomped back in.

Pearl followed his instructions, just as she had followed Nell's, but at the doorway, she executed a graceful two-step, glanced back, and winked.

Nellie folded up her camera and tripod and followed the two into the saloon. Total black met her until her eyes adjusted. Along the left wall was a long bar made of split timbers and varnished so thick and shiny it might have been glass instead of wood. Backless stools were mostly filled with rough-looking men, their faces shadowed from several days' growth of beard, their clothes dusty, and their boots worn from age if nothing else. Two of the men were young with only downy hair on their chins. Tables filled a large space to the right and at one of them sat Gwynn, deep in conversation with another man, the only one in the room who looked as if he had bathed in days. The man's salt-and-pepper hair was neatly combed and his face, anchored by a clean-shaven square jaw below a forehead that verged on being too narrow, was shaped like a pear. His clothes were black but clean and he wore a belt with a large silver buckle. All this Nellie took in with her photographer's eye in a few seconds. On black boots, he wore spurs, which made Nellie smile. No cowboy she'd seen yet had worn spurs. This man must be a dude.

Gwynn saw her and stood up as she made her way to the table, carrying her equipment. "Lassie, how'd you get here?" He held out a chair for her and placed her camera gear on the fourth chair. "Meet Cable O'Donnell." The dude stood with a grace that his age and size belied. He was the tallest man Nell had ever seen. She came to the middle of his chest. "This is Nellie Burns, Photographer," Gwynn said.

"How do you do?" Nellie said, extending

her hand. Mr. O'Donnell, instead of extending his own, took hold of hers as if to kiss it. Nellie quickly retracted it, embarrassed, and sat down. Gwynn grinned at her, apparently pleased with her discomfiture.

"Nellie's new to the West, Cabe, not used to courtly ways. She's from Chicago where all them gangsters live."

Nellie wanted to kick him under the table but forced a laugh instead. "Nice to meet you, Mr. O'Donnell. Indeed, I am not used to such good manners. I've been spending my time with sheepherders and fighting with cowboys. The cowboys in particular have shown evidence of no manners at all."

What had been a slight smile on Mr. O'Donnell's face dropped away. He sat down and she saw that his face was as pale as any woman's who had never been outdoors, and that his eyebrows cut across above his eyes in a salt-and-pepper line. "Have my cowboys been bothering you, Miss Burns? If they have, I'll see they pay for it." His voice was soft, with a dead quality to it because of the lack of any inflection.

"Oh, they have," she answered, then turned to Gwynn. "Alphonso is fine. So are the sheep. Sheriff Azgo came up yesterday to begin his investigation, and he took me

133

to gather up my automobile this morning. He'll be along shortly." If Lulu knew of Domingo's death, then so did everyone else. "My cowboys" could only mean that this man owned the cattle being herded up Fourth of July Creek. Nell wondered how many of the cowboys at the bar worked for him, too. Although most of them had turned when she walked into the room, they no longer paid her any attention.

Pearl sidled up. "Drink, Miss?"

Mr. O'Donnell began to say something to Pearl and Nellie interrupted him. "Yes, Pearl, I would like a seltzer please, if you have one. Also, I'm hungry. Do you serve food?" She had noticed shot glasses in front of the two men. She smiled at Mr. O'Donnell.

"Sorry, Lassie, I should have ordered for you. How about a steak? I bet you're full up to your back teeth with mutton." Gwynn motioned for Pearl to bring food to all three of them. "And bring some of that rotgut wine back with you and two glasses. If you'd order in some Basque wine, it'd be better for everybody." When she left, he turned to O'Donnell and continued. "I figure you only drink whiskey, Cabe." He laughed.

"What was Azgo doing at your sheep camp, Gwynn? He belongs in Blaine

134

County, not Custer." He picked up a bottle from the floor and splashed liquid into his shot glass and Gwynn's. "I don't want him snooping around in my country."

"You ain't got nothing to worry about, Cable, unless you killed my sheepherder," Gwynn said. No laughter softened his words this time.

"I'm not worried. He's the one who should be. A strange lawman in these parts might provoke some of the . . . residents." Again, that flat voice, cold and menacing.

"Did Azgo find anything worth talkin' about?" Gwynn asked Nell.

Even if the sheriff had found the killer, she wasn't certain she'd say anything in front of the cattle man. "Not that I know of. He keeps to himself." She almost added, "as you know." She would tell Gwynn about the other troubles — the tearing up of the camp, Alphonso's apparent tussle with someone, and the moving of the camp — for later. She leaned forward. "Do you know Pearl? Isn't she stunning? Why is she working here?" She didn't mean to sound snobbish but realized that was how her words could be interpreted. "Not that here isn't as good as any other place, but with her looks, she could be a magazine model or movie star."

"Some folks don't think a woman should get above her station in life," Mr. O'Donnell said.

"Oh, and that would be . . . ?"

"Takin' care of her husband and children." O'Connell's bland expression dropped for the barest of moments, becoming hard and bony. He forced a sham laugh and a smile.

"Is she married?"

Gwynn interrupted. "Not so's you could tell. Goodlight is supposed to be her husband from what I've heard. But that cowboy Tanner hangs around a lot. I even seen her goin' up to that dude campout a couple weeks ago, said she was takin' up some 'entertainment.' They're thick as thieves if you ask me."

The subject of their conversation arrived with plates filled with food — steak, bread, and beans. She took bottles of sauce from her apron pocket and plopped them on the table. "Anything else?"

"Don't forget the wine," Gwynn said. He kept his head low.

Her interruption gave Nellie a chance to hide her feelings. Knowing Pearl and Tanner were an item disturbed her, maybe only because she herself had been attracted to the man. She would have thought his depredation of the sheep camp and the ewe had

136

destroyed any attraction she might have felt. Apparently, it hadn't. Nor had her friendship with the sheriff kept her from some dreamy speculation about living on a ranch, with both cattle and sheep. In one short space, she had learned Ned Tanner didn't own the cattle he was herding and he was having some sort of affair with a bar girl, a married one at that. Nell looked for a wedding ring on Pearl's hand and saw nothing on her left hand. Her right one carried a band with her namesake — a round, creamy pearl mounted between two green stones. Were they emeralds? An expensive piece of jewelry.

"Your ring is quite lovely," Nellie said to Pearl before she could walk away.

"Yeah?" Pearl lifted her hand to show it off better. "That's a pearl. A friend gave it to me." She studied it herself. "Those are emeralds, to match my eyes."

Nell looked at Pearl. She wasn't sure she'd call the waitress's eyes green. They were more like Nell's own, hazel. Perhaps they changed too with what she wore or depending on the weather.

"I've seen Mr. Goodlight several times since we ran into each other at Lulu's store," Nell said, "where I first saw you."

Both Mr. O'Donnell and Pearl sharpened

137

their attention to Nell.

"He was at the Smiley Creek store, then with a group of campers and then with Ned Tanner and some cattle. He certainly has a lot of different jobs, it seems."

Did Nell imagine it, or did Mr. O'Donnell's interest wane immediately? Pearl's didn't.

"I wondered where he'd gotten to. He was supposed to come home that very night after I dropped him at the store, said he'd catch a ride with someone else after he took care of some business." She turned to go, then came back. "I'm surprised he was with Ned. They don't get along too well. Still, money's money." She shrugged and left them.

Her absence left a gap of silence at the table. Gwynn filled it with some sheep stories, but both Mr. O'Donnell and Nellie had little to say as they concentrated on eating the food in front of them, notable only for lack of taste. Nell preferred the generously herbed and spiced mutton. She mulled over the words "come home." Surely that meant Pearl and Goodlight were married? And that she was just friends with Ned Tanner, that good-for-nothing cowboy.

By the time they finished eating, Sheriff Azgo still had not arrived. O'Donnell took

138

his leave, lifting Nellie's hand once more, not shaking it, and telling Gwynn to stay in touch. They had common business interests. He stopped to talk with Pearl on his way out. Nellie watched. The man said several sentences. A brief splotch of color burned in Pearl's cheeks, and then she said something back, shaking her head and lifting her chin. The cattle man briefly responded, and Pearl's face turned pale as her name. She kept her mouth shut, turned, and walked away.

"I wonder what that was about," Gwynn said.

"Maybe it had to do with what you mentioned — Pearl and Ned Tanner being thick as thieves." She told Gwynn about meeting Tanner on the trail with the cattle, the mess she'd found at the camp, and what she and Alphonso had done. "Maybe Tanner was stealing those animals."

Gwynn laughed out loud. "Wish I'd a been there, Lassie. No, Tanner works for O'Donnell. I didn't know Goodlight did. That's interesting, too. Goodlight moonshines up one of those draws, I'd swear on a Bible. Never been caught, but I've seen him cartin' sugar out of the Galena Store more than once." He plunked some cash on the table and stood up. "Where's Charlie Azgo?"

"I'd like to take a photo or two in here. Do you suppose that bartender would mind?"

"Doubt it. I'll go talk to him. That's Sam. He's a good ole boy. Crooked as the day is long, but otherwise, not too bad." Gwynn strode to the bar, his head half obscured by a layer of blue cigarette smoke, and had a word, then motioned for Nell to join him. "This here's my friend Nellie Burns, Sam. You don't mind if she takes a few pictures of your bar, do you? Might make you famous back East. She's doin' a big job for the railroad."

The bartender still looked ornery, and his long handlebar mustache gave him a slightly evil countenance, but he nodded his head. "Fine with me. I could use more business, payin' business." He scanned the group of cowboys at the bar with a small sneer on his lips. "Hey, Pearl. Get out here."

Nell jumped at his shout. Pearl sauntered through the doors from the kitchen. "You call me?"

"This here lady wants to take some pictures of my place. You ain't doin' anything. Give her what she needs." Then he turned to Nellie. "And if you want Pearl in 'em, that's okay, too. Didn't know you was a famous person."

"Thank you." Nell smiled briefly, trying not to laugh. She exchanged a quick glance with Gwynn. His eyes sparkled. The door swung open behind him and she saw the sheriff stop to let his eyes get used to the gloom, too. "You've got company," she said, and headed back to the table to retrieve her camera and tripod. They could sort out all the troubles by themselves.

CHAPTER 6

Late-afternoon light beamed through a dirty window to the left of the bar, lighting several faces, shading others. With the door ajar, more light reflected off the shiny bar surface, so Pearl propped it open, while Nellie situated her back to the window with her camera facing the seated patrons and the barkeep's back. Apparently Sam told the men what she was about because one of them straightened his hat and another twirled the end of his mustache to make it pointier. One fellow at the end of the bar turned in his seat so his face wouldn't be in the photo. Setting up took longer than usual because Nellie wanted as much light directed on the cowboys as possible. She pulled her dark cloth around her head and the camera to focus, then, dissatisfied, folded the cloth over the top and moved the camera, more than once.

The level of light called for a slow shutter

speed, which would mean she might get some motion. The longer she took, the more the men became involved in their own conversations and drinks, which was what she wanted. Pearl became impatient and strolled to the bar to position herself between two of the men. Nellie again viewed the scene through the camera, black cloth blocking out all light around her focus. The bar girl's hand rested on one man's neck in a gesture of familiarity and even affection. The man's profile struck a chord in Nell, but no name surfaced. She concentrated on waiting for the exact moment of maximum light and minimum motion, then released the shutter and moved to yet another position.

In the meantime, she was also aware that the sheriff and Gwynn had seated themselves at the same table where Nell had eaten. Their voices rumbled, but no words were distinct to her. One of the drinking patrons turned his head toward them just as she was going to release the shutter again. "Darn," she whispered to herself, took a deep breath, and waited a moment, but the head didn't swivel back, so she took the photo anyway.

In the doorway, she took up another position, hoping for a different cast of light.

While she was under the black cloth, two sets of boots thunked up to her, so she pulled her head out and grew aware that her hair was messed and that she must look tired. The sheriff and Gwynn stood to her side, trying to see what she was focusing on with her camera. "Do you want through?" These two men together would have made an interesting portrait themselves — one white-haired and aging but still containing a measure of power in his physical stance and strength; the other dark, almost moody, in presence, and straight-backed with a hawk's demeanor, softened for the moment with a hint of a smile in his eyes, if not on his lips.

"In a minute. Finish what you're doing," the sheriff said.

Nell forgot what she was doing when she looked again through the camera, so she stood, released the shutter, and began to close up the tripod, preparatory to moving it again. "Would you two mind if I took your photo outside?" She shrugged, wanting to impart that it wasn't important, which was exactly the opposite of what she felt. "Won't take but a minute, and might fit in with what I'm doing here in Stanley." Then she preceded them out the door, as if their answer was an automatic "yes." When she

144

turned back to see if they were coming, she saw Pearl stumble away from the man she had been fondling as if he had flung her off. She headed for the door into the kitchen.

"We're going down the road a piece, Lassie. Got no time for picture-takin'."

Nell wondered if Gwynn just didn't want to be photographed with the sheriff. In spite of the fact that they shared the love of two boys, no friendship marred their antagonism. "Won't take but a minute," she responded and proceeded to set up her camera again as quickly as possible.

"Where do you want us?" the sheriff asked. "Won't hurt you, Gwynn. We're doing the lady a favor."

"Next to the auto, standing as if you were discussing . . . Domingo's death. I want you serious." Both of their faces hardened and their aura of power evolved into menace. Perfect. "Hold still."

One exposure was all she was allowed. When they climbed into the sheriff's auto, she walked over to it. "Can I come?" The sheriff didn't bother answering. Gwynn leaned forward to talk to her, but the auto began to back up. He opened the window and called, "Be back in an hour or two — give you time to take lots of pictures."

Abandoned outside the saloon, Nellie

looked around. Several log cabins on either side sagged on their underpinnings. Up the street, a clapboard structure that needed a coat of paint and clean windows to appear habitable advertised "Rooms." She hoped that was not the only place to stay. Most of the buildings sported boards across windows and doors, hardly inviting photographs for railroad brochures to attract tourists. She remembered Moonshine was still closed in her own auto and she let him out. He sniffed around and marked territory at what was once a hitching post along the front of the bar. Then he looked inquiringly at Nellie.

"I don't know," she said. "Let's explore." She hoisted her camera bag to her shoulder and carried her tripod over the other shoulder. The mountains looming over town made a picture postcard all their own. If she walked down the road, a photo with log cabins in the foreground and mountains behind would be romantic enough. She debated whether to include the "Saloon" sign, not certain if the railroad man would want to advertise an illegal activity. She decided to take one photo with and one without it. She had plenty of film with her and she expected to be able to charge the railroad for its cost.

Too bad there wasn't a horse around. That would be even more enticing.

As if conjured up by her thought, a horseman clip-clopped around the corner and stopped beside her. His head was right in front of the sun as she peered up to see if he was any one of the horsemen who had passed by the sheep camp. All she could see was his cowboy hat and a shaded face above a red bandana. He might have ridden off of a moving-picture screen. "Oh, you're perfect," Nellie said. "Can you stay right there while I move down a ways to photograph the scene?"

"Didn't think you'd want a sheep-killer in one of your pictures," came the reply. "But sure. My friend Luke can use all the dude tourists he can get. Maybe he'll even pay you for a photo himself."

Nellie's good spirits died away. Ned Tanner. He was like a bad smell, as her mother used to say, turning up everywhere. "Hello, Mr. Tanner." Moonshine barked once, but held his ground next to his mistress. If he remembered attacking the cowboy the day before, he didn't give any sign of it. "The railroad won't know you're a sheep killer," she said, "even if you and I know it." She turned to walk down the street. "Stay right there, please. This will take a moment or two."

The distance of half-a-block away gave her the right perspective, although the term "block" could hardly be applied to the space. There was neither rhyme nor reason to the placement of the cabins and the few other structures. The cowboy sat his horse and rolled a cigarette. He was too far away from her for that detail to turn up in the photo, which Nellie regretted, but she decided to ask him if she could take a close-up as well. Everything about him, from his leather chaps to his tall, lean figure, to his scarf and hat reflected every eastern-er's view of the American cowboy. Too bad he didn't have a Colt .45 slung around his waist. The rifle, sticking up at the back of the saddle, would have to suffice.

The sun was lowering in the sky. The scene was partially backlit and Nellie was worried she would get flare in her lens. An early-morning photo session, with the sun shining directly onto the peaks, would have been more conventional, but less dramatic. When she walked back to the waiting cow-boy, who had been remarkably patient, he had dismounted and sat on a rickety chair by the door of the saloon. "Will you be around in the morning?" she asked.

"Can't get enough of my company, is that it?"

Nellie blushed and cursed herself for doing so. "I'd like another photo with the sunshine directly on the peaks and you, if you'd care to help again. I'll give you copies for your family, or girlfriend, or —" She stopped, remembering Pearl was his rumored girlfriend.

"Sure, I'd be happy to help out a lady."

His "aw shucks" tone irritated her. Maybe one of the cowboys in the bar had a horse available and would cooperate with her. Just before she could say "Never mind," he added, "It'll have to be early, though. I got to get back to the cattle."

That reminded Nellie of her lack of a place to stay, although the sheriff must have had something in mind when he suggested she come to Stanley. Driving all the way back to Galena Store for the night and returning in the morning didn't seem feasible. "Is there a place besides that —" she said and pointed to the "Rooms" sign, "where one can stay the night up here?"

A lazy smile played around Ned Tanner's mouth. "There's the Rocking O bunkhouse, up the road a piece. Only a couple of us there for the night and four or five empty bunks."

She waited. He couldn't be serious.

"And there's an old roadhouse in Lower Stanley, down by the river. It takes paying customers in the summer." He pointed to her auto. "Hop in. I'll tie up my horse and ride with you to show you where it is. We'll be back in two shakes of a cow's tail."

That phrase made her smile. "All right. Let's go. Come on Moonshine. Into the back."

They traveled the quarter mile to the main road and turned north, or left. Nellie hadn't known there was yet another town in this valley, but when she drove up in front of the so-called roadhouse, she saw there was no "town." With fewer buildings than the regular Stanley, it looked even more derelict. Even so, the roadhouse, another log building that had seen better days and probably a number of hard winters, appealed to her more than the "Rooms" place. Inside, the main entry area was filled with overstuffed furniture, which gave it a cramped but also comfortable feel. No one was in the room. Ned followed her in and shouted, "Hey, Beans!"

A small, round man came in through a door along one side. "What can I do you for, Ned? This here another lady friend of yours?"

Nellie watched Ned blush before she answered for herself. "I'm a photographer from Ketchum. I'd like a room for the night."

"Your name Miss Nellie Burns?" The man opened a book on the desk.

Surprised, Nellie responded. "Yes, how did you know?"

"Sheriff stopped in earlier, said you'd need a room for the night, maybe two nights. I already got you signed up. Cabin 4." He turned to a peg board behind him and took down a large piece of bark with the number 4 painted on it.

"Oh." She held out her hand for what she thought was a key. "Cabin 4." She wanted to ask where the sheriff was staying, but didn't. The clerk told her anyway. "Sheriff's in Cabin 3. I gave you the best one. Thought you might like a picture of the river. Plus, you're a woman. It's right underneath the back porch." He came out from behind the desk. "I'll show you."

Her small bag in hand, Nell followed the clerk and Ned Tanner followed Nell. "I have my dog. Will it be all right if he stays with me? He's very well behaved."

The man scratched an itch along his side. "Ain't no dogs allowed." Then he grinned. "Sheriff told me you'd want that. Sure.

Can't nothing hurt these cabins. If they can survive gold prospectors, drunks, cowboys, and other fools, they can survive a dog."

Ned Tanner cleared his throat, but the clerk kept talking. "Only place to get dinner is back at the Saloon. Same with breakfast. All I got is rooms," he said as he opened the door to Cabin 4. As near as Nell could tell, there was no lock and then she realized the piece of bark only carried a number, not a key. She held it up.

"What's this for?"

A loud guffaw exploded from Beans. "Just for show. If you have it, then I know you're in your room. If I have it, I know you're not. We don't lock much around here. When you're inside, you can lower the wood piece here. If you want anything kept safe, you gotta bring it inside to me. And I can't guarantee it 'cause I got work to do." The cabin smelled musty, as if it had been closed for some time. Sounds of water running caused both of them to raise their voices. He crossed the small room with a small bed and a small chair and pulled aside a cotton gingham curtain. "This here's the river."

The rushing sound as they had entered the cabin filled it, but when Beans opened the opposite door, the rushing turned into a roar. The river wasn't two steps away and

152

down about four feet. White water boiled and spray lifted, drawing out any smell from the room. She could easily have decided to step out to see the view and dropped into the water.

"Hope you don't sleepwalk," Beans shouted, and laughed from the belly.

"Will my bag be safe here while I go back to Stanley?" She had to repeat herself before he understood her question. They stepped back in and he closed the door; the water roar dulled.

"Sure, long as it don't hold gold or coins or moonshine. One of them might disappear."

This time, Nellie laughed. "Nope. Just a few clothes. All my treasures are in the auto with Moonshine."

The clerk stopped laughing and stared at her.

"My camera. That's my treasure."

"You're carrying moonshine? Here I thought you was a real lady."

"No! My dog is named Moonshine."

Nell had turned to leave and saw Ned roll his eyes and shake his head at Beans. "Busy night at the old roadhouse, Beans. What's the sheriff doing here? Out of his territory, isn't he?"

"Seems someone got kilt up Fourth of July

Creek. He's in hot pursuit." Beans leered at Ned. "You got any evidence to turn over?" He laughed again and didn't wait for an answer, but scooted out the door.

Alone in the room with the cowboy, Nell felt uncomfortable. Up close, he exuded maleness along with cigarette smoke and a leathery smell. He stood so much taller and broader than when he was safely distant in a saddle. There was also an air about him, as if he were coiled to spring and it might be at her. She'd felt the same kind of threat when setting up her tent at the sheep camp, that something out there would hurt her, but she didn't know what. At the time, she had shrugged it off as her too-active imagination. It was probably just a wild animal, one that wouldn't venture near the camp with its dogs and horses and men. "Well. I'll take you back to the saloon and to your horse."

Ned sat down in the small chair, his knees considerably above his hip line, forcing her to come back. "I'm sorry about the misunderstanding in the mountains, Nell. Sometimes my temper gets the better of me." His grin widened his face and the threatening air disappeared. "After you take more pictures in the morning, how'd you like to go to the Rocking O Ranch and take some of a real western cow ranch?" He held his hat in his hands and circled the brim between his fingers. "The railroad might like that, too. Or Old Man O'Donnell might. He'd pay good."

Whatever anger she still felt dissipated. "All right. Yes, I'd like that very much. Thank you for offering." She didn't know what else to say. "Shall we go back to the saloon?"

"Can I buy you dinner tonight?"

In spite of her softened feeling, she felt pressed by him. "Thank you, no." She turned and placed her bag on the floor near the bed, just now realizing that she was in a bedroom with a strange man. "I think Gwynn Campbell and the sheriff expect me to dine with them." She knew no such thing, but hoped that was the case.

"How about tomorrow night, then, if you're still here?"

Again, the feeling of pressure. "Let's wait and see what tomorrow brings. I may drive back to Ketchum. I have lots of negatives to develop." She moved toward the door, opening it wider and holding it so Ned would go out before she did. She noticed the sun had slipped considerably toward the mountains and sunset wouldn't be long. The long evening twilight presented another opportunity for photos, perhaps one across the river and valley.

Nellie was aware of Ned watching her drive and shift and she became so self-conscious about it, she ground the gears once and almost drove off the side of the road trying to get the shifter into the right slot. To cover up, she asked questions. Where was he from? How long had he been a cowboy? Did he get lonely up in the mountains?

His answers were short, but they gave her a picture of him she hadn't expected. He had grown up on a farm in central Oregon where his family raised dairy cows and alfalfa. He'd been too young to go to war, but his older brother had enlisted and then died at Verdun. His father never recovered from that shock and committed suicide by hanging himself in the barn. His mother couldn't stand staying on the farm, so she sold everything — farm, stock, equipment, and Ned's horse — and moved to town, a small place by the name of Prineville, buying a house only big enough for her and Ned's two sisters, both of them younger. He was old enough to leave home by then and headed east to Colorado, and then north to Wyoming, then west again to Idaho. He'd found work at the Rocking O, due in part to his ranch experience while young and his riding experience in rodeos during the course of his travels. The thing he liked best was the camaraderie of other cowboys and the knowledge that he was helping supply meat for the whole country.

Ned's story was too intimate in one sense, but glibly presented in another, as if he'd told it often over the years. By then, they had returned to Stanley. Nell looked for several photo scenes facing east across the valley, but the lighting no longer satisfied her. Darkness began to settle in. Ned, who had watched what she was doing and helped carry her camera on its tripod from one location to another, Nell directing where to place it and Moonshine following, repeated his offer of dinner. Because Gwynn and the sheriff still had not shown up, she agreed and they moved inside the saloon. There was a lull in business, as it was almost empty of patrons. The bartender took their order. He didn't object to Moonshine coming in and lying down at Nell's feet. Pearl was nowhere in sight.

"Now it's your turn, Nell. How did you get here?"

Fair was fair, so Nell shared some of her background in Chicago as a portrait photographer in a studio, her unexpected loss of that job — she didn't tell him she was fired — and her decision to travel west herself. "After I lost my job, I decided to venture out on my own, but first I haunted the library, looking at collections by great photographers — Edward Curtis, Steichen, Stieglitz." Ned didn't know the names, but he listened. "They each had a specialty. Even Imogen Cunningham, one of the few famous women, specialized. I decided that was what I must do if I ever hoped to make a name for myself." She didn't mention that Cunningham worked mostly with portraits, something Nellie did not want to do. Landscape would be her metier. "Photographers traveled the west, in California and the Southwest. I didn't see or read anything about the inner west, so I picked those as possibilities. I wanted vistas without people, but vistas no one else was working with. When the train traveled through Wyoming, it looked like a total wasteland. One of the conductors told me how stark and strange Utah was and how scenic Idaho could be, especially north of Twin Falls. After a short foray into Salt Lake City, which was not a suitable place for a free-thinker like I am, I came north. And here I am."

She realized she had been talking nonstop for quite a while. The saloon was beginning to fill once again. It was past nine o'clock at night and still no Gwynn or Charlie. Time to retreat to her room by the river. Whatever energy had kept her going all day deserted her, and she wanted to lay her head on the table and sleep. Ned was rolling another cigarette, his third or fourth, she decided, wishing she had one.

It was then Pearl marched through the kitchen door with a platter topped by foaming glasses balanced on one shoulder and one hand. She glanced toward Nellie and Ned, stopped midstride, stared at them, placed her second hand on the rim of the platter, and heaved everything right at Ned's back. He didn't see it coming. Fortunately for him, Pearl was far enough away that none, or only one, of the glasses hit him, but the wave of beer splashed him from head to shoulders. Part of the onrushing foam splattered on Nellie and she jumped up to avoid any of the flying glass.

"You witch!" Ned leapt out of his chair, screaming, and headed for Pearl. Beer still foamed down his back. "What're you doing?" The bar patrons had all turned toward the room and most of them were cackling like a band of jackals.

"You two-timing coyote!" Pearl screamed back. She ducked Ned's rush and scooted back into the kitchen. The swinging door hit Ned, giving the bartender time to intercept. The cowboy practically bounced off his stomach, and the patrons' laughter redoubled.

Nell could hardly help a smile herself. She left a dollar on the table to pay for her share of the meal, called Moonshine, and they slipped out the front door. Although muffled voices were still audible behind her, the stillness of the night soon quieted her. The Milky Way was a shining swath of carpet across the whole of the sky. She decided not to wait for the sheriff and the sheepman. The sheriff, at least, knew where she would be, although the odd thought occurred that he had not told her to go to Lower Stanley. It was the cowboy who directed her there. Still, the proprietor said the sheriff had arranged her lodgings.

Back in her small cabin, Nell made notes about the photos she had taken, then unloaded the exposed film in the dark and secured it in a lightproof box. She reloaded the film carrier into the camera pack along with her camera and placed it and the tripod on the floor on the far side of the bed, out of sight. The light-tight box she buried in her bag and shoved it under the bed. The previous winter she had been forced to hide negatives so they wouldn't be stolen and she had formed the habit of carrying exposed film separate from the rest of her gear.

Moonshine had eaten parts of Nell's dinner that she surreptitiously fed to him under the table and he seemed content to lie near the foot of the bed and watch. She peeked outside her door, saw a tiny structure with a dim light over a door marked "washroom," and headed for it. It was little more than an outhouse with a sink and running water that spurted rust and air. The whole affair smelled of lye and sewer, so that she readied herself for bed as fast as possible, breathing in shallow, quick breaths through her mouth. On her return to the room, she began to undress, but stopped, thinking there was a different smell in the air, sour but yeasty, one she didn't remember. She checked her camera — still there — and her bag — still there. Moonshine lay asleep on the floor. Imagining things. Even so, she decided to sleep in her clothes, just in case she had to get up quickly. Yawning broadly, she slipped into bed and turned off the lamp on the table. Deep velvet surrounded her in the same way the river noise did. Far from disturbing her, the sound began to lull her to sleep until she remembered she hadn't secured the wood piece on the door. She climbed out, lowered the two-by-four slat, and snuggled again into the bed and slept.

A change in the quality of rushing water awakened her. The night was so dense, she could see nothing, and before she could reach out to pull the chain on the table lamp, Moonshine uttered a low growl.

"What is it, Moonie?" she whispered.

She sensed rather than saw Moonshine leap toward the door over the river. At the same time, the door banged open and shattered the window behind it. The river noise roared like an oncoming train. Nellie screamed and saw the barest shadow of her dog, a streak blacker than the black around him, leap through the door, and, she knew, straight into the boiling cauldron. "Moonshine!" Did he bark?

Nell dashed into arms that waited to catch her and throw a blanket over her head and around her shoulders. She kicked with stocking feet, thrusting elbows and knees in all directions, scoring one hit against a soft face or belly, evidenced by the expelling of a curse word, but the blanket tightened until she could not move. Still, her mouth was free to scream and she tried. "Charlie! Help —" A hand covered her mouth from the outside of the blanket at the same time a

162

blow landed on her head. A brilliant flash ended all sensations except a final image on her eyelids — her dog tumbling like a piece of flotsam in the river, about to drown.

CHAPTER 7

Gwynn Campbell's pickup tore up to the Galena Store porch, scattering dust and gravel. Lulu heard him from inside and came out in time to see the storm settle and the old sheepherder jump out, just as if he were a young man.

"Lulu! Where's Nellie?" he called before he reached her.

"Nellie?" Lulu shrugged her shoulders. "I thought she was meeting you in Stanley. Did you lose her already? You and the sheriff?" She laughed and was ready to turn back into the store, thinking that the young woman probably shook off her older chaperones. New stock had arrived the day before in preparation for high summer tourists and she had work to do. Then she noticed Gwynn's mouth. He wasn't laughing and indeed, his color wasn't very good either. "What's wrong?"

"I don't know. We left Nellie at the saloon,

taking pictures like she does, and were late gettin' back. The sheriff had an idea about somethin' back up Fourth of July Creek and wanted another man with him, not a girl. When we got back, no sign at all." Gwynn sat down on the chair as if standing took more strength than he had left. "There'd been a dust-up in the bar between Pearl and Ned Tanner — Nell'd been eatin' with that scurrilous cowpoke — and she slipped out. Nobody seen her since."

"What about her auto? She couldn't just disappear. Besides, she'd wait for you or the sheriff, I'm sure of it." Lulu grew concerned about Gwynn and said, "Wait here. I'll get you some water."

"Don't want water," he yelled. "You got anythin' stronger? I need a toot. I been drivin' like a maniac."

She came back out with a seltzer and a pint-size brown bottle. "Here, take a draught of this seltzer. Then you can have a swallow of my 'medicine.' " Fondness for the old coot filled her. He took care of his sheepherders and his sheep, unlike some of the other ranchers in the area and certainly unlike the cattle ranchers. With his passing, which looked too close if she didn't settle him down, the sheep trade would change.

"Calm down. Did you check around the

area? Maybe she camped out nearby." For a city girl, Nellie Burns had more gumption than most women who passed through Galena. Lulu grew weary of their high-pitched giggles and pretended helplessness. They weren't all like that, but enough to grate on her nerves. She was probably in the wrong business — she'd rather cater to the men who came through, even the cowboys. "What about the roadhouse down on the river?"

"We checked there. Beans told us she took a cabin in the afternoon and he thought she'd driven in later, but her auto wasn't there. The room was empty — no bag or camera or anything. Broken window was all."

"Where's Sheriff Azgo?"

"We both ended up stayin' at the roadhouse 'cause it was late when we found all this out. Then he went back to the saloon and was headin' for the Rocking O Ranch." His hand reached out for the brown bottle and Lulu handed it over. Gwynn took a quick drink and wiped his mouth. "I run into Cabe O'Donnell yesterday. Thought maybe Nellie might have headed to the ranch to take more photos. But soon as I saw her auto wasn't there, I hightailed it here, thinkin' she might have come back to do her hocus-pocus on her film." His breathing had calmed, but he rested his head in his big scarred hand, his elbow propped up on the arm of the chair. "If I've lost that little lassie, I'll —" He lapsed into silence.

Not certain what to say, Lulu remained quiet. Her mind raced, though, thinking where Nell could have got to. She said she wanted her own auto up in the Basin so she could leave whenever she decided. Maybe she'd driven in the night past the store and on to Ketchum. "I'll go in and telephone Goldie. Nell might have gone on to town, as you say, to do something with her photos. She must have a slug of them after all this time up in the Basin. Don't worry, Gwynn. I'm sure she'll be all right."

On her way back to the porch to report no news from Goldie, Lulu saw an auto speeding down the road from the Pass. One driver and one dog. "Uh-oh."

Gwynn's head swiveled up to Lulu and then to the road. "That's Charlie." He dragged himself up off the chair in a series of crank motions, as if his joints had frozen while he'd been sitting.

From "that blasted sheriff" to "Charlie" marked a huge leap in attitude. Lulu wondered if Nellie's disappearance had caused it, or something else. "That's her dog, but I don't see Nell."

"She won't go no place without her dog," Gwynn said. "Maybe she's lying down in back, hurt." He stepped down from the porch, gradually moving more like a person than a rusty hinge, and waited for the sheriff to stop. The dog leaped over the sheriff's lap and out the window, barked twice, ran up the steps and into the store. When he didn't find his mistress in there, he came back out and looked up at Lulu, his head angled to the side, his brown eyes asking the question, Where is she?

"Oh, dear." Lulu squatted to Moonshine's level and hugged him. "I don't know where she is. How did you get separated?" She turned to the sheriff as he trudged up to Gwynn, his eyes as sad as the dog's and lines etched down either side of his mouth.

"The dog found me," Charlie Azgo said. "I went back to the roadhouse and looked through the cabin again. I found a bag under the bed — Nell's clothes and a box. I want to send it down to Twin to that photographer fellow there. Maybe he can give us photos that will tell us something. It will take a few days. After that, I drove north from there a mile or two. Pulled over to check an automobile parked down among some trees by the Salmon River. Empty. Then this animal came out from behind a big rock, just like he was waiting for someone he knew." He reached the porch, looking as discouraged as Gwynn.

"Was it Nellie's Oldsmobile?" she asked.

"No. I hung around a while and a man came walking down the road, carrying a fishing rod. Said the auto was his. He had not seen the dog before or anyone else."

"He was lying!" Gwynn said. "I woulda arrested him, brought him in for questioning."

"No. He was not lying. His creel had four good-sized trout in it, all fresh-caught. The dog stayed by my side, wasn't even curious about the fellow. Just a fisherman driving up from Twin Falls for a couple days to fish. Showed me his tent, which was down from the road."

"Maybe he saw something. How did Moonshine get so far from the roadhouse?" Lulu didn't want to sound like Gwynn, but finding the dog without his mistress was mighty strange. As little as she knew Nell, she'd seen the affection between the two, more like friends than dog and owner.

Charlie shrugged. "I do not know. By the river is all I can piece together. He was not wet, but he wouldn't be if he had been out of the water for even a few hours. You know how dry it is this time of year."

The three of them stood on the porch, thinking their own thoughts, and then Moonshine barked.

"He wants action even if we don't know what to do," Gwynn said. "Find anything at the Rocking O?"

"No, only two cowboys — Ned Tanner being one of them. He said after his set-to with Pearl, he went back to the bunkhouse and he'd been there ever since. Not sure I believed him. He looked as beat-up as I have ever seen any cowboy look, but he offered to let me into the bunkhouse and I took him up on it. No one there except another cowboy cleaning his Winchester. No one I knew."

"Maybe he hid her in the ranch house. Was O'Donnell there? He's a cool customer. I never can tell whether he lies all the time or just during the week." Gwynn's color was coming back. "I had a whiskey with him — I mean a soda pop — at the saloon and he told me how many head of cattle he was running up in the hills and how much property he owns there in the Basin. To hear him tell it, he's richer than Croesus." The lines of his face sagged even more, if that was possible. Lulu thought he looked older than Croesus. "I tackled him about Domingo, said I thought one of his cowboys had played too rough — mighta been an accident, but my man was dead."

"Who is Croesus?" the sheriff asked. He had removed his hat and the sun shone on his black hair where it rippled from his fingers brushing through it. The day was heating up and it wasn't even noon yet.

"Oh some Greek guy with enough gold to sink a mountain," Gwynn said.

"Too hot out here for me," Lulu said. "Come on in. I'll rustle up some lunch for the two of you while you decide what to do next. I don't think Nellie came by here, and Goldie says she didn't come home. I think I'd have heard her on the gravel road if she'd gone by. Didn't sleep too well myself last night. Heat's building up on this side of the Pass. No cool night like you probably had in the Basin." She glanced up the hillside across the road. "Coming on to fire season is what I'm thinkin'." Moonshine followed her into the lodge kitchen. She poked her head back out. "If you want to send something to Twin, get it ready, and I'll see that it gets at least to Goldie."

While Lulu worked building sandwiches from newly baked bread, slabs of ham, and slathers of mustard, she listened to the men

171

talk and fed scraps to the dog. They apparently didn't care if she heard or maybe they'd forgotten about her. Moonshine gulped down the ham pieces and then lay down near the table and fell asleep, his head on his paws.

"How 'bout the saloon? Did you check back there?" Gwynn sounded as if he thought he should have done the checking, that the sheriff didn't know how to do a good job of policing.

"Sam came out the door when I drove in. He said he hadn't seen Miss Burns since dinner the night before. He also said Pearl ran out on him last night, too, after she spilled a tray of beer onto Tanner. 'Not the first time,' he said, and he did not expect it to be the last time. Pearl lives in one of those shacks with a man, supposedly her husband. He pointed it out to me and I checked it out, too. No one there."

"Did you break the door down? I woulda."

Lulu served a platter of sandwiches and several colas and decided to put away stores there in the kitchen. She wanted to hear what else went on. She gave the sheriff a piece of paper so he could write a note to Goldie.

"No, Gwynn. I did not break the door down. I scouted around. There was no

Oldsmobile and no trace of anything related to Nell." He took a bite of sandwich and said, his mouth full, "But I did look through all the windows. Not much of a housekeeper is Pearl."

Lulu turned to see if he was joking or laughing. That was as near to a sense of humor as she'd heard from the sheriff. He saw her and winked. She smiled and finished stacking cans of beans on a middle shelf where they'd be handy.

"Maybe she went back up to find Alphonso. And stumbled across the —"

When Gwynn interrupted himself, Lulu turned again and saw him looking at her. She tried to make it look as if she were merely glancing around the room preparing for the next job, and then she picked up another case of canned goods — peas — and slammed it on the countertop, making noise, hoping he would continue.

"— still we found." His voice was lower, but carried almost as well. "I know it looked deserted when we was there, but that don't mean some of them moonshiners ain't hiding out somewhere nearby."

The sheriff finished up his note, retrieved a box from a bag in his automobile, and handed it all to Lulu. She nodded and stuck it behind the counter.

"I say we go back out Fourth of July Creek. That's the only place she knows in the Basin." Gwynn shoved his chair back. "Maybe her auto broke down and she's stranded. Al's too far back up in the mountains by now for her to find him without one heck of a long walk. Hard to do without food and water." The plaintive note in his voice trembled.

Lulu couldn't keep herself quiet. "There's a creek right there, Gwynn. And fish. She's no helpless ninny. If her auto broke down, she'd come back to the road and wait for someone to come along."

Before Gwynn or the sheriff could answer, they all heard an automobile drive along the gravel road leading to the lodge, turn in, stop, and doors slam. "Maybe that's her right now," Lulu said, and dashed out into the main store. Two couples, dressed as if for a city outing, walked in, asking questions, wanting supplies for an overnight campout. She hoped her disappointment didn't show and began waiting on her customers. The men in back must have heard the voices and known Nellie's wasn't one of them. As she was finishing up with the people, giving them instructions and warnings about fire and animals, Gwynn and the sheriff came out of the back room.

They were so obviously men of the country that the two women gawked as they walked through, their boots heavy on the wood floor, their Stetsons stained from wear and work, their shoulders broad, and their clothes well worn. Moonshine kept close to the sheriff's feet.

"Who are they?" one of women whispered to Lulu after they reached the porch.

"One's the sheriff and the other is a sheep rancher. They're westerners." Lulu could hardly keep the pride out of her voice.

"Look kind of dirty to me," one of the men said. The women stared at him, but he was oblivious, squatting to check out some cowboy boots.

Lulu decided she could trust her customers not to steal her blind, and she left them in the store to follow the men to their autos. "Where are you going?" She wasn't certain they would tell her. "I need to know in case Nellie shows up here and I can send word to you."

Charlie Azgo opened the passenger door and Moonshine leaped in, just as if he knew his place. The sheriff walked back to his side and opened his own door. "We are driving back to the Basin. Gwynn is going to the Rocking O to scout around again, and I will try Fourth of July Creek. We saw some structures up there yesterday that I want to investigate."

"A moonshine still? They're all over the back-country. So you're back to your law work, I suppose." She didn't think he'd give up on finding Nellie so soon. "But I think I'd check out Smiley Creek first, Sheriff. That's where they hang out and cook up their plans, you know. What about Nellie? Are you just going to let her go missing?"

Gwynn had already backed out and headed for the Pass. Charlie climbed into his auto, folding his long legs with care, closed the door, and turned on the engine. The dog gave Lulu a long soulful look from the side window.

CHAPTER 8

Her head split when Nell tried to sit up, so she ceased trying, hoping the pieces would knit together again. At first, she thought a blanket still covered her head, but she could breathe, so she was mistaken. Dark enveloped her. Was it night? Yes. No. No carpet of stars lit the canopy. A rocking motion held her in its sway, and then changed abruptly to bouncing, jouncing, rattling. She wanted to hold her head but couldn't find an arm or hand to protect it from the stabs entering through her ears, her temple, her neck. A moan. Hers? She slipped back, thankfully, into a deep oblivion.

The next time she was aware of herself, her head ached but no longer did needles shoot into her skull. Still dark. No motion. Once more, she pushed to lift her head and shoulders. Her head stopped her. Her legs were curled up and cramping. With as much care as if she would break them, she began to stretch one. It stopped at an obstruction. Where was her arm? She thought doggedly of each part of her body, naming it and wiggling it — a foot, a leg, her shoulder, her chest, her head — no, she couldn't remember where her arm was. A smell like kerosene clogged her head, making her eyes water.

Either she was growing used to the black or something was beginning to cast a delicate glow into the space around her. A feeling not unlike snow blindness assailed her, but no white obscurity this time. It was all dark and she couldn't decide if she were prone or vertical. Maybe her foot had stopped at the floor. What was up? What was down? She'd lost her arm. Tears welled. What direction? She felt damp running down the side of her face into her hair. She was lying down. Gravity never lies. Pleased with her deduction, she stopped crying, but was reminded of her father's admonition, "Only sissies cry," and water ran again. She was a sissy.

Time passed, or didn't. She wasn't certain. Everything was black but not everything was silent. She thought she heard voices, then a latch scraped, a cover lifted, and a light shone into her eyes, blinding her.

"What have you done?" a voice demanded

to know. "Are you crazy?" Even with eyes closed, Nell could identify Pearl. Her screech resembled nothing so much as an outraged magpie, the same tone she had used when calling Ned Tanner a two-timer.

Mumbles answered.

"Well, she knows me, you stupid —" Pearl removed the beam from Nell's face, placed the light somewhere else, and leaned in. "Oh, Nellie, you poor thing! Can you move? Let me get this blanket off you. Careful now, your legs'll cramp if you move too fast."

A comforting arm slipped around Nell and helped to lift her. She heard herself moan again, then gritted her teeth. When the blanket slipped from underneath her, she discovered her arms and could help boost herself from the trunk of an auto, which was where she had been. Not her own, she could see. This was a large touring car, all black and, in the ambient light, appeared to be covered with mud, as if it had raced through puddles and ditches. Maybe it had. She remembered feeling as if she had been in a wash-tub.

Pearl placed the blanket around Nell's shoulders and bade her stay sitting on the edge of the auto for a few minutes. Then the flashlight and the woman moved away and once again Nell was surrounded by night, but this time, the smell of sagebrush and fir trees scented the air. Above, familiar stars shone: cold beacons oblivious of life on earth. And she was alive. Had someone wanted her dead? No, she wouldn't be sitting on a car edge if that were the case.

She breathed deeply, trying to reorient herself, and at the same time gingerly touched a painful goose-egg on her head. What had happened? She remembered the wash-room and placing her exposed film in the lightproof box, the film carrier in her camera pack — where was it? She leaned back and felt around the boot of the auto. Nothing there. And Moonshine. He growled, then leapt at — no, through the doorway. Her camera and her dog, gone. Sobs threatened, but she closed them down. First things first. Where was she?

Because it was still dark, she couldn't be too far from Stanley. It had been close to midnight when she switched off the bedside lamp. The sagebrush told her she was on a south- or west-sloping hillside. The smell of pitch told her the north slope wasn't far away. A glow almost too faint to register pointed her east. There was something else, a familiar smell, tantalizing her senses, but she couldn't place it. She stood up, wrapped the blanket tighter, and took several steps. Her legs still worked, but her feet were covered only by socks. Maybe her camera was inside the auto. She stumbled over a rut, caught her balance on the top of the auto, and moved along the side until she reached a door handle. Her hand was still numb, but she managed to open it, lean in, and feel along the seat and the floor. Just as she came in contact with canvas, she heard Pearl coming back. At least she hoped it was Pearl.

"Nellie? Where are you?" The flashlight beam swung one way and then another, stopping on Nell, where she leaned against the now-shut door of the car.

"Where am I? Pearl, how did you get here?" With her throat as dry as it was, Nellie's words sounded scratchy. "Could I have some water?"

"Here, I brought a canteen. Drink from it." Pearl lifted a round canister and Nell grasped it, holding it to her mouth. Except for a slight metallic tang, the water tasted pure and clean. She offered it back.

"Keep it. You'll need it again." Pearl paced back and forth, her light flashing on brush, a few trees, a dirt road. They seemed to be in the middle of nowhere, although the woman had approached Nellie from behind the auto. Whoever had driven her to this place was no longer around. Or was he hiding, listening?

"Can you take me back? I was staying at a cabin in lower Stanley. I need my things, my camera —" she stopped before she said, "my dog." "I'm sure there was some mistake." She took another drink and remembered the sheriff. "Sheriff Azgo will be looking for me shortly. Surely, you don't want a run-in with him — or your friends don't. I know you wouldn't have done this to me." No response. "Would you?"

"I got to think," Pearl said, stopping several yards away. "The sheriff. The sheriff. Why'd you bring him to the saloon?" She paced again.

"I didn't! He's looking for a murderer. We just happened to be traveling to the same places. I'm a photographer, trying to make a living. You know that." The canteen had a strap and Nellie placed it around her neck and shoulder and stepped toward Pearl. "Help me, Pearl. I'll never say anything about your — your —" What could she call it? Complicity in kidnapping? What was going on? "Ow!" She had stepped on small rocks. "I need my boots."

"Hush!" Pearl turned off the flashlight. The night was no longer totally dark; a fringe of light outlined the hills behind them. She grabbed Nell's arm and pushed her back to the rear of the auto. "Sit there, like you're having trouble getting up."

The sound of boots swishing through brush made Nellie follow directions. Pearl might be her enemy, but she might also be her friend. A man's voice called, "Pearl." Only the one word. The woman moved toward the sound, using her flash to guide her. Nellie watched her progress, hoping to see the man. He stayed behind several small fir trees. From a low rumble of words, she could pick out a few. "Get her . . ." and then ". . . loaded . . ." and then ". . . deal with her later." After a minute or two, Pearl was back. "C'mon," she said and led Nellie to a path.

"But my camera. I think it's in the auto." She stumbled, almost falling, then deliberately sank to the ground, trying to delay her departure from the auto. It felt safer than being led off into the woods. "And I'm in my socks." She deliberately mouthed a small moan.

"Damnit." Pearl's oath was low and vicious. She strode to the auto, opened the back door, lifted a bundle, and began to close the door.

"And my tripod," Nell called, trying to

183

keep her voice low. "I need it, too." The door groaned open again and Pearl almost disappeared inside. "And my bag," Nell said at the same time the door slammed shut. Two boots came flying toward her. She donned them immediately. They were hers. "I need my toothbrush."

"Pearl!" Words from the man in the bushes. Nellie tried to place the voice and couldn't.

By now, Nell could see most of Pearl's features. Her eyes flashed white as they turned to the source of exasperation, and she hurried her step. "Here," she said to Nellie, thrusting the pack and the tripod at her. "Get moving," she warned. "These men don't play games."

With dawn brightening, Nellie found her way behind Pearl more easily. They followed a rough path that wound through sagebrush, over rocks, up and down hard-packed earth. Their direction was south so the road must have traveled east and west. The faint scent she'd smelled earlier grew stronger. Burnt sugar. That's what it was. A sharp sting of memory — she and her mother baking cookies in their kitchen in preparation for a visit from her grandparents — made her stumble once more. Tears blurred her way and she wished with all her heart that she were back in Chicago, safe, taking portraits, and sharing her evenings with her mother, who stitched handwork while Nellie read, each at one end of the couch, a warmed teapot between them on a low table. What was her mother doing now? Perhaps arriving at her job in the library.

Gossamer strings of clouds, like angel hair, began to turn pink, then deepened to fuchsia and several shades of lavender, then changed to gold and finally to white as the sun burst from behind the mountaintop above them. A rainbow had slipped from its moorings and splashed itself across the sky. From rabbitbrush a scant ten yards from the path, a meadowlark serenaded, and scarlet gilia, its trumpets glowing, grew in random patches across the hillside, interrupted here and there by yellow balsamroot and white lupine. Nellie stopped. Safety or glory. She had chosen glory. No time for regret now.

Her guide, perhaps jaded with the beauty of Idaho, did not stop or look around, but plodded on, her slim figure clothed in a long canvas coat that caught on sage branches from time to time. From the back, she might have been a small man, so sturdy were her shoulders and straight her neck and head, only half-covered by a cap into which her hair had been tucked. Nell hurried along. The way was not so clear that she wouldn't get lost if she didn't keep up.

The path curled around and it wasn't long before Nell decided they were moving in a large semi-circle, roughly back to a point not far from where they began, although she could see no road or auto in the distance. Trees and a long ridge cutting from high left to lower right cut off her view west, so she couldn't find mountains as a beacon to where she might be. They entered a grove of widely spaced aspens intermingled with fir, and, rounding a bend, arrived abruptly at a large camp area, near the edge of which sat a huge metal pot with a coned top and a coil extending from it to another pot. An almost smokeless fire burned beneath the larger pot and the burnt sugar smell, now mixed with the odor of yeast and something else, permeated the air.

No one else was about, but someone must tend to that fire. Nell craned her head around to see, felt more shooting pains, and decided it was time to sit down and rest, whether Pearl liked it or not. A likely spot invited Nell: a bench built around the base of a large pine tree. She swung her pack carefully to the ground, laid her tripod on it, and lowered herself, not wanting to jar

186

her head in any fashion. The canteen, which had been bumping on her side, furnished more of the cold water that tasted so good. A continuous, soft, rushing sound she identified as a creek running over rocks, probably falling water.

She didn't need a guide to identify what was going on in this glade: moonshining. Nor was it a small operation, such as she'd heard about in the woods around Hailey and the draws north of Ketchum. Large crocks were lined up near the pots. Three tents, wide enough to hold several men who could stand upright, formed a quarter circle at the end opposite the pots — she assumed this was a still — and the falls. A big black pot hung over a fire pit in front of the tents, but no embers burned to cook whatever might be in there.

While Nellie caught her breath — the hike took more out of her than all her days with Alphonso — Pearl entered a smaller tent set off to one side and closest to the trees, brushing aside the flap as if it were home and without a backward glance at her captive. The grounds in front of the tents were filthy, littered with bottles, piles of wiring, metal pipes, dog excrement, empty tin cans with torn labels or shorn of identification and flashing silver in the sunlight. The smell from the still probably covered up worse ones around the camp. Whoever lived here and made the moonshine was messy and neglectful.

Time passed and the sun moved higher in the sky; no motion or sound came from the tent where Pearl had disappeared. As far as Nell could determine, no one watched her. Why not just walk away? She had rested and could hike to a promontory to find out where she was. Rather than head back along the path they had followed to get to the camp, Nell studied the area around it, found a well-used trail to the water, which she would need to replenish, and to one side a stock of goods in crates upended to serve as shelves. A knife would be useful, as would food. She crept from her perch and found a rusted paring knife, which she placed in her pack, along with two large pieces of jerky. It was dusty and held little appeal, but she knew it gave energy. The dogs in the sheep camp had virtually lived on it. She noticed a box of matches and grabbed a handful and stuck them in her pocket. She tried to think of anything else that would be useful if she could escape. The goods were too heavy.

The trail to the creek was short. Nell filled the canteen and slung it over her shoulder again, lifted her pack, and slipped her arms through the straps. The tripod she had already strapped to the pack. She was ready to explore and make her escape.

"Nell!" Pearl's voice was low and urgent. "Where are you?"

Nellie hesitated. Would Pearl pay for losing her captive?

"Come back," Pearl said, raising her voice only slightly. "If you can hear me, come back. They'll send the dogs after you."

Fear leaped in Nellie's breast. She'd seen the dogs at Smiley Creek. Cowpie was one. There had been others. Then she remembered the dog with Wolfman Pitts. Was he part of the group that stayed in this camp? Judging by how he had looked then, she could imagine that he was one of the men who lived like animals in the mountains. Worse than animals. She wished Moonshine were with her, then decided it was better he was not. He could swim. He had to be alive! But those dogs could kill him, and no one would feel any compunction in such a death. Maybe they would feel as little about Nellie. Even as she wavered, a commotion made its way up the path — dogs barking, men talking, horse hooves striking on rocks. She had not acted soon enough.

"I'm here." She walked back to the edge

189

of the camp and Pearl, whose face no longer looked like a Greek goddess. It was cramped and taut, like an older woman's whose nose and chin were gathering to meet each other. At Nell's appearance, it settled back to its usual expression, boredom mixed with wariness, like a fox's, ready to react if threatened. "I waited too long," Nell said.

Pearl nodded. "Go in my tent. The dogs know they ain't allowed in there, but there's a box of cayenne pepper, if one forgets."

Nell scrambled toward the flap and then turned back. "Find out why they want me. I'm no good to them for any reason I can think of, and the sheriff will be after me soon. That won't be good for anyone here." Then she ducked through the flap, relieved to be out of sight. There, neatness reigned. A sleeping bag was rolled into one corner, and several blankets were stacked in another. In a crate at one end, clothes were neatly folded. Two pairs of shoes were lined in a row along one side, both crusted with mud and both flimsy as dancing slippers. Nell slipped off her pack and placed it near the door, tripod facing the inner part of the tent space, so she could grab it and use it as a weapon, if necessary. The only reason anyone would want her would be for photos — either ones already taken or ones to be taken. A groan almost escaped her when she thought of all the exposed film in the lightproof box in her bag. Had they taken and destroyed those? Two weeks of solid, good work.

The commotion arrived outside the tent. One man yelled to the dogs to shut up. Another yelled to Pearl. "Where is she? You didn't let her go, didja?" This voice Nell recognized as Dick Goodlight's, Pearl's supposed husband. Any hope she had of keeping Pearl on her side and helping her escape drained away.

"She's in my tent. And she's gonna stay there 'til you tell me what's going on."

Footsteps near the flap. Nellie scooted to the back of the tent, grabbing her tripod and the cayenne pepper box that she found near the front. If it worked on dogs, it might work on men.

"Get away from there, Dick." Pearl's voice was low. She must not have wanted the others to hear her. "I'm warnin' you."

"It's my tent, too," he snarled back at her.

"Not now, it ain't. Not 'til you tell me what you think you're doin'. Bringin' that eastern sissy out here in the wilds. Are you crazy?" Her voice came closer and was somewhat more conciliatory. "That sheriff'll be here anytime. Your friends there don't exactly sneak up on a person. And you can smell this camp a mile away."

"No one found it before now. It's safe, unless that snoop took pictures when she was up here with the sheep." His voice didn't sound any closer.

The reference to the sheep elated Nellie. They must be up Fourth of July Creek! She knew either Gwynn or Charlie would think to come up this way, supposing that Nell might have gone back to the sheep camp, unless these kidnappers left her auto at the motor lodge. Then what would they think?

"That sheriff don't want moonshiners," Pearl said. "He sat right there in the saloon, big as you please, and didn't disturb nobody. They was all drinkin'. He even drank some wine. He wants the man who killed that — the Basque fellow." She stepped away from the front of the tent. Nellie could still hear her voice, but not her words.

"Bring her out!" A different man's voice, and one that made her own hackles rise. The man at the summit, Wolfman Pitts.

Pearl leaned in, her eyes unreadable, but her face tight again. "Be careful," she whispered. "Act dumb."

Nell stood as upright as possible. She didn't want to crawl on her knees in front of anyone, and particularly that man. She clutched the cayenne box in one. It might be useful. With as much courage as she could muster, she stepped out in front of the tent. "What do you want with me?" she demanded, speaking as carefully and as firmly as she could, hoping no one would notice her fright. "Take me back to Stanley."

Three men besides Goodlight and Pearl stood around, one tending the fire under the still. Three dogs had been tied to trees, including Cowpie and the wolf-dog. The latter strained at its rope and growled, teeth bared. Nell recognized Wolfman, who looked even filthier than he had at Galena Pass, but he didn't seem to be drunk this time. His leer remained the same.

"Maybe you'll sing a different tune this time, you witch!" Wolfman reached out to grab Nell, but Pearl moved between them, seemingly unafraid of him.

"Don't you touch her, you dumb —" She had gloves in her hand and swiped them at him. He stopped, his face turning a splotchy red. Nell feared for Pearl, but she stood her ground. "You want the whole two counties and all the feds in Idaho after you? Get what you want and let 'er go."

Wolfman pushed Pearl away and leaned so close to Nellie's face, she could see large pores on his nose and smell his breath — a combination of cigarettes and rotten teeth — but he didn't touch her. Nellie couldn't step back because the tent was in the way. "Gimme that pack with your picture-taker."

"Why?" Her camera was Nellie's most precious possession. She wanted to look at Pearl, but didn't turn her head. "Act dumb" she'd warned.

Wolfman's arm came up as if he were going to hit her. She tried not to flinch, to be as brave as the saloon girl.

"I want them pictures. I saw you settin' up here and there and actin' like you owned the land around. Gimme it, or I swear I'll kick you to a pulp." His voice was hoarse and low. His dog's rumble matched it. "And Pearl, too. She's gettin' too big for her britches."

She ventured a glance toward Pearl, who closed her eyes slowly and opened them again, a signal to do what he said. Everyone else in camp had crowded closer and watched and waited. Nell felt surrounded by the glittering eyes and dripping teeth of an animal pack. Knowing this man had watched her photograph raised gooseflesh along her arms and legs.

"All right," she said. "I'll get it." Carefully, she eased backward into the tent, not losing sight of Wolfman or the other men, grabbed her pack and her tripod, and lifted the pack forward, letting the tripod lean against the canvas wall, just outside the flap, hoping it wouldn't sag to the ground. She wanted it at hand. Then she placed the pack in front of her, at her feet. Wolfman didn't take the bait of leaning down.

"Open it," he ordered. "Gimme the box you was using."

No no no no, Nellie repeated to herself. My camera. My precious camera. She squatted beside the pack, undid the top flap, and lifted out her Premo camera box, clutching it to her chest.

"That ain't it!" Wolfman stomped his foot. "The thing you was usin' had a bellows on it. I saw you, prancin' around that fool sheepherder and followin' them maggots." He kicked at the pack, lifted the flap, and saw there was no other box in it. "If them dudes hadn't come along, I'd 'a got you then." His leer was back in place. Lechery looked less deadly.

"This does have a bellows. Here, let me show you." She unlatched the box on the ground and pulled the bellows from one end. "See?" She pointed to the other end and said, "I look through here, place the film in here, and move the bellows back and forth to focus." Maybe her explanation

195

would forestall and calm Wolfman. "Would you like me to take a photograph of you? Maybe you have a family somewhere who would like to see your picture."

Without warning, he kicked at the camera and it slewed away from Nellie and the tent. "Gimme the pictures," he growled.

"They're not in there," she screamed at him and lunged at his leg to keep him from kicking it again. "Leave my camera alone!" As she tumbled forward, a small pop sounded in the man's leg. Only she heard it because her ear was next to his knee.

Wolfman Pitts screamed and fell to the ground, tangled up with Nellie. His free leg swung against her shoulder and a sharp pain skittered down her arm. His dog lunged at his rope, barking and growling. The other men laughed and shouted to Wolfman. "She's after you now, Pitts. Gotta watch them eastern ladies."

Nellie rescued her camera and scrambled back to the tent, pushing her camera inside. "The pictures aren't in the box. They're on film." Before Wolfman could recover himself and kick her because she knelt on the ground, she felt around in the pack for her film carrier. "They're in here." She held the small box firmly against herself and sank back on her heels. "Don't open it, please.

All my work for two weeks is in there." She lowered her face, waiting for his leg to strike her. The dog no longer lunged, but barked furiously. Nothing happened, so she glanced sideways.

Slowly, Pitts pushed himself up, first to one knee and then to his feet. Lines etched his face, whether from anger or pain, she didn't know. She must have hurt him. While her fear mounted, she glanced the other way. Pearl stood in front of Dick, both hovering nearby, neither of them laughing, but also making no move to protect Nell, or rather, Dick had Pearl's upper arm in his grasp, as if he were holding her back. The laughter of the other two men eased off, and the one who tended the fire moved toward it. She heard the scrape of his boot across the dirt, the cry of a raven in one of the trees, the bounding of water on rock, and her own quick breathing. Even her heartbeat sounded loud in her ears.

Wolfman limped back to her. He held out his hand. "Gimme it. I won't touch you, but my wolf-dog sure will." He pointed. "He ain't eaten today. You'll be dinner."

Pearl's eyes widened, and she took a step toward the side of the tent, shaking off Dick. Nell whimpered. "No. They're my work." But she unwrapped her arms and gathered herself up, unsteadily, and only a quick grasp at the tent kept her from falling back. "Please."

Her enemy took several steps toward the dog. He would release it. Nellie saw it in his eyes. He might even prefer that she continue to defy him. How many times had he seen his dog attack a person, kill a person? If Domingo had not had a bullet hole in his head, Nellie would have been certain that Wolfman Pitts had killed him. She held out her hand with the film carrier in it. "If you open this, all the pictures will be ruined. I could take them to my darkroom and find the ones you think are dangerous to you. I'm sure none of them are. I was taking mountains, trees, sheep, Alphonso, and then the saloon. I never saw any of this." She swept her arm around, the same one that held the carrier. "I swear it."

"Ha, ha, ha." His laugh was forced and guttural. He grabbed the carrier, flung it on the ground, stomped on it, but used his hurt leg. He screamed with pain. The film in the carrier flew in all directions, black pieces of celluloid, empty, Nell knew, of anything.

Then Wolfman Pitts took a knife from his belt, flipped it open, and limped back to his dog. With a stare fixed on Nellie, his arm dropped, the knife sliced through the rope, and his wolf-dog leapt forward. Its teeth ripped toward her face.

CHAPTER 9

In terror, Nellie searched for the cayenne
pepper. It had spilled on the ground, a red
splash where she had fallen with Pitts. Pearl
screamed. Nellie dove sideways, trying to
escape the dog and grab a handful of pepper. A gunshot boomed and, on her knees
and covering her head to protect herself
from the oncoming brute, Nellie heard the
echo off the mountainside behind the camp.
The part wolf, part dog slammed onto the
dirt at Nellie's side, a pile of filthy, matted
fur. Blood, wet and scarlet, gushed from its
head. From the corner of her eye, she saw
Pearl reach for Dick and Dick push her
away.

As if tied together, everyone stared at the
animal and then their heads swung around
to the source of the shot. A rifle rested care-
lessly in the crook of Dick Goodlight's arm.

"You killed my dawg," Wolfman Pitts
cried. "You killed my dawg." The pitch of

his voice rose with every word.

" 'Bout time someone did," Goodlight answered. He turned to Nellie. "Pick up your gear," he said, gesturing with the rifle to the broken carrier and the scattered film, "and get back in the tent. Pearl, you see to her."

Nellie trembled so hard, she had difficulty moving. With a quick glance at Pitts, who still stood stunned by the fact of his dead dog, she scrambled to pick up the carrier pieces and destroyed film. None of the film was of any use now, but she wanted to do what Goodlight told her to do. Behind her, he ordered the other men to take the dead dog and bury it far from camp. "Don't want no coyotes pickin' around here." The two dogs still tethered to trees whined, the sound a welcome relief from the barking racket.

"C'mon, Wolfman. We got a delivery to make. Move." Goodlight pulled down on a lever, ejecting a shell, and pulled the lever back up. Even she could hear another shell fitting into the chamber. The rifle wasn't pointed at anything, but the threat hung in the air. Pitts must have felt it, too. He kicked his dog, spit on the ground, and followed Goodlight out of camp. Nellie ducked into the tent with her belongings. She stuffed the camera back in the pack, grabbed the tripod from outside, and then collapsed against the rolled-up bag at the other end, wanting to remove herself as far away as possible from the cruelty of the men and the dogs, and hugged herself to stop shaking, covering her mouth so she wouldn't cry out.

Silence descended on the camp, and the sun, a high golden glow through the canvas, warmed the air. Dust motes hung suspended in the heat. She heard a gunshot and then another and another. They didn't move closer or farther away. Someone practicing? For the moment, she felt safe enough to rest and plan what to do. Goodlight's brutal action had saved Nellie, she knew. What she didn't know was why he did it. At the moment, it didn't matter, but the reason might be important. Nell rolled out the bag and lay down on it, too tired to poke her head outside the tent to see where Pearl had gone or investigate the steady rhythm of gunfire.

Through the afternoon, Nellie dozed off and on, her head still aching, but she was aware of the burying detail returning, the end of the shooting, the sounds of a fire being replenished, a pot being stirred, wood being chopped, a dog's desultory barking and a command to shut up. Voices, male and female, drifted in and out of her consciousness, not as words, more as an accompaniment to the tumbling creek water. The soporific heat lessened and she sat up, aware of pain in her shoulder. Her canteen still rested by the dancing shoes, so she took several draughts of now warm water and turned to her pack. Her camera was safe, but she situated it carefully, packing the ruined film around it. No reason to keep the broken carrier, but she tucked the separated wood parts in a side pocket and found the knife she'd taken and the jerky.

What else could she use? Matches, more food, more water, more clothes. She sorted through the items folded in the box and found a sweater and a wool hat and stuffed them in her pack, re-stacking the remainder so Pearl wouldn't see anything amiss. As hot as the days were, the nights were cold, even in July. She stuffed the long coat in, too.

A vague plan had formed while she dozed. If this was Fourth of July Creek, then Alphonso was somewhere on the mountainside with his sheep. She could find him, although how, she wasn't certain. Eventually, the camp supplier would return and she could return to town, to Charlie, even to Gwynn and she hoped, Moonshine. Despair flooded her. All of them had become much more precious to her in the last several hours. And what were they doing? Were they worried? What happened to her dog? She took a deep breath and stepped out of the tent. Somehow, she had to get away while it was still light, not difficult in the long twilight, unless a guard had been established to keep her there. The first thing she spied as she exited the tent was Cowpie, still tethered, but pacing at the base of a tree. The other dog slept.

Pearl stirred the pot over the fire, looking up as Nell appeared.

"I heard shooting."

"Target practice," Pearl said. "That was me."

"Is there an outhouse or somewhere —" Nell let the question dangle. Her need was urgent, but she also wanted to scout out as much as she could without being sent back to the tent.

"Down that way." Pearl pointed with a big wooden spoon toward a grove of trees behind the tent. " 'Member what I told you about the dogs."

Without speaking, Nell walked slowly in the direction indicated, limping as if she were still sore. She found a smelly pit with a makeshift bench with a hole in it straddling a vile mess. She couldn't. Instead, she walked a little farther to find a private spot in the woods and squatted there, using a tissue she'd brought with her. Then she explored the area quickly, knowing she would be missed if she took too long. On her way back, she stopped at the tent to see how firmly the lower edge hugged the ground, and found it tight. If she reset one or two of the stakes around which the tent ropes were wound, the canvas could be lifted enough to push her camera pack, tripod, and maybe herself out the back. But moving the stakes presented a problem when she tested one; they'd been hammered into the ground. Still, she tried wiggling one back and forth, and gradually, it shifted. The earth was so dry, the dirt crumbled around the wood.

"Nell," Pearl called.

"I'm here." She stepped from behind the tent and strode toward the other woman. "That place was awful. I went farther into the woods. Is there a wash basin?"

Pearl gestured toward the creek. "That's it."

When Nell returned, she offered to help Pearl cook. Clearly she had been handed the women's work part of the chores, and she didn't like it. "I wait bar with a bunch of rowdies, and then I gotta do the same up here. Cussed men." She offered Nell the spoon. "Stew. That's all I know how to cook in a pot like this. They don't care, long as their guts are filled. Then they drink their own corn likker and pass out." She stamped her foot. "Ain't so bad when we got someone playin' an accordion and we're celebratin' a good batch. Then I get to dance." A slow blush moved from her neck up to her face. "I'm not a dancin' girl, understand, or anythin' cheap like that. I only do it up here, not down at the saloon." A thought checked her. "Well, once I did it —" Pearl turned to walk away, then looked back. "Put that metal lid on, then some coals on top, and it'll cook itself."

After the stew was bubbling away in its pot, Nell ambled around the camp, moving closer to the back of the tent. She wiggled at the stakes, sauntered to the creek, then back again. No one seemed to notice either because they were working themselves — one man carried water to the large pot and the other chopped wood, rested, and chopped again. Pearl sat on the bench around the tree, doing nothing, just staring at the ground. Her foot tapped to some beat only she could hear.

By early evening, Nell had worked the stakes to a standing position, which allowed her to lift the canvas from the inside and push her pack and tripod outside. She just had to trust to luck that no one would notice them under the couple of pine branches she'd found to lay on top. Other pine branches broken by winter winds or snow had fallen around the camp or been tossed aside. Pearl had donned a pair of the dancing shoes after brushing them clean while she sat on the bench.

Because neither Pearl nor Nellie had done anything else about serving a meal, one of the men made up some biscuits and cooked them in another pot on the fire, reminding Nell of how Alphonso usually did the cooking in the sheep camp. She missed him and his calm efficiency. This camp cook swore and blustered, and managed to drop the dough twice on the ground before he finished. "Come and get it," he called.

The other man and Pearl dug into one of the boxes for metal plates and Pearl handed one to Nell. "Better eat up," she said and winked. "This here's Long John," she said, pointing to the erstwhile cook, "and this here's Bob."

Nell mumbled a greeting. Dressed in dirty overalls with unkempt hair and beards, they looked virtually identical. Neither said a word to her, but Long John plopped a serving of stew on her plate along with two dingy biscuits. Log rounds served as seats near the fire and Nell claimed one. She ate with gusto. Her fear had chased away her appetite for most of the day, but when the stew began to smell of cooked meat and potatoes, hunger had resurfaced. She had not eaten since the night before at the saloon. Already, it seemed days ago, in another life.

The other three ate as if famished also, but talked desultorily about making moonshine — whether the corn mash needed replenishing, whether the temperature of the fire was hot enough, whether the wood would give out, how their compatriots were making out with their deliveries, which Nell determined had gone north rather than to Hailey or Ketchum. The towns of Challis and Salmon were mentioned. Mining took place at the former, she thought, but Salmon was a cow-town. Probably a good market there. Long John said he'd heard there were federal agents in Salmon, and Goodlight and Pitts and The Boss had better watch their tails. If he, personally, saw any strangers around the camp, he was hightailing it for good. He had no plans to spend time in the penitentiary at Leavenworth.

"Why don't you pull out that ukulele, Bob?" Pearl asked. "I'd like to hear you play." She made the request shyly, as if she had never done so before.

"Me?" His voice was almost as high-pitched as a woman's. Nell wondered if that was who she had heard earlier in the day, rather than Pearl talking with the two men.

"You." Pearl stood up. "I saw the handle sticking out of your gear. You play, don't you? Seems to me Dick said you strummed a lively tune. You never done it when I was around."

Bob stammered a minute, then Long John joined in. "Don't be so shy, Bob. You play that uke whenever you think you're alone up here, but we all heard you, one time or t'other."

"Get me somethin' to wet my whistle," he answered, "and I will. I surely will."

Pearl fetched a big cup, filled it from a jug over by the still, and handed it to Bob. "Here you go. Now you do your part."

The man took a huge swig from the cup, probably downing half of its contents, and letting some of it dribble down the hair on his face, a scraggly beard matching the thin patch of hair on his head. He strode over to some gear outside one of the tents and pulled his musical instrument loose. For the first time, he glanced at Nell. "You object?"

"Of course not. I'd love to hear you play." What did Pearl have up her sleeve? This was obviously not normal routine. Even she had mentioned a celebration. There was nothing to celebrate tonight on their part, although Nell was happy to celebrate the absence of the other men. Even the dogs had been quiet all afternoon, as if they knew they were off duty.

Bob strummed his ukulele and to Nell's surprise began to play what she thought of as a Hawaiian melody. To her even greater surprise, Pearl began to dance. She moved her feet softly back and forth on the dirt and moved her hands in complicated patterns. Long John drank heavily and watched the show, slumping lower and lower against the log end he leaned against. Soon, he was snoring gently and on his side. Bob stopped from time to time to take another giant swig, stretch his fingers, say a few words to Pearl, mostly about what song to play, took another swig, and continued his strumming. Pearl never flagged, dancing slower or faster depending on the songs, swaying her body as if it had been wound up and was winding down again, humming from time to time. None of her movements were crude or suggestive; rather, she turned like a doll on a music box, somewhat mechanically but still gracefully.

Even though Nell had not been drinking any of the moonshine, she began to feel as if she were being hypnotized by Pearl, like a cobra in a basket in India. She shook her head, stretched her limbs, stood up and saw how dark it was beyond the fire circle, nodded to the others, and ambled back to the tent she was sharing with Pearl. Maybe Pearl would be so exhausted and the two men so drunk, they would never hear her leave. If she had a long enough lead time, the dogs might never find her track. But how would she see? Some stars already twinkled in the vast spaces above, but not enough to light her way. Nevertheless, if she moved carefully and followed the creek, she could get some distance by the time the moon came out. Then the going would get easier. She listened to be sure the music continued, but it did not. Neither did she hear any voices. Were they all asleep?

Just as Nell had decided to escape under the back end of the tent, someone scooted in the front, the aroma of cologne announcing it was Pearl. The thought of striking the other woman over the head with her tripod entered her mind, but she couldn't bring herself to do it. It was outside anyway. "Shhhh," Pearl whispered as Nell opened her mouth. "Get your stuff. We're sneaking out. Now." She grabbed a bag of sorts from behind the shelf, stuffed some clothes in it, dragged out a long flashlight, then changed her shoes back to her boots with hardly a sound. Quickly, she rumpled up the sleeping bag and the blankets to make it look as if two people slept in them. Then she thrust her head out the front flap, holding one hand up behind her, and motioned to Nell.

Both women tiptoed out of the tent, turned immediately toward its back. Nell shouldered her pack with the camera and tripod, slung the canteen across her chest, and stayed close to Pearl, who had turned on the light, but held her hand over the front of it so only a pencil-thin beam of light led the way. They followed the path toward the latrine but angled off to meet the creek. Here, they could no longer move as quietly because branches and rocks littered the ground. Each snap and gravel rasp frightened Nell, certain they would be heard back in the camp. Nothing stirred, not even the dogs. She remembered Pearl giving them dishes with water, but maybe it had been moonshine, not water. Men and dogs — pie-eyed.

When they reached the creek, Pearl turned to follow it down the hill. Nell pulled at her arm and stepped up close to the girl's face. "No," she whispered. "I think we should go upstream. They'll think we went down and take longer to follow." She was reluctant to say anything about Alphonso yet. Pearl seemed to be in league with Nell now, but she couldn't be certain.

Pearl paused and looked down and then up the falling water. "Maybe you're right." Still, she didn't move. "But what then? We'll be trapped 'cause they'll be between us and the road."

Caution told Nell, again, not to mention Alphonso. And yet, what could he do? He was armed, but he was only one man. Maybe Pearl was right. "When do the others come back from their delivery?" she asked.

"T'night. Maybe early mornin'."

"If we go down, how far is the Rocking O Ranch? Could we get there before the men return? We'd be safe then with cowboys and people around." Nell wanted to move. Standing and arguing by the creek was dangerous.

Without another word, Pearl headed back up the creek. "Stay close," she whispered. Their progress was slow. Brush was thick

213

near the creek bed and branches whipped their faces and arms. Often, they walked in the water to avoid the willows alongside, wetting their boots and legs up to their knees. The night was cool, but their efforts were strenuous and sweat dampened the small of Nell's back and her neck. If they stopped to rest, she felt the chill immediately. The creek twisted and turned. The rocks in the bed were slippery and more than once, one of them stumbled and grabbed at a branch or each other to keep from falling. A bright, just-past-full moon rose and lit their way when they escaped the brush in short stretches, so their need for the flashlight diminished.

When the creek at last intersected with the road and a rough bridge, they stopped. Nell brought out the beef jerky and unscrewed the top of the canteen, offering both to Pearl first. "I'm tired. Here, have something. How far do you think we've gone?" She feared not far, but she didn't whisper anymore. She thought she could still smell the burnt sugar and mash, and hoped the smell came from her own clothes, not the air.

A long sigh was her answer. Pearl chewed on a strip of jerky, drank from the canteen, and handed it back. "I don't know. I'm thinkin' we should have gone downstream. What're we gonna do up in these mountains?"

Nell no longer thought her plan was a good one. Indeed, what would they do? How far was Alphonso? As she chewed her own piece of jerky, she became aware of sounds in the night. They had stopped in a small grove of aspen and the leaves were clattering. A breeze had begun to riffle them, a familiar, comforting sound during the day, but at night, it seemed threatening. Was a storm coming in? A rock rattled over by the creek. Had one of them destabilized it or was someone walking behind them?

Pearl's head leaned against a white aspen trunk. Nell couldn't tell if she had fallen asleep or if she was listening, too. As she sat there, trying to interpret every sound, Nell became aware that she was shivering. All of her seemed wet. She dug into her pack and pulled out the sweater she had stolen from Pearl and pulled it on over her clothes. If Pearl could see her, she didn't say anything. Nell dug into her pack again and brought out the long canvas coat and handed it over to Pearl. "This is yours. I took it." Once again, she spoke in a whisper. The moon had cleared all of the trees and the mountainsides angling down sharply on either

215

side of them.

Loud yips startled them both so much, they grabbed each other. A chorus wound up and down an off-key musical scale, stopped, then began again with first one howl and then another.

"Coyotes," Pearl said, her voice shaky. She unclutched Nell and stood up. "We better get movin'. I'm cold." She grabbed the coat and donned it. "Thanks. Glad you was carryin' it and not me. It's heavy."

"But the coyotes. Will they attack?" Hearing coyotes when she had been camping with Alphonso had frightened her at first, but she'd grown used to it. They had represented a danger to the sheep, but not to her, then. Alone in the wilderness with another woman increased her feeling of vulnerability. With no sheep around, maybe the coyotes would want people. The two of them had no dog or gun to frighten them away. Once again, she felt keenly the absence of Moonshine.

"Nope. Wolves might, but I ain't seen any around here. Pretty much they been killed off by the cowboys." Her rustling and matter-of-fact voice calmed Nellie's fears. "C'mon."

They began their trek again, this time walking along the road in the moonlight and making faster progress. The yips stopped when the moon slid behind a cloud, but then Pearl had to use her flashlight again. The sound of their footsteps on dirt and rock — an uneven scrunching and scraping — was much too loud to Nell's ears. Surely, anyone looking would hear them.

A sharp, shrill scream pierced the night, rising and then falling to a strangled cry that etched the night and hung in Nell's ears like a firecracker's image on the eye, long after it had died away. She held her breath and heard her heart pound. Pearl, too, had stopped short. She swung her flashlight around, no longer bothering to cover most of the light. It flashed off grass, aspens, rocks, logs, pock-marked road, sagebrush, wildflowers drained of color in its bright light. No animal.

"Go back! Go back! The logs!" Nell stepped from the road toward what she thought she had seen in the quickly moving light.

"What d'you mean?"

"Flash around again. I saw some logs. Didn't you?"

This time, Pearl moved the light more slowly. Up against a talus slope, logs again appeared in the light and she stopped its motion. There was the log structure Nell had photographed in what seemed like a different country and long ago, during her sojourn with Alphonso. "It's a half-built cabin. I know where we are now." She couldn't keep the triumph out of her voice. She stepped off the road to make her way to the rough cabin.

A second scream, sounding even more like a woman being tortured and strangled than the first one, shattered them. The sound might have been ten feet away and came from behind. Pearl began to run. Nell almost gave in to panic, too, her whole body one big goose bump.

"Wait. Stop!" Nell called. "It's a mountain lion. *Don't run!*"

Pearl must have heard the urgency in Nell's voice because she stopped and then stood as if paralyzed. "Flash the light around again," Nell ordered.

Nothing happened. A heavy rustling and then pounding through sagebrush warned them of the presence of an animal. At that moment, the moon slipped from behind clouds and a stag deer, its antlers a tall, branched crown reflecting golden light, leaped past between Nell and Pearl. His large, long body with huge ears and then his white tail sprang up and down like a flag, rapidly, but also gracefully. Nell held her breath, waiting for the mountain lion that surely followed it. She wanted to squat down, make herself small and hidden.

The deer crashed through the trees and brush near the creek and they could hear his progress until the sounds disappeared. Nell and Pearl waited. No lion appeared. When silence reigned again, they stepped closer to each other.

"If the mountain lion killed a doe or fawn," Pearl said. "If so, it won't be hungry." She shivered. "Let's climb into that half-cabin. I'm tired and cold." She took a step toward it and when Nellie didn't follow, added, "It's gettin' light. We better hide ourselves."

The faint glow of dawn back-lit the ridge above the road. The moon was beginning to fade as morning approached. "All right," Nell said.

The pounding sound of another animal running stopped them in their tracks. Once more, Pearl lifted the flashlight and turned. This time, the light shone full on into the yellow eyes of a mountain lion, long and golden, that stopped and shied back, momentarily, then crouched, just like the feline hunting position Nell had seen in pictures of the veldt in Africa.

"Stand still," she whispered, and one slow

step at a time, she moved next to Pearl. "Keep the light on his eyes."

The lion's back muscles flexed.

"Lift your arms slowly," Nell said, "and when I say so, wave them up and down and yell."

The cat and the women stared at each other.

"Now!" Both women hollered and flapped their arms. The animal raised itself to a standing position, took a half step back, and then bounded away.

"Well, if that don't wake the dead and anyone else on this mountain, nothin' will," Pearl said. She looked at Nell and they laughed. After a moment, the edge of hysteria disappeared.

"Let's go hide," they both said at the same time and laughed again. Nell led the way to the logs.

CHAPTER 10

The cabin was not a true cabin, only half-built with no roof. The floor might once have been cleared, but now brush and grass grew and animal scat told the two women that others had occupied the space before them. Nevertheless, it served as a shelter of sorts in that several of the logs had fallen and created a cubbyhole large enough for the two of them to sit or lie in. Until she sat down and stretched out her legs, Nell didn't realize how tired she was. She ached all over from the exertion of the night, the tension of hurrying and not making noise, the fear of the mountain lion, the many scratches from sagebrush and willow branches. Her pants had been ripped in several places.

"Now what?" Nell's question wasn't directed so much at Pearl as at herself. She was regretting not heading for the main road. Alphonso was a long ways away. The night she and the sheriff and the sheepherder had moved the wagon, they had traveled for hours along the road. Since then, Alphonso could have traveled even farther away.

"You were right about comin' uphill," Pearl said. "We ain't been followed yet. That means they think we took to the road going down."

"I was just thinking the opposite, wishing we had gone your way," Nell said. "How do you know they returned already?"

"They was due back about midnight. I figure they drank a while and didn't check on us except to poke nosy noses into the tent. It woulda looked like we was still there until Dick tried to get in with me. Then they'd know."

Nell giggled.

"Are you laughin' at me?"

"No. Just at how well you know him. I wonder if I'll ever have a man to know that well."

For a moment, Pearl was silent. Then she leaned toward Nell and patted her shoulder. "Sure you will. You're pretty and smart. Some men don't like that. But some men can't resist it. Take that sheriff of yours. . . ." She let her voice drop to nothing. "Hush."

Nell realized with a start that it was daylight outside, although they sat in dark shadows. She followed Pearl's example and rolled over to peer through a chink in the logs. "What?" she whispered.

Then she, too, heard something, the clip-clop of a horse's hooves. She raised her eyebrows at Pearl, who motioned with a finger to her lips. Stay still. The horse came into view from a direction she didn't expect, moving at a steady pace, not hurrying, not lagging. Nell recognized the rider instantly, the cowboy Ned Tanner. She moved one leg under her to stand up and call. Pearl grabbed her arm and held her with a strength that astonished Nell. She made a sound, something like a squeak.

The rider turned his head, but in the direction opposite the cabin. His horse turned its head and seemed to look directly at Nell through the logs. Whether Ned heard her or not, he didn't stop his progress and, in a moment, he was out of sight and the sound of his horse ended. Pearl released Nell and Nell felt as if a vise had been removed from her arm.

"What's wrong? Why didn't we tell him we were here?" Nell still whispered, but she might as well have been shouting, so angry was she.

Pearl raised herself to a sitting position. "He's dangerous, that's why. And a dunderhead besides." She didn't look at Nell.

"I don't understand. He could have helped us. Taken us to one of the tourist campouts, or —" She stopped, still reluctant to mention Alphonso. "You think I'm interested in him? Well, I'm not. We were just having dinner because he knew I was alone." She wanted to add, "Besides, you're married," but didn't. "I think you're jealous!"

"Wouldn't matter if you was interested," Pearl said. "Smart women scare him." She rolled away, pulled her satchel from her shoulder, wrapped her coat around her, and laid down, using the bag as a pillow. "I'm gonna get some sleep. You better, too." She closed her eyes. "And I'm not jealous. You ain't that pretty."

Nell snorted. What a stupid situation. "Pearl, he was headed downhill, not up. What does that mean? Where was he coming from?"

The other woman shrugged. "How do I know? Probably a cattle camp of some sort. He don't tell me everything he's doin'."

Meaning, Nell guessed, that he told her most of what he was doing. He had told Nell that he would go back to the cattle the morning after they had dinner. Her mind was fuzzy. Was that yesterday? So why was he coming back down again? She decided

224

to try and sleep too, but knew she wouldn't. She had to plan what to do. When light finally reached the cabin, she sat up and watched the scene through the logs. A squirrel with a black tail scampered into the clearing, rustled around near what was an old fire ring, sat on its haunches and chattered, and then ran away. Birds flitted in the treetops, small brown ones, and then a couple of robins. A deer and a fawn crossed the road and ambled toward the creek, the doe's head turning one way and another, alert to danger. The sun climbed higher and their hiding place grew warmer.

As the deer moved through the aspen trees, Nellie saw something familiar, carvings in the white bark. She studied the woman beside her and decided she was sound asleep. As silently as possible, she rose, opened a pouch on her pack and retrieved the rusty knife and a couple pieces of the broken film carrier, then crawled out of the cabin and crossed the road. Her idea was truly a long shot, but, knowing the sharp eyes of both Gwynn and Charlie, she could leave a message of sorts in case they came this way. No camp-tender would see it, but Alphonso might when he came down, which would be weeks. Discouragement almost stopped her. Weeks would be too late. Wolfman Pitts wanted her gone, and how it happened didn't seem too fine a question for him. Even the thought of him made her stomach jump.

At the tree nearest the road, she carved h-e-l-p. Under it, she added her initials: cnb for Cora Nell Burns. Then she realized neither man knew her first name was Cora. Too late. They could figure out the "nb" part. Then she carved the month, day, and year. To her, the information jumped out from the white bark because it was so unlike the old carvings of names and dates, which were lumpy and edged in black from age and part of the tree itself. Finally, she cut an arrow pointing east, toward where she thought Alphonso might be. With three of the wood pieces from the carrier, she formed another arrow at the base of the tree. At the nonpointed end, she built a small cairn from pebbles, something that might attract them if they were looking.

Back at the cabin, Pearl stirred when Nellie entered. "Where'd you go?" she mumbled.

"To the woods." Nell sat down again and looked through the log chink for her handiwork. It jumped out as if she had posted a red flag. What would Pearl do when she saw it? "Don't you think we should move on?

226

Maybe now we should circle around and head for the main road." She almost hit her head. Stupid idea. She'd just drawn the arrow pointing the other way.

"No, you're right about the dude camp. That'd be safer since Ned ain't with 'em."

"What's so dangerous about him? He seemed perfectly pleasant to me when I was taking his photograph. Aren't all cowboys supposed to be courteous and helpful and brave?"

"You been readin' too many books." Pearl's voice was cold. She sat up, straightened her hair, and said, "I'm hungry. Where's the canteen?"

Nellie handed it over. She had filled it while she was out, and she dug into her pack for more jerky, broke the last big piece, and offered half to Pearl. "That's it, I'm afraid."

Outside, Pearl looked up and down the road. She didn't seem to see the carving on the tree. "We better stay off the road, walk alongside so's we can jump into the brush. We'll hear an auto if it's a comin' but not necessarily horses."

"Do you think they would follow us on horses? I didn't see any around the camp."

"If they're leadin' dogs, they'll have horses. Ain't none of 'em wants to walk."

"Pearl, I've been thinking. Why would they follow us? They have what they wanted — all my photographs are gone." The lie didn't trouble Nell. For the moment, they were gone because she had no idea where her bag with the box was. Maybe they had it — in the sedan in which they'd taken her away, or somewhere in the camp, although she'd not seen it.

A troubled look crossed Pearl's face. "Then why didn't they just let you go? I think Wolfman Pitts has more business with you." She turned to walk up the side of the road. "And Dick has some with me." She paused and began to walk. "Now you know where they cook up the hooch, you might spill what you know. There's that sheriff followin' you around."

"But I told you, he's after —"

"Don't matter what you said. They think he's in cahoots with the revenuers."

Something Pearl had said earlier came back to Nellie. "Did you know Domingo? The Basque sheepman." Nellie couldn't imagine any circumstances in which Pearl might even know Domingo.

The two of them walked along the verge of the road, although "road" exaggerated the track it really was. Two ruts with grass in the center climbed steadily through a forest of lodgepole pine and alpine fir, accompanied by the thrum of water in the distance. Nell, behind Pearl, wasn't certain the saloon girl had heard her question or just didn't intend to answer it.

"The more I tell you, thc worse . . . be for you. They . . . think you know. . . ."

Pearl's words drifted back, as she didn't slow her pace and the crunch of rocks and dirt under their feet made Nellie wonder if she heard correctly.

Who was "they," besides Dick, Wolfman, Bob, and Long John? Not one of them planned the whole moonshine operation, Nellie was sure. The man who spoke to Pearl in the woods during the night must be the leader. Who was he?

"Domingo was a drinker, I heard." Nellie persevered. How would "they" know she knew anything unless Pearl blabbed. Pearl already risked danger just by helping Nell to escape. Or maybe Pearl had escaped, too. That dreadful camp and those men. Still, the men had not threatened or belittled Pearl in any way, and Dick Goodlight had saved Nellie's life. "Why did Dick shoot the wolf dog? I know he hates me. I've seen it in his face."

Again, a long silence, then Pearl mumbled an answer that Nell couldn't hear or one she didn't understand. She reached forward to touch Pearl's shoulder, wanting her to turn around. The woman immediately swung around, her arm raised. "Don't you touch me!"

Nell stepped back. "I'm sorry. I didn't hear what you said." Surprised by Pearl's obvious anger, Nell wanted to take the question back, but she couldn't. "Something about Dick?"

"Where is this blasted tourist camp?"

If Pearl was going to ignore her question, Nell decided not to ask it for a third time. "I don't know. I just know they came through here. By a lake, maybe. The cowboys and their cattle might be up this way, too." Her jaunt with Alphonso to frighten off the cattle had been through the sagebrush hills lower in the valley, and she hadn't truly known where she was.

"Nah. You can tell when cattle have moved through an area." Pearl's mood settled back to its normal insouciance. "There's cowshit everywhere."

A sound Nellie had dismissed as water spilling down rocks grew louder. Either they were nearing a waterfall or something was coming up the road. She reached out to grab Pearl's arm, but thought better of it. "Pearl!" The woman stopped. "I think I hear someone coming. Listen."

They stood with their ears cocked. Pearl's expression changed from tired boredom to concern and then to something else. "Let's get away from the road. Quick."

The evergreens grew in thick groves on both sides of the road, but all the trunks were skinny, offering no immediate hiding place. Pearl looked one way and then the other, paralyzed.

"To the right," Nellie ordered. She led, hurrying through the trees. Branches reached out to catch at her clothes and hair. "Hurry, Pearl!" Behind her, Pearl had similar trouble; wood cracked and swear words erupted. A long dead bone of a trunk, larger than the live ones surrounding them, offered cover. Nellie jumped it and hunkered down.

Sound carried long distances in the dry air and both women had time to lie flat on the lumpy ground behind the white, aged remnant. Here, they huddled close, Pearl no longer minding that Nell touched her. Unless someone stopped and stood up to search the woods, they would not be seen. They heard an automobile labor over the track, but neither dared risk a look. As the whir of the motor began to fade, Nellie crawled up to sit on the log.

"We gotta stay off the road," Pearl said.

Nell studied the trees and the slope leading down to the course of Fourth of July Creek. Few aspen grew in this altitude, so her view encompassed deep green mottled by lighter green shrubs. Purple lupine and red Indian paintbrush splashed a palette of colors among the dead wood littering the forest floor. She wanted to stay right there and rest. Travel along the water would be slippery because it was high this time of year and broken limbs, brush, and snags would hinder them. But what choice did they have? The auto would return, sooner or later. "All right. If we follow the creek, we'll probably end up near the campout. They need water."

"I'm hungry. All that dried old jerky did was make me thirsty. Let's go catch us a fish." The farther from the moonshine camp that Pearl traveled, the cheerier she grew, as if she had loosened a tether. "We can be like that man who got stuck on an island. Make our own way." With that, she scrambled down the rest of the slope and Nellie hurried to catch up, puzzled.

"An island," she said. "Oh, Robinson Crusoe!"

Pearl flashed a big crooked smile back at Nellie.

"I hope we're not abandoned though. I've

232

got my —" Nell stumbled over a tree root and nearly fell. Thank goodness, she thought. She'd almost let out that she still had negatives to develop. Maybe. She hoped her bag was still under the bed at the road-house.

At the creek, they found a deep pool. Both of them took off their boots, soaked their feet, and admired the delicate lilies growing in the shadows. When something like a feather wound around Nell's legs, she pulled them out. "That tickles."

"Fish. We need a sharp stick. Then we could catch us something to eat."

"I've got a knife. It's rusty, but might work to make a point," Nell said.

They set about sharpening a willow branch. Pearl stalked a few trout, finally jabbing one. Out it came, flapping at the end of the stick. With quick, sure moves, she grabbed it, slammed the back of its head on a rock, and held her hand out for the knife. "I'll clean it. See if you can get a little fire going. Use dead twigs. Over there on that flat rock. We don't want no smoke showing, and we sure don't want to set the woods on fire." She studied the sky and the road. "Do it quick."

By the time Nellie had a small fire started, Pearl had caught and killed three more small trout. The half-cooked fish satisfied their pangs of hunger. Nell licked her fingers. "You know how to do a lot of things, Pearl. How'd you get to Stanley?" She meant, "How did you learn them?" but didn't know if such a question would be prying.

Pearl wrapped two fish in leaves and handed them to Nellie to place in her camera pack. The saloon girl seemed disinclined to add anything to her own satchel. "I grew up on a dirt farm." She snorted. "My pa farmed dirt and best I remember, nothin' ever grew. Then he left. I tended a passel of kids for a while, then hightailed it soon as I found a ride to somewhere else. That turned out to be Stanley." Her shoulders heaved in a large sigh.

Nell thought of ten more questions about Pearl's mother, whose "passel of kids," and who offered the ride, but decided on what she hoped was a safe one. "Where did you learn to dance? I've never seen anything quite so lovely as what you did last night. It was as if you stepped off an exotic stage."

A shy smile lit Pearl's face. "From an old darkie woman — part Chinee, part something else — in a mining camp." She ducked her head, but not before Nell saw a tear slip down. "Saloon girl" was no longer an apt description for Pearl.

"Where'd you learn to take pictures with that big machine?"

"In a studio in Chicago. A friend of my mother's helped me get a job there. Mostly I helped the main photographer by posing his subjects seated and keeping the darkroom — that's where film is developed into negatives and then into prints — supplied. But then Mr. Scotto, he was my boss, began to teach me about cameras." Those days seemed long ago and easy and simple.

Nell cleaned the knife on grass and tucked it in her pack again. Those days were gone. "We better get going. That auto hasn't returned. Do you suppose they're waiting for us around some bend?" An involuntary shiver made the hair on her arms stand up. As carefree as the two of them seemed catching and cooking trout, Nell knew danger lay ahead if they were caught. Better to focus on finding the campout or Alphonso. Either place would be safer than here in the wild stretches of the Stanley Basin, vulnerable to four-legged and two-legged creatures alike.

Their hike took them over piles of brush, fallen tree limbs and trunks, and rock piles. Always, they climbed. The creek wound back and forth, sometimes far from and sometimes too close to the road. They scuttled through those areas as fast as possible. In the late afternoon, they rested below a talus scree against boulders that placed them out of sight of the road.

"Are you afraid of Dick?" Nell asked. She wanted to get to the bottom of why Dick had shot the dog. His actions seemed so erratic. Maybe Pearl would open up a little more. They'd been fairly easy with each other since the last scare of the automobile and their Robinson Crusoe cookout.

"Why should I be afraid of him? He's in love with me." Pearl didn't sound happy about that fact. She twisted long pine needles around a finger, then held up her hand to show Nell a green "wedding band."

"Are you married to him?" Nell hesitated to ask, but knowing the relationship between the two might be helpful when they all met up again, which was almost sure to happen, whether here in the mountains or elsewhere. She felt like a snoop, burrowing for information the sheriff could use in his investigation of murder.

Pearl shrugged. "Not really. He likes to say so, and I don't say much against it. Comes in handy, sometimes, havin' people think we're hitched."

"And other times? What about Ned Tanner. He seems taken with you." Nell wanted to mention the rancher, Cable somebody, but sensed Pearl would clam up if questioned about that relationship. Something wasn't quite right there, from the way Pearl had reacted in the bar when the rancher talked with her. Was it fear or anger that had caused the young woman to turn so white?

"Oh, Ned. He likes anything in skirts. Even you." Pearl laughed and added, "Except you don't wear skirts!" Her laugh faded and her expression turned serious. "Watch him, Nellie Burns. He ain't what he seems."

"Dick doesn't seem to be, either. Shooting that dog to save me. I wasn't sure he had a good side, the way he talked to you at the Galena Store and acted at Smiley Creek. But if he loves you and if he'd saved me — there must be a tender side to him that he doesn't let show, except maybe to you."

Pearl stared at Nellie. Two bright red spots flared in her cheeks. "You mind your own business." She stood up, started to walk, picked up a small, sharp rock, and then turned back to Nellie. "Dick didn't shoot the dog. I did. He grabbed the gun to save me." Pearl was practically shouting at Nellie. She looked at the rock in her hand and dropped it. "Why do you think I been practicing so much with the gun?" Pearl clamped her mouth shut and strode forward again.

"But . . . he . . . you . . ." Nell had seen with her own eyes Dick holding the gun in the crook of his arm. So had everyone else. Wolfman's rage had been directed at Dick, not Pearl. Nellie shook her head and hastened to catch up. Maybe Pearl was crazy.

Then Pearl leaped for Nellie, grabbed her by the arm, and pulled them both down again behind a large bush and a boulder. "They're comin' back," she whispered.

Nellie couldn't hear anything but the river below and one raven cawing to another, one across the road from the other. She spied the first raven in the top of a scraggly fir tree above where they hid. Then she, too, heard another auto, but coming up the hill, not down, this one making the grade more easily than the first, and so more quietly. What they both feared, happened. The vehicle stopped just short of where they lay hidden. A door opened. A man's voice said: "Someone else motored this way. A while ago." A mumbled answer and another door opened. A dog barked.

Pearl grabbed Nell and pulled her head down as Nell began to get to her knees. She knew that voice and she knew that dog. The sheriff and Moonshine! From nowhere it seemed, Pearl dragged a gun and pointed it at Nell. Shut up, she mouthed, then leaned over to whisper in the slightest of breath, "Or I'll kill your dog, too."

CHAPTER 11

Nell froze. What if Pearl weren't crazy and she had shot the wolf-dog? That meant she was an excellent shot. And a quick one. Target practice. Now she understood. Nell would endanger herself; she already had, but she wouldn't endanger Moonshine, or indeed, the sheriff. Her face was almost smashed into Pearl's leg. She could feel the tension and strength in it as she waited, trying to figure out what to do. If she wrestled with Pearl, the noise would draw the dog closer. If she could pull away and run toward the sheriff, she didn't think Pearl would shoot. Or would she? Seconds passed, then a minute. A muffled conversation drifted over to the two women. Neither moved.

Sheriff Azgo called the dog. Doors slammed. The auto started again, traveling up the road and winding out of hearing. Nell wanted to cry with frustration. Rescue so close! And relief. Moonshine had survived his leap into the roaring river!

"Why did you do that?" Nellie pulled herself out of Pearl's grasp and sat back on her haunches, glancing along the road, knowing it was empty. "They would have taken us back down to safety! How could you be so stupid?"

Pearl stood up, her face caught between anger and relief. "Safety for you, maybe. What about me? If I show up with the sheriff anywhere, I'm a dead cookie."

"I can't believe that. You're just dramatizing everything." Even as she said it, Nellie wavered. The memory of Wolfman Pitts's rage and his deliberate cutting of the dog's rope told her enough about the nature of at least one of Pearl's companions. "Besides, the sheriff would make certain you were safe. You could come to Ketchum, stay with me."

"If he stays around up here, he'll be dead, just like that other sheriff. Just like your precious sheepherder. Dumb Basque." Pearl stood up and brushed accumulated sand and dust off her clothes, not that it made any difference. "You say you're from Chicago. I heard there were gangsters there. Now you've met the Idaho kind." She gave Nellie a twisted smile. "And what would I

241

do in Ketchum? Be your helper?" She shook her head. "Not me. Find another flunky." She tossed her head again and her hair came loose, a cascade of blond, not as pale as earlier because of dust and grease. She tucked the gun in her satchel and plaited her hair into a braid, wrapped it on her head, and pinned it up with bobby pins taken from the satchel. "Let's go." Abruptly, she moved up the road.

Nellie followed, thinking furiously. Domingo was killed by this troop of outlaw moonshiners, that much was clear. And Pearl knew who did it. Nellie couldn't help worrying what would happen when the first auto that passed turned around and met the sheriff and Moonshine and probably Gwynn. They might be in grave danger. The sheriff was armed, she knew. But what about Gwynn? Who was in the first vehicle? Was it the sedan? She guessed not, judging by the way it had labored up the road. It must have been an older automobile with narrow tires.

Hiking along the road sped the women's progress. Nellie knew how tired she was from clambering over obstacles along the creek and welcomed the relief of easy walking, while fearing the return of either auto. Hunger gnawed at her; surely Pearl must be hungry as well. They carried two fish and could get more. Pine cones from the lodge-pole trees abounded. Maybe she could find nuts inside them. She picked up several as they strode along, side-by-side.

"What're you doing?"

"I thought I'd see if there were nuts or seeds in these cones. I'm hungry. Aren't you?" The sun had dropped behind the steep mountainside in the canyon, so they walked in shade but still plenty of daylight. "How far do you think we've come?"

"Maybe a mile or two, if that, along the creek. That's too slow. If we're gonna make the campout by dark, we've got to move along."

"Maybe we'll run into both autos meeting each other. Then what?"

"Then we watch the fireworks, from a distance." Pearl laughed. "I'd like to see that!" She almost skipped ahead.

"Wait for me," Nellie called. Her feet ached; her head ached; her stomach ached. Her camera pack burdened her shoulders like a pack of rocks and she longed to leave it by the wayside. Little sleep for two nights running and little food over the same period was wearing her down. She wondered at the strength and resilience of Pearl.

They traveled again through thick forests of short, skinny trees. From time to time, a meadow appeared either to the right or the left. Wildflowers grew in a riot of color. Nellie wanted to stop and look at and smell the profusion of purple, red, white, and yellow. She knew quite a few from a book Goldie showed her, and some bore slight resemblances to domestic flowers. The leaves in which the fish were wrapped had grown below small white blossoms, like lily-of-the-valley. "Wait. I want to look at the flowers." She wanted to rest.

Pearl stopped and waited, then grew impatient. "We can't lollygag." She sat on a broken tree trunk, gray, twisted, and gaunt as if it were older than the forest itself, much larger than anything they'd seen growing. She closed her eyes and her whole body sagged. "We're not gonna make it tonight. We better think about where we can hide and rest and maybe catch us another fish or two, before it gets dark."

The creek was smaller but noisier because of the pitch of the hillside and the number of rocks in it. The uneven thrum of water lay off to their right. "If we go back to the creek, we'll miss the 'fireworks' as you say," Nellie said. "Where do you suppose both autos went? I'd have thought at least one would have returned by now."

"The road ends up there a piece, and then

there's a horse track to the lake, two lakes. Maybe they all hiked in, thinking that's where we'd be."

"We know the sheriff is looking for me. We don't know who was in the other one. Maybe it was someone bringing up supplies."

"Hmph. You don't know outfitters, that's clear. If they don't pack it in on their horses, too bad."

A depressing thought occurred to Nellie. "Maybe there isn't any campout going on right now. Maybe no one is at the lake except . . . and then the sheriff will show up with Moonshine. . . ."

"It will be chaos," Pearl said, discouragement in every line of her body and every syllable of her words. "We better hope Luke or Joe or somebody is up there with a passel of tourists."

"Let's go a little farther and keep an eye out for something that might work as a shelter. I doubt we'll find another half cabin, though," Nellie said, thinking of the protection those walls had given them, whether real or only perceived. They walked in silence for a while and then rounded a bend. Three automobiles were parked at the end of the road: the sheriff's car, which Nellie recognized, and an old Model T Ford, which she didn't. Both were empty. The third auto was an Oldsmobile: Nellie's own. She dashed over to it.

"This is mine. This is my auto." She touched and patted it, then turned to Pearl. "How did it get here? Do you know?"

Pearl shook her head and turned away. Nellie was certain she did know. The door opened easily. There was no key in the ignition, but nothing seemed harmed inside. She wished she knew how to start the vehicle without the ignition key. Surely, anyone who stole automobiles knew how to do just that. She closed the door, feeling frustrated and sad that she had the means to escape, but not the knowledge.

"All right. Now what? It's going to be dark soon. The sheriff and my dog must be at the campout, thinking I'll be there, too, because my auto is here. Whoever came up in that Model T must be at the campout, too. You don't want to be seen with the sheriff. I want to go home."

No sound came from Pearl; she chewed on her lip instead. "I don't know what to do. Seems like there'll be a big brouhaha up in that camp. Maybe it's goin' on right now."

They both listened. Only a slight breeze at treetop level disturbed the silence, and then the scolding of a squirrel. Nell noted the lack of birds; not since the ravens when they'd been hidden down by the scree had she seen anything flying.

"I say we keep hiking as long as we can see. How far is the lake?"

"Maybe a mile. Maybe a tad more." Pearl kicked at the dust, clearly undecided.

"There are tourists, we hope. We should both be safe no matter who is there. Your outlaw band isn't going to hurt a bunch of tourists, are they? The sheriff is looking for me, not the moonshine men. My dog —" Her heart ached at the thought of him. "He won't take on anyone as long as he's with the sheriff, I wouldn't think." Except whoever had stolen her from the roadhouse cabin. Wolfman Pitts, maybe. Her skin flinched at the thought of that man wrapping her in a blanket and knocking her out.

"All right. But you go first. And remember I have this gun." Pearl patted her bag. "Don't you do anything to tell the sheriff you're on the trail, or I'll shoot your dog."

"But what if we run into them? I can't help that." Nell was eager to begin the trek up the rough track, but she didn't want to endanger Moonshine or the sheriff.

Pearl chewed on her lip again. "Go. If they're fightin' with each other, we'll hear that."

The dusty trail, spotted now and again with horse manure, wound up and through the trees. By now, Nell figured the altitude was quite high; she felt how much harder she had to breathe, and she'd spent a couple weeks at the sheep camp. Pearl must feel it even more. The forest was less densely packed, but ancient trunks and stumps still littered the floor, looking like ghosts in the deepening twilight.

"I can't see anymore," she complained in a low voice to the woman behind her. "We're going to have to use the flashlight if we want to continue." She sat down on a huge old log and Pearl sat beside her, breathing harder than usual.

Nellie knew her pace was slow, but she also felt she'd walked five miles since they left the vehicles behind. Many nights Alphonso had come back late from his rambles. How had he seen? And where was he now? For some time, Nell had realized that the direction the two of them had been climbing was not the same direction that Alphonso, the sheriff, and she had taken that night they moved the camp. And yet, the Fourth of July Creek splashed down the mountainside in a narrow canyon with few side canyons, if any.

It would be easy in this dense forest to

pass by Alphonso and the sheep if they were only a hundred yards off to either side. Still, she would have expected to smell the lanolin or smoke from a campfire, or hear the bell of a lead ewe or the ping of a horseshoe on rock. Instead, the dark silence of the forest surrounded them. It seemed unnaturally hushed, as if waiting for something to happen.

As if on cue, a gunshot cracked and echoed. Then a second one.

"Omigod. They're killing each other!" Nell stood, preparatory to fleeing down.

"Hsst!" Pearl was standing too. "Listen!"

In the distance, voices swelled, then diminished. To Nellie, the sound came from all directions. "What is it?"

"Huntin' is my guess. They shot a bear or an elk. Maybe a mountain lion." She cackled. "That'll get 'em in deep doo with the sheriff, I'd guess. There's rules about when you can hunt and when you can't. 'Course the outfitters don't care." Her spirits seemed very much improved. "Let's go. We're almost there. We can say we was stranded when our horse shied at a lion and ran off without us. Them tourists believe any such story, even if the outfitters don't. They're no never mind anyway."

"What about the sheriff?"

"What about him? It'll be clear I ain't with him. You, neither." She swung around and faced Nellie. "You can't leave with him, though. If we go down with the tourists, then I'm not in no trouble with Dick." She pondered that statement. "I don't think. I'll just tell the boys I followed you up here and couldn't stop you. But if you go out with the sheriff, then —" She sat down again. "Oh, it's too complicated. Why did I ever go with you? I'm in Dutch no matter what I do here."

Even in the dark, Nellie knew Pearl was crying. She was young and troubled and in danger, not the tough cookie she portrayed herself, capable of handling any circumstance. Tentatively, Nell placed an arm around the young woman's shoulder. "Let's just see what's going on up there. We don't know the moonshiners were in that Model T. There'd be no reason for them to hike to the lake, would there? I'm sure you're right. They would have gone down to the road and out, looking for us that way."

When Pearl didn't flinch under Nellie's touch, she ventured another proposal. "Don't kill Moonshine, Pearl. I'd never forgive you if you did, and it isn't necessary, no matter what. Moonie is just an innocent dog, an animal that loves me, even if I've exposed him to danger. It wouldn't be fair." She wanted to ask for the gun, but she didn't know how to use it anyway. Next time she saw Lulu, she'd remedy that lack.

Pearl snuffled, a loud, guttural sound. Then she dug in her bag and pulled out the long flashlight. "We better use this, but cover up everything except a teeny beam. Just in case."

The two of them inched along, Pearl in front, Nellie walking in her footsteps as much as possible. No one jumped out at them. The voices grew louder, interjected with laughs and an occasional woman's squeal. Finally, through the trees, they could see a large flat meadow and a campfire surrounded by men and women, outlined in profile or visible in the leaping flames. To one side in the light of a flashlight held by someone not visible, a man worked over a pile of fur. Several canvas tents stood in a row behind the fire. The scene looked like what it was: tourists having an adventure in the Wild West.

From where they stood, Nellie recognized no one. She didn't know whether to be relieved or frustrated once again. Where were the sheriff, her dog, and Gwynn? "Do you recognize anyone?" she whispered to her companion.

251

In answer, Pearl doused her light, stuffed it in her bag, and strode forward. "Howdy, everyone," she called. "Thank goodness, we found you!" The gaiety stopped as two of the men and one of the women stood. "We got thrown from our horse. Scared by a polecat. We heard a gunshot and all the laughing and figured we was gonna make it up here alive!" She tittered, an actress through and through. She turned back to Nellie and motioned her forward. "Better think up a name," she whispered.

Everyone talked at once, but a tall man in a Stetson came forward. "Wal, glad you found us, little lady."

Nellie recognized Luke's voice with the questionable southern drawl. The outfitter she'd met her first day in the sheep camp. Would he remember her? And surely, he must know Pearl. They all lived in or around Stanley in the summertime. If he did, he didn't let on. "Come sit around the fire. You and your friend shouldn't have been out in these hills alone. We just shot a bear. Scared the cub off into the woods. Likely he'll grow up to eat wandering ladies like you."

Pearl managed not to give him a dirty look, instead gushing, "Oh, thank you. We lost all our gear. We're so hungry we could *eat* a bear."

Two women rose to greet them and made room around the fire, retrieving two camp chairs from a stack near one of the tents. They clucked like hens, found two plates, and dished up beans and mystery meat for the wanderers. Nellie accepted her plate and tried not to gobble, nodding and smiling around.

Pearl was doing enough talking for three people, describing an encounter with a mountain lion, being chased through the woods, losing their lovely horse — a true 'Paloosa that belonged to her uncle and how angry he would be, maybe they could go search for it in the morning — stumbling through the dark, falling into the creek, being frightened half to death by the gunshot. Nellie quit listening and studied the people around her. Luke was the only one she recognized. He listened, and she could not tell from his expression whether he believed the story or not.

"Then you're not the lost woman the sheriff was here asking about," Luke said, cutting into the flow. "He didn't say there was two."

"Where is he?" Nell asked, realizing too late how abrupt she sounded. "We saw an automobile down the road a ways and wondered if the owner would ever get back."

Pearl cast daggers with her eyes. "Sure did. But we didn't know if it had been abandoned or not and we didn't want to wait all alone in the dark. Why, we heard growls and rustles and banshees, I can tell you." And she was off on another story. The women at the fire hung on every word, as did one or two of the men. A fairly portly gentleman fetched coffee for Nell and Pearl, asked if they were cold, and rounded up two blankets to put around their shoulders. He took extra time with Pearl, which she played to the hilt, grabbing his hand and thanking him, "Kind sir!"

Nell wandered over toward the man with the pile of fur, but veered off when she realized he was cleaning and skinning the bear. In the firelight, she saw horses rounded up in a makeshift corral off to one side of the meadow, but it was too dark for her to venture there. Mostly, she wanted to lie down and sleep.

Luke joined her at the edge of the group around the fire. "Aren't you that sheep lady I met a couple weeks ago?"

Not sure just exactly how to respond, Nell said, "Sheep lady? What makes you say that? Do I smell like sheep?" She laughed, feeling as phony as Pearl sounded.

"You sure look familiar." He wasn't going

to let it go. "I thought I met you at a camp down the canyon. There you were, tending sheep all alone." He smiled and his eyes reflected the yellow flames.

"Oh, yes, I visited the sheep camp back a while. Were you the one leading tourists through? This night has been so . . . so discombobulating, I can't remember much of anything. Do you have a spare tent the two of us could use? I'm very tired." If she could just get some sleep, she could figure out what to do next. The sheriff had not returned to his car. Had he been waiting, hidden in the woods? If so, he now knew where Nellie was and that she was with Pearl.

"Hank," Luke called, startling Nellie with his loud voice. "Did you bring up a tent with the other gear?"

An affirmative answer came back. Luke turned to Nell. "We had some additional guests come up in an auto this afternoon. They packed in more gear. O'Donnell seems to think we can't get our fill of greenhorns up here." He snorted. "We'll round up something for you two. A couple of the men can get a feel for the 'real West,' sleepin' on the ground."

So the Model T didn't hold moonshiners, just more eastern adventurers. O'Donnell.

The man in the saloon with Gwynn. He was a cattle rancher. Did he also run "greenhorns," as Luke called them? A man of many interests.

Before long, another tent joined the line behind the fire, a little off because the ground had swelled next to the last one. Soon, all the campers had left the fire and retreated to their tents, except the two men who agreed to sleep under the stars. They acted gallantly, saying they didn't mind at all, and after all, wasn't that the true Western experience, just like cowboys on the open range? Pearl snorted as she rolled herself into the blankets Luke had brought to them.

Nellie never found a way to bring up the sheriff again, although she heard two of the women campers mention how handsome and friendly he had been. Nell would never have called Charlie Azgo friendly, so he must have been acting like Pearl did: adopting a facade to get what he wanted. Where had he gone? And where was her dog? One of the outfitters mentioned another lake farther along the trail, about a mile away. She couldn't follow it in the night, not even with the aid of moonlight, but in the morning, she vowed to wake herself early enough to explore. She assured herself with one foot that her camera lay near her. Her companion snored slightly, but it didn't keep Nellie awake.

True to her word, Nell woke up and inched toward the flap. Outside, light barely illuminated the camp — the tents, the dead fire, long lumps near it. Steam rose from the lake or, more likely, fog. As quietly as she could, she eased out the canvas opening and stood up. Across the lake and above it, rock ramparts like medieval castles guarded the cirque in which she stood. What she wouldn't give to be able to photograph the scene. Her celluloid film was ruined, but she carried several rolls of unexposed film she had hoped to experiment with, using the new roll film back for large-format camera. Her camera — it lay in the tent. If she tried to get it, she might awaken Pearl.

The outlines of the camp were filling in as dawn approached. Nell made her way to the trail on which she and Pearl had entered the camp, passing near the horses. To her dismay, a figure stepped out to meet her.

"You looking for the facilities?" he asked. It was one of the hands, the same one who had been skinning the bear.

"Yes, please."

The man pointed along the path she was following and told her to veer right. There were outhouses for the accommodation of the campers, one for women and one for men. He spoke quietly and went back toward the horses, to Nellie's relief.

Horse droppings led the way along a trail she hoped would take her to the other lake. If the sheriff and Moonie weren't at this camp, they may have tried the upper lake, knowing Nell's auto sat at the end of the road. Night overtook them and they camped out themselves. The air chilled her and she wished she had brought along one of the blankets to wrap around her shoulders. Brisk walking soon achieved what she needed, warmth. Her footsteps along the rutted dirt and rocky path sounded loud in the morning stillness and startled several deer grazing in another meadow along the way. A rocky cirque in the distance suggested where the upper lake might be, but it did not draw closer as she continued. Maybe it was more than a mile.

A low, dark animal appeared out of the woods in front of her. The darkness of the trees in the faint early light obscured her vision of it. Was it the cub and would it attack? She stopped. Turning and fleeing back to the camp wasn't a good option. Thanks to Alphonso, she already knew that running away would cause a wild animal to give chase. This one hadn't seen her yet, she was sure. If she stepped off the trail and hid, it might pass on by. It could smell her humanness, though, reminding her of how dirty she felt. She couldn't remember the last time she had washed.

A larger shadow loomed up behind the low one. Fright welled up, raising hackles on her neck and gooseflesh on her arms. She took two steps sideways and stumbled over a root. As she fell, the lower shadow leaped toward her. With raised arms, Nellie protected her face and head and hunched over, waiting to be ripped into shreds by curved talons or razor-sharp teeth.

CHAPTER 12

A wet tongue lapped at Nellie's hands. She moved them and Moonshine licked her face and wiggled with pleasure. "Moonie!" Nell trembled as she wrapped her arms around her dog, overwhelmed with relief and release of fear. When Sheriff Azgo stepped into her line of sight, she almost leaped at him. He held her close, saying nothing, letting her calm down. Moonshine barked once, but at a motion from the man, sat on his haunches and opened his mouth but kept quiet. He might have been smiling.

"You're all right," the sheriff said, in a half-question, half-statement.

Nellie nodded. Words flooded her head, but what came out surprised both of them. "I know who killed Domingo." She stood away from Charlie. "I mean, I don't know, but Pearl knows. It's someone from the moonshine group. That's who took me. Where did you find Moonie? I was sure he drowned in the river. I should never have named him Moonshine, now that I know how evil those people are, and how filthy, and —. My bag! Did you find it under the bed? My exposed film is in there.

"Where were you? How did you know I needed a room? Pearl helped me escape. She's back at the camp and I have to return. I can't let those men think she —. Where's Gwynn? Is he all right? Do you have the ignition key for my auto? Can you start it? I've been trying to find Alphonso. Where did we take him that night?"

The sheriff waited until her stream of questions ran down. He walked her along the trail until they reached a downed log and then he sat her down. "First, Gwynn is fine. He stayed with the auto at the beginning of the trail. You must not have seen him, or he you. Next, I found Moonshine down the river from Stanley several miles. He either swam or was carried by the current, but pulled himself out. He was tired, but fine, and he's been with me ever since. Now, it sounds as if you didn't drive yourself up here."

"No. I was taken from the roadhouse in the middle of the night. One of the moonshiners put me in the boot of a motor vehicle and they took me up the road to

261

their camp. It's somewhere near our first sheep camp."

"Who is 'they'?"

"I don't know for certain. Someone wrapped a blanket around my head and then struck me. When Pearl opened the boot, she was mad as blazes. The men in the camp were Dick Goodlight, Wolfman Pitts —" she shuddered but continued, "— and two other outlaw-types. There was another man near the sedan that carried me, but I never saw him and I didn't recognize his voice." Doubt crept into Nellie. Had she recognized that voice? "They brought my camera because they wanted the photos I took. I gave them my blank film. Did you find my bag?"

The light was bright enough for Nellie to see the sheriff smile. "Yes. It was under the bed. Probably a good thing. I found a box in it —"

"You didn't open it, did you?"

"And violate all the stern warnings of 'DO NOT OPEN'? Of course not. I sent it off to Jacob Levine in Twin Falls. I didn't want to be responsible for it." He raised his hands in mock horror.

"Laugh, now, Charlie, but when that film gets developed, we will know who murdered Domingo, I'm certain of it. Wolfman Pitts is probably the murderer. He was going to —" No need to go into that yet. "The men at the moonshine camp left to deliver their, their 'hooch' and that night Pearl and I escaped. We've been traveling this way ever since. I wanted to find either the campout or Alphonso."

"Didn't you see or hear me along the road? I saw your sign. That's how I knew what direction to follow. Otherwise, I would have stopped and turned around."

"We saw you, but Pearl said she'd shoot Moonie if I made a sound. She thinks if she's seen with you, the moonshiners will do something terrible to her. They all think you're out here to find the illegal still and shut it down, that you're in cahoots with the revenuers." Nellie shut her mouth. She was beginning to sound like one of them. "They killed the other sheriff already. Domingo must have found their operation, too, and maybe threatened one of them."

"Domingo would have joined in," the sheriff said. "He liked his liquor too much. More likely, he didn't pay for what he drank."

"And they'd shoot him for that?"

"Maybe. Now," he said, standing up. "What are we going to do with you and your dog? And Pearl?"

"Our plan was to find the tourist group, stick with them, and return with them. Then, Pearl won't be in trouble with Dick and the others. She'll say I escaped and she followed and stuck with me. Once we get back, I can return to Ketchum. She can do what she wants."

Sheriff Azgo lifted his hand to stop Nell, but she kept going. "In the meantime, I'm fairly certain I can find out who killed Domingo and I can get that information to you. If you do want to shut down the liquor operation, I can tell you where it is. But there's that other man. Pearl knows him. Maybe I can get that information, too. I'll be a sleuth for you."

"I want you to come back with me."

"No! Then Pearl will be in real trouble. Without her — She rescued me and I can't desert her now." She rubbed Moonshine's neck and ears. "The still lies next to the creek in a bend that dips back a long ways from the road on one end and isn't too far from the road as it turns toward where Alphonso and I were camped, but it's lower, not higher. At least I think that's the case. There are only evergreens and no aspen trees in the immediate vicinity. Maybe they've used them all to keep the fire going under the, the pot."

"And if Goodlight and Pitts and the others catch up with you? What then?" He wouldn't be deterred from scaring her.

Even the thought of the one man frightened Nellie. Pitts was an animal. "We'll be with the tourists and the outfitters. That should be safe enough." She sounded confident, but she didn't feel that way. Pearl had a gun; Nellie wished she did, too. Asking the sheriff for his didn't seem like a good idea.

Sheriff Azgo held out his hand and Nellie took it. She'd held his hand before, but she knew he offered it to bring her to her feet. His skin was warm, his fingers rough with calluses, as if he worked physically as well as mentally.

"You should know this about Domingo's death, Nellie. The bullet to his head came from a rifle, so whoever did it was a distance from him. You saw how roughed up he was. Either before or after he was shot, I believe he was pulled by a rope behind a horse in heavy brush, probably sagebrush. There were rope burns around his wrists. Whoever killed him, tortured him as well. If Pearl knows the murderer, she also knows about the rest, is my guess. Maybe she rescued you. Maybe there was a plan to get rid of you in the forest where you'd never be found."

Sobering thoughts, but Nellie believed the sheriff was wrong about Pearl. There had been many chances for Pearl to "get rid" of her along the way. The only threat had been to Moonshine. Still, so far they had not been followed. The reason might be to give Pearl time to do her job. Nellie knew she herself was naive about people she met in Idaho.

The morning light had grown stronger while they talked. "If I'm going to get back before the others are up, I'd better go."

"You're too late. The hands will have breakfast ready, so you better think of something to explain yourself. I'll let you return, but not without Moonshine. He can be your guard until you get back down to the valley. Gwynn or I will be waiting for you, either at the Rocking O or at the saloon in Stanley."

"The Rocking O? Why there?"

"O'Donnell loans out the horses for the campouts, for a price, and some of his hands work as outfitters — not for him, but to make ends meet. He's not a generous man when it comes to wages. He brings people in from the East from time to time to pretend like they're cowboys. I don't know what his game is there." They began to walk back toward the camp. "The outfitters will likely take the tourists back to the Rocking O to return the horses."

"My auto. I forgot about it. How will I get it back to the highway?" She didn't want to lose her means of transportation.

"Gwynn and I will take care of that."

"But the ignition key —"

"We'll take care of it. But if the moonshine gang sees us driving it, that may not be good for you and Pearl. It must have been one of them that drove it up here in the first place." He placed a hand on Nellie's shoulder. "Nell, I do not believe this is a good idea."

"Leave the automobile there, then. We can drive it down to Stanley later." Later, she meant, when all the mysteries were solved and the bad people were jailed and she was safe and Pearl was safe. "Now, go." Then she left the secure feeling his hand on her gave her, and ran lightly toward camp, calling Moonie to come.

As soon as she saw a person, she shouted. "Look. I found Moonshine!" She ran a few more steps. "Pearl, I found my dog!"

Pearl sat with the other tourists around the fireplace, a metal plate in her lap. Her face changed from a gaunt paleness to one with color, as if a paintbrush dipped in pink had washed over her. "Nellie!" The plate clattered to the ground as she stood to greet Nell, wrapping her in a bear hug and whispering, "I thought they'd gotten you." Out loud, she laughed. "I thought you'd fallen in. Where you been?"

"I took a walk up the trail a ways. When I saw this animal, I thought the bear cub had returned, looking for its mother." She glowered at one of the hands who tended the fire. "But it was Moonshine. I worried he'd run away forever last night when the mountain lion scared our horse." She knelt down to her dog and hugged him. "But here he is. He must have followed our scent to find our camp! Smart dog," she crooned.

The expression on the other woman's face was halfway between relief at Nellie showing up and exasperation about the dog. Pearl knew Moonie had been with the sheriff. Once the two of them were alone, Nell would have to tell her something approximating the truth. To forestall that moment and give herself time to think, she said, "I smell breakfast. Can a visitor get a bite to eat? I'm starving!"

The same two men who had brought coffee the night before showed up with a plate heaped with fried potatoes, sausage patties, muffins, gravy, and two eggs. "Oh my. I haven't eaten this much in a week!"

Luke showed up as well. "I don't allow dogs in camp. The horses get nervous and dogs scare away the animals the campers come to see."

And shoot, Nellie thought, but didn't say. "This one is well behaved and I'll keep him by my side." She dug in to her food and turned toward the two gentlemen. "You're so kind!" she said, echoing Pearl from the night before.

Pearl and Nellie let the touring women talk them into staying with the group, at least for the day and another night. They hiked together around the lake, then walked up to the higher lake, Washington Lake, accompanied by Moonshine who stayed by Nellie's side as if stuck there. Some of the men headed out with guns intent on bagging another bear. Nellie wished them bad luck. The day was warm and the scenery beautiful. Except for chatter from time to time, Nellie enjoyed the sounds of scolding squirrels and ravens calling to each other. One of them changed its call to a metallic "krr-poing" sound. Perhaps he was courting. The rock cirque around Washington Lake was largely talus, a stark contrast to the trees beyond Fourth of July Lake. Nearly every sound elicited a faint echo, as if in an amphitheater.

More than anything, Nellie wanted to bathe in the lake. She proposed that she and Pearl remain behind when the others began to ready themselves to return to camp, embellishing Pearl's story from the night before by adding a day of wandering and little food and no water except a creek, which was being fished in by a bear, so they'd avoided it. The women tittered and warned them to return before dark. They would guard the trail ahead so no men would venture upon them while they were in the water.

Once they were alone, Pearl confronted Nellie about the dog and the sheriff. Nellie told her about the meeting in the woods and that the sheriff had left the area, returning to the Basin. Both of them stripped and tiptoed into the icy water. Neither stayed in long, although Nellie noticed Pearl watched her satchel as closely as Nell watched her camera pack. Moonshine waded into the water with them and then lay down by the pack. Nellie would have liked to wash her clothes too, but had not brought any soap. Nevertheless, after hesitating a few minutes, she grabbed her pants, shirt, and underthings and swished them through the water. Even getting off the dust and surface dirt and blood from scratches would make her feel cleaner.

"Now you have to wait for them to dry," Pearl pointed out. She stood on a rock on the shore, her skin rosy from the chilly dip.

"Yes, but we're not going anywhere anyway." Nellie brought her clothes out of the water, wrung them, and spread them to dry on the hot rocks around the lake. Naked, she felt vulnerable and wondered if Pearl felt the same way. If she did, it wasn't apparent. Pearl waded back into the shallows and stepped from one smooth rock to the next. Nell gathered herself together on a large flat rock and decided now was as good a time as any.

"Pearl, who killed Domingo?" It was a stark question, and Pearl seemed not to have heard it. She leaned over and inspected a piece of white rock, quartz perhaps. Just as Nell thought she'd ask again, Pearl stood and faced her, looking as if she had just stepped out of a French Impressionist's painting, one Nell had seen at the Chicago Art Institute.

"I did." Her face crumpled. "I didn't mean to. They put a rope around Domingo and pulled him through the rocks and sage. Just because they thought I'd —" She turned away and back again. "I didn't. I just

271

danced because he played music on his flute." She blushed. "I screamed. They stopped. Then Wolfman let loose that wolf dog, just like on you. I reached into the camp and got the Winchester and shot it in the air. I thought that would stop the dog. But it didn't. It tore into Domingo. I shot again, but I didn't hit the dog. I hit Domingo!" Her voice ended in a wail.

Nell didn't know what to think. Was this another act? "Who pulled him with a rope?"

Pearl squatted and dragged her hand through the water. "The Boss. Wolfman and Dick were with him. Dick started it all, saying I shouldn't have been at the sheep camp, and that I'd been fooling around with the sheepherder. Then the Boss said they'd have a little fun with the maggot-herder. He was a pain anyway. I went along because I thought I could stop them."

"Who was the Boss?"

Pearl stood and skipped a flat rock across the still surface of the lake. Both of them counted the skips: ten before it sank. She stepped over to her pile of clothes and dressed herself.

"I'm taking a walk." Subject closed.

Would Nell ever get any more information from Pearl? Nellie remembered her own scrape between two dogs at Smiley Creek.

She shuddered to think someone would have fired a gun then. And the wolfdog when it charged her at the moonshine camp. Was it really Pearl who killed it then or Dick who cradled the gun? Domingo's clothes had been torn and his body scraped. She had photos — maybe.

Nell found a grassy place a few steps away from the shore, carried her pack to it, and laid down with her head against her camera. "Here, Moonshine. Keep me warm." The dog curled up next to Nellie, who closed her eyes and felt her skin gradually warm. Her brief shivering slowed and ended. In spite of all the questions she had about Pearl's confession, drowsiness overtook her.

A low rumbling from Moonshine awoke Nellie. "What is it?" she whispered, frantically groping around for her clothes. "Pearl." No answer. Nellie rolled to her knees and glanced around, seeing her clothes with relief, and no person. Quickly, she donned her shirt and pants, still slightly damp along the seams. Moonie stood facing the trail from the other lake, the hair on his neck straight up, the rumble almost too low to hear, but continuous, more like a cat's purr than a threatening dog sound. Nellie's own hackles rose. She grabbed her camera pack and Pearl's satchel, which still lay by the shore, and moved toward several large rocks, hoping to hide herself before whatever her dog growled at appeared along the path.

A boulder as tall as Nellie rested near one of the trees and she hurried toward it for cover. Just as she reached the rock, Moonie's growl turned to both barking and snarling. A man leaped up onto the top from behind it, a movement so rapid Nellie could hardly stop herself in her own haste. He prepared to jump down on Nellie, his body hunched in its buckskin, the fringes still dancing from the movement, his hands grasping and his face a rotten-toothed menacing grimace. Wolfman Pitts. "Now there ain't no one to save you. I'll murder that dog of yours soon as look at 'em." He pulled a knife from a strap near his boot. "And you, too. Comin' along to ruin me."

"Heel," Nellie ordered and Moonshine moved back to her leg, growling low and crouched as well. "The outfitters will get you, Mr. Pitts. They're just down the way. Leave me alone." Her voice quavered and her knees felt like water. She took a step backward, still clutching her camera pack and the satchel. The gun. Was it still there? "And I didn't ruin you. I don't know what you're talking about. What do you mean?"

While she talked, she slipped one hand into the satchel, groping blindly, found a metal tube and pulled on it, then realized it was the flashlight.

"A knife's quiet. It slices without a sound. No outfitters gonna hear me, just your screams, and that'll be too late." He crouched even lower and Nellie could tell from his eyes that he intended to do what he said. "That skunk of a sheriff'll find my still, but he won't never find you. The varmints'll take care of that."

"He doesn't want your still. He wants the murderer — th . . . the man who killed Domingo." She gripped the flashlight hard. "I have a gun. I'll shoot you just like your dog was shot."

The man's red-rimmed eyes widened and he snarled like a coyote and threw himself toward Nellie. She dodged to the side away from his knife, but his other arm caught her as he landed and whirled her to him, the camera pack caught between them, but protecting her from the knife hand that slashed a tear in the pack. She ducked her head and rammed it up against his chin and stomped on his foot. Still, his arm squeezed like a vise, even as he almost fell backward. Moonshine attacked the man's head, his teeth bared. A bloody rip appeared along one cheek. By then, Nellie had the flashlight out of the pack. She beat along the upper arm holding the knife and was sure she broke it, but he continued to slash, finally slashing her upraised forearm. Even as she dropped the flashlight, the sunlight off the blade almost blinded her. She pushed against the man with all her strength and knew this was the same person who had stolen her from the roadhouse. Never had she felt so helpless against such iron strength. Then Moonshine gripped the man's shoulder above the knife arm. His teeth sank into the buckskin, sank deeper, and the dog shook his head, bracing his feet on the man's back. Wolfman Pitts screamed, released the knife, and let Nellie go. She stumbled backward and fell sideways, her head striking a rock, although not hard enough to knock her out.

The wolf-man dove to the ground, rolling over, and Moonshine released his grip. The man scrambled to his feet, again in a crouch, like a mountain lion's. His hands curled and he swiped toward the dog, but Moonie was quicker. He leaped once again, this time at the throat of his enemy, his snarl deadly and loud, his muzzle bared, his teeth sharp. Pitts dodged just enough so that the dog only grazed his throat, but the man fell, grabbing onto Moonshine as he went down. Over and over they rolled, crunching against rock, dust flying. Blood splattered, landing on stone and leaves.

Nellie crawled to her hands and knees, trying to clear her head. Dizziness swarmed her eyes, her ears. The knife. If she could find the knife, she could kill Wolfman Pitts. She scrambled toward the large boulder and hurriedly searched the ground with her hands and her eyes. There it was, a red stain on the tip of the blade. She scooped it up and gripped it in her right hand. With her left, she grabbed the flashlight, still a good weapon, and scuttled toward the raging man-dog rowl. As at Smiley Creek, she couldn't get at one of the pair without risking hurting the other, Moonie. Just like Pearl.

As she circled, the twisting, snarling man-and-beast clump came to rest against another boulder. The man grasped the dog with both hands and lifted him in the air. Nellie dashed around to the side and shoved the knife into Wolfman Pitts's left shoulder. She felt it meet gristle and bone. Sickened, she shoved harder. He screamed and tossed the dog ten feet to land on its back in a loud *whumpf.* Moonie lay still.

"Now you ain't got no help." The man

panted. Blood poured down one side of his face. He reached around to his back, clutched the knife handle, and, with a sharp yank, pulled it out, tossing it into bushes alongside the rock. "I'll get you with my bare hands. Watch you strangle, your tongue turn purple, your eyes bulge."

Nellie didn't wait. She clambered to her feet and began to run, leaving her pack and her dog. The trail was trampled and dry so that she could move fast. Her pursuer might be strong, but he was hurt and losing blood. He had to weaken. It was less than a mile to the camp. "Help!" she called, knowing her voice carried no farther than the next bend. "Luke! Pearl!" She tried to make her voice deeper, but she needed every breath to keep placing one foot in front of the other without stumbling.

A gunshot barked from behind her and echoed off the rocky cirque. "Oh, no." Nellie fell to her knees. He shot Moonshine! She hung her head a moment, then realized if the man had a gun, he would have used it sooner, wouldn't he? She stood and turned in the path, waiting for the monster who followed her. Only a forest quiet greeted her. No pounding, no snarling, no rocks cracking against each other. No birds or squirrels either. One slow step at a time,

Nellie retraced her steps, wondering if she were walking into gruesome death.

At the lake, Moonie stood next to the leather-clad figure lying along the shore. Nellie moved cautiously forward. Wolfman Pitts didn't move. Was it a trick? Moonshine wouldn't stand still if Pitts were alive, she reasoned, so she approached in a circular fashion, finding a gun along the edge of her path as she crept up behind the man's head. She picked it up and she, too, stood over the man. A bleeding hole in his temple told her all she needed to know. She resisted the strong desire to shoot, to place another hole beside the one already there.

The water lapped quietly, barely moving. Her hand trembled. Her mouth filled with saliva. Think! The gun in her hand was Pearl's, Nellie was certain. When Moonshine was the target of the gun, Nellie had a good look at it. This was the same kind. Where was Pearl? Even as she looked around, she realized that this young woman had saved her once again. So much for the sheriff's theory that Pearl intended to "do her in."

Thumps along the trail made her heart beat faster. She prepared to run again. Were the rest of the moonshiners coming now, intent on finishing what Pitts started? No time. Nellie raised the gun with both hands and aimed it toward the path, her finger on the trigger. Moonshine braced himself against her, his growl reactivated. They had faced down one enemy together. Perhaps they could do it again, this time with a real weapon on their side.

The noise became a horse trotting rapidly and then the animal itself with Luke in the saddle. He reined in as soon as he saw Nellie pointing the gun at him. "The women heard a scream. I heard a gunshot. Are you all right?" He jumped down and walked slowly toward her. "Are you aiming that at me?"

Nellie was wary of any man after what she'd just been through. Luke didn't seem dangerous, so she lowered the gun, but not all the way. "It depends. Who's with you?" Her voice sounded tinny to her own ears. Another horseman appeared, this one riding bareback. Hank, the man who brought up the Model T. The man who did errands. He reined up, too, but remained on his horse, staying back in the shade of the trees. When he turned and looked behind him, Nellie realized she knew him, or rather, had photographed him. He had been sitting at the bar in the saloon and had shaded his face when she readied her camera for the long row of cowboys drinking.

Only then did Luke see the prone man behind Nellie. "Who is that? What happened here?" He stepped toward Nellie. "You're bleeding," he said, gesturing toward her arm with the slashed sleeve, her left arm. "Miss Burns, let me help you." Moonshine crouched, ready to spring on the outfitter.

"It's all right, Moonshine." She lowered the gun the rest of the way and turned back toward Wolfman Pitts, deciding in that moment what to do.

"I shot him," she said.

CHAPTER 13

Luke and Nellie stood over the body. The face in death still menaced and his eyes stared, a blind gelatinous leer at the world. To Nell, he looked as murderous as when he was alive and she stepped back. A life gone, and she couldn't feel anything but a release of fear. She understood now that she could kill a man. Before Luke could say anything or Nell could sort out why she said she'd murdered Pitts, a long *Halloooooo* sounded from halfway around the lake. "Nellieeeeee. Are you all right?" There was no mistaking Pearl's voice. Nellie looked at the gun in her hand and back up the lake. If Pearl didn't shoot Pitts, then who did?

"Pearl!" she called. "Come back!" She faced away from the grotesque body and turned toward the lake, as serene as if nothing had happened along its rocky strand, her mind filled with waves of words trying to work them into an explanation. "We took

282

a bath in the lake after the other ladies left. Pearl went off exploring. I washed out my things and fell asleep, waiting for them to dry." Nell gestured toward the figure that was now moving toward them, her progress slow and uneven because of talus running from the cirque down into the water itself. "I got dressed and then Moonshine began to growl. This . . . this man —" Nellie decided not to identify him "— came out of the woods and attacked me. Moonshine tried to rescue me." Her voice broke and she knelt down and hugged her dog, murmuring as she ran one hand along his neck and his back to see if she could find any cuts. The other hand still held the gun. The weight of it was beginning to feel comfortable, as if it did indeed belong to her.

"So you shot him in self-defense," Luke said. "Where'd you get that gun?" He reached for it, but Nellie held onto it. She wasn't giving it up to anyone.

"We carried it. For protection."

By then, Pearl was narrowing the gap and Nellie ran forward, her own breath coming in short gasps as if she, rather than her companion, had been clambering over rocks and whitewashed logs. "He attacked me. I shot him. While you were gone."

Pearl grasped Nellie by the shoulders.

"Are you all right? I heard a scream, that dog barking and snarling. . . ." She let her words drift, then reached for the gun, just as Luke had done. Nellie twisted out of the other woman's grasp, which hadn't been all that gentle, and said, "He tried to kill me and Moonshine both. He came out of the woods and threatened to . . . he had a knife . . . I tried to. . . ." Calm down, Nellie told herself. She had already explained what happened, and by her own false admission warned Pearl. More words might make the story change. Until the two of them were alone, she couldn't talk about exactly what happened. She had been certain Pearl had fired the gun, but now Nell's lie became the story.

"What do we do now?" Nellie directed her question at Luke, who was already dragging the body by its arms over toward Hank's horse, who shied away. "Hold that nag still. We gotta take this madman back to town. May as well be you." Hank dismounted and helped Luke roll the body over and lift him across the back of the horse. His curled lip showed what he thought of his assigned task. Luke continued. "I'll get the girls on my horse and walk back with them. Don't take the darned body into camp. No need to scare everybody. Keep an eye out. This son-of-a . . . so-and-so don't usually travel alone. For one thing, he's got a half-dog, half-wolf that'll kill you."

While the men performed their task, Nellie rounded up her camera pack and stuck the gun into a side pocket, strapping it shut. Her arm hurt and she saw that it oozed blood along the line where the knife cut. She needed to get it wrapped. She exchanged glances with Pearl, who picked up her satchel, hefting it to show how light it was now. "I'll walk," she said.

Nellie found the long flashlight, its glass broken and the mechanism probably useless, and handed it to Pearl. Luke's warning to Hank finally penetrated. She glanced toward the woods from which Wolfman had leaped onto the rock. Were Dick and the others out there? Maybe one of them had shot Pitts, not wanting to create more trouble for themselves than they were in already. All she could see were the trunks of trees and the whitish remnants that littered the forest wherever they traveled. If other men skulked in the woods, they were gone now. "I'll ride," Nell announced to Luke. He helped her mount, wanting her to give him her camera pack, which she refused to do, while she stood with one leg on his cupped hands and, when he lifted, swung her other leg over the horse's back. This horse was taller than any she had ever ridden, but as they began to move down the trail, she discovered it was also the most comfortable, like riding in a rocking-chair.

Hank led the group and moved at a faster pace, soon disappearing around bends in the trail. His burden's legs and arms flapped and it was a relief to see him go. Luke walked beside Nellie; Pearl strode along the other side. Nellie's arm throbbed and she wished she could bind it up soon. Although the ride was smooth, she felt blood run, then stop, then run again.

As soon as Hank was out of sight, Luke reached for the horse's bridle and stopped the procession. "You better tell me what happened. That was Wolfman Pitts. Pearl knows him, so don't pretend you don't. That cock-and-bull story last night about falling off a horse and losing your way didn't make sense then and it still doesn't. What's going on?"

Nellie avoided looking at Pearl. Each waited for the other to speak. Neither did. "Are you both involved in the moonshine operation? Are they after you because of that?"

"Moonshine?" Nellie said.

"Moonshine!" Pearl said.

The dog barked. He had been following the horse and trotted now to the front of the line. "I don't know anything about moonshine," Nellie said quickly, "except for my dog here. That's his name. What we told you last night was true. We were lost in the woods. But I knew there was a dude camp-out going on up this road, so we searched for you and we found you!"

"The sheriff was looking for you, Miss Burns. You two don't fool me." Luke eyed Nellie for a moment. "You can keep it to yourself for now, but you killed a man back there. You're gonna have to answer to the law for that one, even if you murdered him in self-defense. There ain't no witnesses but you. I can tell the sheriff what you looked like — like a wild animal attacked you — but you better be thinking about how this happened. And where you found that gun." He glanced over at Pearl. "And the two of you better get your stories straight. Right now, I'd say there's a bunch of holes in them." He released the bridle and began walking. His horse followed, and the three of them spoke not another word until they reached camp. Then Luke muttered, "Blast it! Now you tell these dudes that you fell off a rock into the lake or some such and scraped yourself up good. I don't want them scared and tellin' their friends not to come here."

Nellie suspected that the tourists would be thrilled with a story of what really happened and that would attract even more tourists, hoping for an adventure of their own. But she followed Luke's orders, as did Pearl. Soon, the women were treating Nellie's arm with an ointment — Mrs. Pinkham's Treatment — and binding up her arm, and in truth, it helped. The bleeding stopped, as did the throbbing. Around the campfire, she spun a tale about exploring the shore, standing on a rock, hearing a huge bear behind her, and falling in. Pearl swore there was no bear, that it was only she looking for berries to eat, and the two of them bantered back and forth. One of the hands told a ghost story, and soon enough, everyone had retired to their respective tents, except for the two men who were supposed to sleep on the ground. Nellie wondered if they regretted their gallantry, especially when it began to rain as she settled into her blanket. The candle she had lit and placed just inside the tent flap comforted her; she was reluctant to blow it out. Pearl rolled herself into her blanket and faced away from Nellie, not saying a word.

"We've got to talk about this, Pearl. As

Luke said, we'd better get our stories straight."

"What stories? You killed Wolfman Pitts. You said it yourself, or so I understand that's what you did." She didn't turn around.

"That's your gun. You shot him and then ran around the lake. I said it to protect you."

"Protect me?" Pearl rolled half over to give Nellie a fish-eye stare. Her face was gaunt and almost menacing in the flickering light. "Don't make me laugh. All you've done is cause trouble for me ever since you first took my picture at the saloon."

"I've caused *you* trouble? You and those deadbeat bandits you hang around with stole me away, destroyed my film, nearly killed Moonshine, and scared the life half out of me. You've got your nerve." What had started out as a whisper had strengthened into a normal voice and was verging on a shout.

"Dick is not a deadbeat bandit. Besides, now you know who killed Domingo. Wolfman Pitts." Pearl's voice was none too quiet, either.

"What? You said *you* did it."

In the silence that followed, both women realized their words could carry all through the camp. Maybe the raindrops muffled their argument. Nell hoped so. She listened to see if anyone stirred or talked in the other tents, but all seemed quiet. Her eyes ached and her arm had begun to throb again. So, now she was a self-admitted murderer, and Pearl was going to lie her way out of everything. Perhaps that was what poetic justice meant. Nell had certainly tried to murder the evil man by stabbing him in the back.

Moonshine, who had laid down just outside the tent flap, whined softly and his paws crept under the canvas. Nell lifted the flap and whispered, "Moonie. Come sleep with me."

"I don't want that dog in here," Pearl whispered.

"Too bad. He's in and he's staying. Just in case your *criminal* friends come back. With luck, he'll tear one of their hearts out." Nellie placed the camera pack against her stomach with her arms around it. Then she remembered. "You said you killed Domingo. Convenient, isn't it? That Wolfman Pitts is lying there dead and your story changes?"

No response.

In spite of the nightmare afternoon, Nellie fell asleep to the lullaby of the rain *thrfft*ing on the canvas and did not dream.

The next morning when Nellie awoke,

Pearl was already up and out. Nell patted her camera pack to make sure the gun was still there. It was. Moonshine was also gone. Sunlight spilled through the tent flap and the smell of bacon frying brought her fully awake. She pulled on her boots, wincing when her arm protested against its use, and joined a group around the campfire.

One of the women asked after her injury, insisted on seeing it, and decided to reclean and resalve it, once again binding it, but more loosely this time. She informed Nellie that all the women were going down a day early so the men could go farther into the mountains hunting for elk. No one seemed to mind, least of all the chatty informant who explained they would be visiting Stanley to see a "real" saloon and stay at a roadhouse along the river. Beds sounded more alluring than sleeping on the ground. She assumed Nellie and Pearl would accompany them and Nellie let that assumption stand. She certainly intended to keep with the group from now on. Pearl could go to hell in her own way.

One of the hands brought over two metal plates heaped with food. She sat on one of the stump seats and ate every bit, wiping up leftover egg yolk with cowboy bread. The thick coffee stimulated her, and she felt much better than the night before. Even her arm felt as if it were healing. The slant of early-morning light caught the smoke from the firepit as it drifted up and over the lake, hanging like a small, blue cloud. The castle ramparts glowed gold and impregnable and Nellie almost wished she were going on the hunt, but not quite. Killing animals for food was one thing; killing them for sport quite another. Civilization, even in the form of the saloon in Stanley, and maybe especially the saloon if Charlie Azgo were there, appealed to her. Once again, she wished she had more unexposed film. She would have liked to photograph the camp, the tents, the cowboys working, the landscape of lake behind the "roughing it" foreground.

Nellie did what she could to take down the tent, roll up blankets, stow utensils in packs. One-handed, she wasn't much help, and finally decided to wait out the breaking-down of camp perched on a rock by the lake. She had not seen Pearl during breakfast and wondered if the saloon girl (a name maybe she did deserve) had left camp already. Being shut of Pearl appealed to Nell too.

As the camp slowly disappeared and the rolling meadow took its place, Luke strode to where Nellie sat. "How are you this morning?" The question was kinder than any he'd posed the day before, both in tone and intent, but he didn't wait for an answer. "We're taking the ladies down to see the 'Wild West' saloon in Stanley and stay a night at the roadhouse. You're coming at least as far as Stanley with us. Your friend, too." He gestured toward the horses where Nell could see Pearl saddling one of them. The girl of many talents. Including, maybe, murder.

A nod seemed sufficient for Luke. "You get around, Miss Burns. From tending sheep to killing a man."

"Yes, well, a photographer can't always choose her subjects with an eye toward beauty. Sometimes, life needs to be shown as life. Or death." Photographing had been the farthest thought from her mind the day before when she was struggling for her life.

"I'm surprised you didn't take pictures up here. I bet you could sell a bunch." Luke had swung one leg up to rest on the rock. Sunshine lightened the top of his head and outlined his profile. In his denim shirt and cowhide vest and chaps, he could have posed for every cowboy picture in eastern magazines.

"I've been out of film for days," Nellie said. Her regret swelled at the thought of selling photos of the camp and the tourists to the tourists, maybe even to the outfitters or O'Donnell, if, indeed, he was the boss of the whole organization.

"Poor plannin' on your part." Luke grinned, his teeth slightly crooked, but his smile friendly. "Gettin' *lost* and all."

"Wait!" Nellie jumped up. "Don't take down those last two tents," she called out, then turned to Luke. "I do have some film. I just remembered. Roll film and a roll back. Can you wait? I could set up and take some photos —" she hoped "— of everyone around one of the tents and around the campfire and with the bearskin." Hypocrite, she thought to herself. "And the horses."

"Sure, we'll wait. Anythin' that makes the dudes happy makes me happy." He frowned and thought a minute. "Almost anythin'." He, too, stood upright and called out, "Hang on there. We've got ourselves a picture-taker. Souvenirs for the ladies to take home and the gentlemen to brag about." Back to Nellie, he said, "But don't take all mornin'. We're short of horses and packin' out is goin' to take a little longer than comin' in, even if it is all downhill. Some of you have to take turns walkin'."

She was already digging into her pack and asked Luke to carry her tripod and one of the hands to round up the tourists for a group photo with the ramparts in the background, "Try that sunny spot over there," she said, while fastening the roll-film camera back onto her Premo camera. She'd never used it before and kept her fingers crossed that she could figure it out and take enough photographs to satisfy the tourists and earn some money. How she would get the photos to them and the money back, she didn't know, but that could come later. One of the women had traveled all the way from Pennsylvania with her husband.

The roll film and different camera back were new to Nellie. She was used to setting up the camera, using her black cloth and focus to get the photograph exactly as she wanted, then sliding in a film holder. Once it was in, she could no longer see the scene, but she would know it was right and could release the shutter. With the roll film and camera back, she couldn't look through the lens at all. The roll back replaced the viewing screen, so to set up the photograph, she could only aim by looking through a small wire viewer on top of the camera. She also had to move the camera farther back than she would for a large-format negative; otherwise, she would only get a few heads of a group photo or a small portion of a landscape. All her efforts would be "by guess and by gosh," a term her father had used to explain how he would get a new job after being fired from an old job, usually for drinking, a term he used before he generally disappeared from the life of Nellie and her mother.

At first, Pearl refused to join the group as they stood and knelt by the tent, but when everyone sat around the campfire, she, too, sat on a stump seat and pretended to eat from a metal plate, then clanked her coffee cup in a toast to the West and then to the cowboys and then to the horses and then to the bear. The women wanted photos of themselves astride a horse, which Nell accommodated, but took them as a group. By then, Pearl helped Nell carry the camera and tripod to a better location near the makeshift corral. Then she wanted her own picture astride a horse, one she and Nellie were going to have to ride together, a closeness that neither of them was looking forward to, Nell was sure.

By the time Nell finished taking photographs and collecting names and addresses and telling the women how much she planned to charge, and turning down cash thrust at her because she didn't know if the photos in fact would turn up on the exposed film, everyone was feeling gay. The men were looking forward to their hunt, asking Nell to come along and record their sure-to-be-success. She declined and the women congratulated her for her good sense. Even Pearl laughed at one of the cowboy's jokes and spent a little time fixing one of the women's hair in the same fashion as Pearl's: braids wound around the top of her head. It was as if leaving the camp loosened everyone's shyness and inhibitions. Nell could understand why tourists liked the campouts, if for no other reason than the camaraderie that developed among them, let alone the stunning landscapes. She felt as if she had been entertaining the women on her "home ground," even if she was a relative newcomer. Their obvious delight in the Wild West pleased Nellie because she was so delighted with her chosen home, too.

The appearance of two men on the trail from the road reminded her that delight wasn't the only thing she felt in this new home. The sun didn't reach the pair, but they wore rough garb and Stetsons shaded their faces. A flash of fear moved her toward Luke, who seemed most capable of protecting her. At the same time, she patted the pack in search of the gun and had almost unstrapped the pocket where it lay when she realized she was looking at the Sheriff and Gwynn Campbell.

Relief surged through her and she would have run to them except for the rough and forbidding mien of their faces. Charlie looked right through Nell as if she didn't exist. Something wasn't right. For the first time that morning, Nell glanced toward Pearl to see what she thought, but Pearl didn't look at Nellie. She looked at her hands on the bridle of a horse.

"Hank Fischer said you'd had a little trouble up here," Sheriff Azgo said as he approached Luke. "Brought down a —"

"Sheriff," Luke interrupted. "Maybe you and I could talk over to the side here? We're trying to break up camp. Don't want to stop progress." His laugh sounded as phony as it was. "No trouble here this morning." He reached for the sheriff's arm, which Charlie shook off. Nevertheless, he took several steps away from the group now hanging on his every word and lowered his voice.

"Go on about your business," he said. "Except you, Miss Burns. Would you step over here with me?"

Nellie wondered if her face was as white as Pearl's. Maybe whiter. She had rarely seen the sheriff so serious and couldn't think if he'd ever turned his official lawman's wrath on her, for that was what he was doing. His job was to uphold the law, and he must have heard that she said she'd broken it in the worst possible way, killing a man. She glanced toward Luke, wanting him to back up her story of self-defense, even if he didn't know the truth — that Nellie didn't shoot that gun. Acting in self-defense surely was acceptable in the west. She'd heard of shootouts, still but rarely in these modern times, in the streets of western towns where the killer "acted in self-defense" and went scot-free. Trying to save herself from a murderer must qualify. And she could tell the sheriff when they were alone that she had lied about shooting Wolfman Pitts. But could she? Pearl was the other obvious suspect and she had been halfway around the lake. Luke and Hank and Nell were witnesses to that fact. She wouldn't admit to the shooting, Nell was certain, and there had been no one else around.

Luke accompanied Nellie to the sheriff's side. Gwynn studied the ground, refusing to look at Nell. "Now look here, Sheriff," Luke began.

"Miss Burns. You're under arrest for the murder of Herbert Pitts. Hank Fischer says you admitted to shooting him in the head and he saw you holding a gun when he and Luke found you and the dead body by Washington Lake. Do you deny this?"

"No, I — I did say that. Wolfman Pitts tried to kill me and tried to kill Moonshine. I was fighting for my life." She wanted to say, "Charlie, it's me. Nellie. Your friend. What are you doing? Of course I didn't shoot him, but I did stab him. He tried to murder me." But she couldn't choke out any words other than those she already spoke. Even speaking those few words brought back the scene, brought back the nausea and fear she had felt.

"Do you have a weapon in your possession?" The sheriff held out his hand. His eyes, dark and wrathful, stared into hers. There was no hint of friendship, trust, compassion, caring. His face could have been cut from the stone of the ramparts behind him. Gwynn cleared his throat, glanced at Nellie and away. His age seemed to have trebled since they had sat around the campfire with the Basque sheepherder.

"Yes. I — it's in my pack." She swung her pack off her shoulder and began to reach for the gun. The sheriff grabbed the pack from her, bumping into her hurt arm.

"Owww." Nellie leaned over with pain. So much for a healed knife slash.

"Sheriff, she's been slashed with a knife."
Luke took a step forward and eased his arm
around Nellie's shoulder. "Let me look at
that arm. It might be bleedin' again."

"It's fine, Luke. Thank you. He just
bumped it." But the throbbing had begun
again.

"Show me your arm, Nellie," Luke ordered, his eyes telling her something. He
reached for her hand and began to unbut-
ton the sleeve.

At the same time, Nellie grabbed for her
pack, an instinctive reaction to protect the
work she had just accomplished. The sheriff
took the gun and knocked Luke's hand off
Nellie's arm. "Step back, Luke. You're
interfering with the law. I'll arrest you too if
you continue to assist Miss Burns in her
resistance." He handed the pack to Gwynn,
who took it as if it were a haunch of meat
instead of a valuable camera with exposed
film inside. "We'll need a horse to take Miss
Burns down the mountain with us to the
road. I'll leave it there for you." He motioned with the gun for Luke to move.

Nellie looked from one to the other, at
first stunned and then realizing she was getting Luke into trouble, but finally understanding what he had tried to do. "My arm,"
she cried. "It's bleeding again." She undid

301

the sleeve and rolled it up. In fact, blood was seeping into the makeshift bandage. "Wolfman Pitts tried to kill me with his knife, Sheriff. You can see for yourself." She tore open the bandage and blood welled along the wound. "Isn't a woman entitled to defend herself in this godforsaken 'wild west'?" Tears filled her eyes. She would *not* cry. She wrapped the bandage around her forearm again, pulled her sleeve down and buttoned it, and held her wrists out. "Where are the handcuffs? I might attack someone else, you know."

The sheriff's expression changed not a whit, but Nell saw a ghost of a twitch around Gwynn's mouth. At least he cared for her still.

By then, Luke had brought a horse over to the trio and the tourists behind were murmuring with excitement. "She's under arrest!" one of the women exclaimed. Nell heard her and glanced toward Pearl, whose back was to Nell, talking to the women in a group. Now everyone had a story to tell when each of the dudes returned home.

The sheriff helped Nellie mount the horse and took the camera pack from Gwynn, who took the bridle and began to lead her away. She felt a prisoner already and regretted deeply saying she had shot Wolfman.

Still, she half turned in the saddle and called to the dudes, "I'll get the film developed soon and send the photos to you. Thank you for taking care of my arm." Gwynn jerked on the bridle to stop her talking.

The sheriff led the way down the trail, his back stiff, the gun no longer in his hand, her camera pack on his back. All the gaiety of the morning had disappeared like morning fog. Nellie turned back again when they reached the junction of trails. The tourists were busy climbing onto the horses. It was as if they had already forgotten about her. The lake was no bigger than a pond and dust from the trail rose to choke her. Above the lake, the ramparts had lost their gold and no longer resembled castles. They were gray, silent stones.

CHAPTER 14

"Charlie," Nell ventured once, but the sheriff did not turn his head. "Gwynn," she tried, but the old sheep man turned to her and shook his head, placing a finger on his lips. "Moonshine," she called. He barked.

The path down seemed steeper than the night she and Pearl had climbed it. The horse lunged once or twice and Nell grabbed the saddle horn, once again tweaking her arm. Although the morning sun shone through the trees, dappling the trail in places, the gloom of the closely spaced fir trees gradually worked into her. Her shoulders slumped. Her tailbone hurt. This horse was no rocking-chair ride, as had been Luke's.

Memories of crisp mornings in Chicago with traffic moving back and forth, crowds of people hurrying to work or to shop, even the faintly rancid smell of the packing plants, almost brought tears to her eyes. The gangsters there never bothered ordinary people, although she suspected she might be wrong in that supposition. Still, they would not have bothered her or her mother. Her sweet mother who, even now, was laboring away in the library where she worked, rebinding dusty books, reshelving those used the evening before, cataloging new arrivals, touching each one as if it were a child who needed tender care. Books had always lined the walls of their apartment, often resting on the floor as well. Her mother read voraciously. Nell read, too, but was more interested in photographic books. Still, she could hardly recall even seeing a book in Ketchum or Hailey or even Twin Falls.

Maybe she had inherited all of her father's bad qualities. She'd lost her job as a portrait photographer in Chicago, and now she was under arrest. How many times had her father been arrested for drunkenness and mayhem? She remembered her mother's white face, her tight lips, her despair when she left the apartment to visit him in jail, to bail him out, to sober him up. The most distressful moment of her life, before Wolfman Pitts's attack, had been to identify her father in the morgue, a duty she took on when her mother took to her bed upon news that he had been killed in a street fight.

The sheriff abruptly stopped and Gwynn pulled on the bridle to hold the horse. Moonie continued to trot, sniffing at the trail, but the sheriff grabbed at the scruff of his neck. Her reminiscences thankfully interrupted, Nell opened her mouth to ask what was wrong. Then she heard a noise of brush breaking, rocks rolling, and a bull elk leaped across their path, followed by two cows and a calf. They disappeared almost as rapidly as they had appeared. Still, Charlie and Gwynn stayed motionless, the former's hand still on the dog's neck.

"What's going — ?"

Three men, two with rifles, tailed the elk and appeared on the path. They were just as startled to see the sheriff, Gwynn, and Nellie on a horse as she was to see them, although her — what? her captors? — didn't look surprised at all. A gun had appeared in the sheriff's hand, and although it wasn't pointed at anyone or anything, it had a life of its own, wavering briefly up and down as the sheriff spoke.

"What are you men doing?" His voice rang with authority.

"What's it to you?" Dick Goodlight answered. "We might ask the same thing of you." By now he had seen Nellie on the horse. "Where'd you find her?" He motioned toward Nell with his rifle, but didn't look at her. "She stole a gun from our camp, along with a few other things."

Nellie wondered if he was referring to Pearl as one of the "things."

"Your camp?" the sheriff said. "It's somewhere along the trail here?"

"Down yonder," Goodlight answered. Again he motioned with his gun, and the other two men with him, Long John and Bob from the moonshine operation, stared at the ground. "We're after elk today. You keep us jawin' much longer and we'll miss 'em altogether."

"Let me see your license." The sheriff's gun still hovered between pointing down and pointing at Goodlight.

"You ain't the fish and game officer. You're just a sheriff from Blaine County. You got jurisdiction here?"

"I do now. The license?" He stared at Goodlight, who stared back.

Goodlight caved. "Left the license back at camp. Didn't expect no lawman up in the wilds. Usually they stay behind their desks — them that knows what's good for 'em. But I got one. You can check with old Rainy Jones at Smiley Creek."

The sheriff's gun quit wavering. It pointed

directly at Goodlight. "Hand me your rifle." He motioned to the others. "Yours, too." They looked at Goodlight to see what he'd do.

"Sheriff, you ain't got no right to take our guns." A shaft of light lit on Goodlight's pale hair, turning him almost wraith-like. His shabby garb appeared even dirtier and more ragged than usual, lit from behind.

"Gwynn," the sheriff said, motioning with his head toward the three men. The sheep man let go of the bridle and stepped toward Goodlight, grabbed the rifle, and ejected a handful of cartridges, which he placed in the pocket of his jacket. Then he handed the gun back. He did the same with the other rifle.

"How am I gonna kill my elk without cartridges?" Goodlight whined.

"Guess you'll have to head back to camp, won't you?" Gwynn answered as he picked up the bridle rein. "Next time, remember your license." His voice mocked, as the sheriff's had not.

Goodlight studied Gwynn. "I'll remember this. You own sheep, don't you? Better keep a good eye on 'em."

"You're in deep cow dung already, Goodlight. I reckon you better steer clear of me." Gwynn began walking down the trail again.

"And her." He jerked his thumb back toward Nell. "If you don't, you'll have hell to pay." He stopped briefly. "You're gonna have hell to pay anyway. If I were you, I'd clear out of this country."

Nellie felt Goodlight's glare on her as she rode past, her back straight again, her eyes looking ahead. She hoped he didn't have another gun hidden somewhere in those ill-fitting clothes. Bob was off to one side, and as Nellie passed, she risked a glance at him. He gave a little wave with his hand down near his hip, and she remembered how his voice blended with his ukulele.

When they reached the road at the trail-head, Nellie saw a jumble of automobiles, but none of them was hers. She recognized the sheriff's and Gwynn's truck. A third one belonged to one of the tourists in the group behind. A horse was tethered near where Hank's old Model T had rested, a pile of straw nearby. Not far up the rough track were weather-beaten shacks, the last remnants of a mining operation at Fourth of July Creek, the reason for the road in the first place. At dusk, neither she nor Pearl had noticed them.

"Now what?" she asked. "Since you think I'm an outlaw, are you taking me to jail? Don't you want to hear my story at all?

About how Wolfman Pitts attacked me, and how he was going to strangle me, turn my tongue purple, he said." Her words began to shake and she could feel the anger grow inside.

"First, we're going to sew up that slash on your arm, Lassie." Gwynn helped her dismount, trying rather clumsily to avoid touching her hurt arm. He led her to his truck and sat her down in the bed at the back. "Stay there. This won't look pretty, but it'll stop the bleeding. I done this to a lot of sheep, and the sooner we get it closed, the better off you'll be. You've got some rough days ahead of you."

"I do?" She looked from Gwynn to the sheriff, who wasn't paying any attention to her at all. He had placed Nellie's camera next to her in the truck, then tied up the horse at a railing near the path and then walked back to his auto. None of his motions were hurried, and yet he accomplished everything in the space of a minute or less. He climbed in the auto and started it up, then backed around. "Wait! Charlie, where are you going?" She jumped down and began to run after the sheriff. "Charlie!"

"Cora Nell, get back here!" Gwynn roared.

Her full name stopped Nellie cold. Moonshine, who had followed and then passed her as if she were playing a game, ran back and licked her hand.

"What is going on? I thought I was under arrest." Her throbbing forearm, her aching shoulder, her tired feet, her bruised body — all these things, compounded by lack of sleep, fear, and then relief — threatened to undermine the determination she'd dredged up from the bottom of her being in the last few days. She slumped back onto the truck bed, as weary as she'd ever been in her life. "I don't understand what's happening."

"Rest your arm on this box," Gwynn ordered. "This is gonna hurt like sin, . . . heck, . . . no, it's gonna hurt worse than sin. First I'm gonna pour some moonshine over that cut. You better drink some yourself. That might help. I'll be fast as I can. If you gotta scream, try to do it quiet-like." He glanced around toward the trailhead. "Don't wanta scare them tourists, and I'm hopin' Goodlight and his scallawags hustled back to their camp. Don't know if they was after that elk or was after you and that tart."

Gwynn handed Nellie a tin cup filled with clear liquid. She sniffed it, held her nose, and took two big gulps before she choked. Fire filled her mouth, ran down her throat, and slammed into her stomach. "Aghhh!

Are you trying to poison me?"

The old sheep rancher ignored her while he opened a box marked with a big red "X." Inside was rolled gauze, gauze patches, a needle and two spools of thread, one white and one black, a tube of ointment that smelled like the goo Alphonso had spread on the wounded dog in the sheep camp, and white tape. Already, her knees were feeling wobbly and she wasn't even standing up.

"Drink some more." Gwynn threaded the needle. His hand trembled as he concentrated. Then he poured more liquid from the bottle standing by the first aid box onto the needle and thread both. When he held Nellie's arm and prodded the wound open with the needle, then splashed some of the liquid across it, she almost came up off the truck bed.

"Works for sheep. Oughta work for you." He took one of the gauze pads and brushed more liquid along the sides of the slash, cleaning off blood and bits of bandage stuck in it.

Nellie looked away and took two more huge swallows of moonshine. It didn't taste as bad this time, nor burn as intensely going down. Still, she preferred the wine served up by Alphonso. Would this make her an alcoholic?

312

"Where did you get the moonshine?" She didn't care, but she needed whatever distraction she could drum up. Another two swallows and she slumped against a thick blanket Gwynn had rigged up behind her. He handed her a stick.

"Found it along the road," he said and chuckled. "Now, I'm told if you bite on that stick, it'll help." He sounded as doubtful about that lore as Nellie felt about it. "You can grab my shoulder, but keep clear of my hands. I'll be neat as I can about this, but if we don't get this cleaned out and sewn up, you're likely to get good and infected and maybe lose a limb. Hard to take pictures then."

Whether Gwynn intended to scare her men's pants off or not, he succeeded in frightening her to her marrow. She took two more swallows and then gripped the stick between her teeth. "Mmm ruddy." She watched as the needle neared the soft skin of her forearm. As it pricked into her, she closed her eyes. The pain was so intense when the needle went in, tears squeezed out, and she clamped on the wood, moaning. She pressed the fingernails of one hand into her palm, trying to create a counter pain, but it was so pale by comparison, she stopped. Almost worse was the feel of thread tugging her skin as Gwynn moved from stitch to stitch, muttering curses whenever the thread stuck.

"Almost done, Lassie. You're doin' all right. You're braver than any sheep I've ever worked on. They squeal and jerk around — takes twice as long. Hold on, honey. I'll be done in a minute." And still the needle pierced skin and the thread pulled and the pain filled her until every nerve ending was burning. When she thought she couldn't last another second, it stopped.

"Whoever fixed you up at the camp did a right smart job," Gwynn said. "You'll have a scar along this arm, but it won't be too bad. Now you keep cleanin' the stitches with the moonshine and then rub salve into the skin around it. I'll give you some from the box here."

Nellie opened her eyes when she was sure he had stopped. Her arm might have been burned in a fire, it felt so raw. The earlier throbbing was a mere bruise compared to the agony she suffered now. And yet, as she studied the neat line of stitches, the burning began to subside. Whether that was because the wound was already healing or the moonshine had finally knocked her senses out of kilter, she didn't know.

"You ever show on a kilt?" Something

about the words didn't come out right.

"You'll never see a kilt on me, Lassie. My old legs would be too embarrassed."

"Qu . . . qu . . . quilt," she amended. "Show." No, that wasn't right. Carefully, she said the word again. "Sew."

Gwynn stopped putting away his supplies and studied her arm. "Good job, huh? Nope, just sewed up sheep and men. Maybe I got a hidden talent." His movements became more hurried. He helped Nellie to the front of the truck and folded the blanket around her back and then over her knees. "Don't want you bouncin' around. Hold this arm —" he pointed to the freshly sewed up forearm "— with this arm." He lifted her good arm. "We gotta get hustlin'." He called Moonshine over and let him in below Nell's knees. He slammed her door shut and stepped quickly around to his side. "I'll fix up a sling if you need it." As he pushed the starter button on the truck, he swore. "Those dudes are comin' outta the woods. Keep your head low."

She couldn't do anything but keep her head low. She was already unconscious.

One sense at a time, Nellie came back to consciousness. There were few sounds except that of water, perhaps, softly touch-

315

ing a beach of sand, flowing in, flowing out. A familiar smell drifted around her. Something green and dusty, sharpened by an earthy scent and softened by something like hand lotion, the thought of which made her aware of her arm, a limb that felt big and bloated and red to the touch. Darkness swaddled her in the same way soft, thick blankets held her, warm but not heavy. Her lips were crusted and dry as was the inside of her mouth. Her tongue, when she tried to moisten her lips, scraped along chapped and broken skin. Something inside her head grunted and then twisted, causing a screech of pain. She heard a short, quiet groan. Afraid someone lurked over her, she tried to push up with the arm that didn't feel bloated and hot. Then the pain ripped down the back of her neck.

A tin cup pressed against her face and cool water spilled along her chin until she figured out how to let it fall into her mouth. Then she sucked greedily, letting the water soak into her tongue and gums and then soften the ridges along her lips. The cup went away and came back and she gulped, finally choking with all the air that accompanied the water, forcing her up, bringing back the piercing of needles at the base of her skull.

Still, the black could not be seen through.

But it no longer threatened, rather comforted and warmed, a place she had visited in the past. Gradually, the water sound, flowing in, flowing out, resolved into soft bleating, now here, now there. Sheep. Nellie closed her eyes, lay back, and slept again.

When Nell next opened her eyes, she watched a slim, dark man light a stove, pour water, stir a pot. Candlelight cast a steady glow on the interior of a small room; dull gray turned pearl through a square at the end. Again, dry cotton filled her mouth, stretched her lips, swelled her tongue. Again, a brief sound brought the tin cup back and she drank. The pain no longer screeched, but throbbed. This time, her arm hurt more than her head.

As the cotton left to be replaced by a normal mouth, tongue, and lips, Nellie sat herself up, aware of the ceiling close to her head. "Alphonso?"

"Si. Como esta?"

"Am I in your sheep camp? I must be in your bed. Thank you for the water. *Gracias.*"

Alphonso went back to the stove and stirred a pot. He sniffed at it closely, made a face, and then opened the door and took the pot outside. Nell heard water spilling onto the ground. He came back in and spooned the contents of the pot onto a square of cloth that he then wrung out into the pot again. With one step, he was at her side, motioning for her arm, which she brought out from under the covers, trying to keep anything from touching it. Not without care, but more roughly than she expected, Alphonso took her arm, undid the packing, opened up the cloth, and laid wet, lumpy and smelly green stuff across the stitches. It looked like cooked spinach. The first contact shocked her with pain, but in seconds, the herbs, or whatever the spinach really was, began to draw out the pain and heat. With more care than the initial slopping of the mixture, Alphonso wrapped the cloth around her arm to hold the stuff in place. He studied her in the candlelight, seemed satisfied, grabbed his hat, and stepped down the short front ladder, causing the wagon to shift slightly. Then all was quiet. He had left the door open, and shortly, the wagon shifted again, and Moonshine came inside, walked over to her, sniffed, licked her hand, turned in circles, and lay down in front of the shelf upon which she lay.

Familiar sounds drifted into the camp: Alphonso's low voice moving the sheep, occasionally instructing the dogs, the cinch of leather on leather and squeak of human on saddle as he mounted his horse, the faint thud of hooves on dirt, the silky sound of sheep moving, and the rising *baaa, baaa, baaa,* as the animals began their daily round of moving to a new pasture, eating and resting. Those sounds were replaced by the twitter of the occasional bird, the *craak* of magpies. She knew she was alone again.

Inside the wagon, the temperature rose. Or maybe it was Nell's temperature rising that caused her to perspire and woke her up. When she raised herself with her good arm, she saw that Moonshine no longer rested on the floor beside the shelf-bed. The door remained open, the usual sign that the sheepherder was out with his sheep, an invitation to weary travelers to sit and rest, get water if need be, and food, but don't abuse the privilege.

Gwynn had instructed Nellie to pour more moonshine on the stitches and rub them with salve. Her arm hurt less than it had since Pitts slashed her. She was reluctant to remove the cloth and the spinach-like goo that Alphonso had spread on it. Maybe she should dampen the whole mess. The question was whether she should use moonshine or water. She sat up, feeling human for the first time in days, and looked around the wagon. Alphonso's living quarters were not neat, but neither were they messy. The wood stove had been cleared of all pots except one iron frying pan with a skim of grease, half-melted, half congealed; the fold-down countertop stood upright against one side of the canvas, held by a hook and eye hammered into the wood frame. A coat and pair of pants hung on a nail near the door. Heavy boots lay toppled over next to the stove with gray socks poking out the tops. Right next to them stood her own boots, looking almost dainty in comparison, although they were mud-coated, scuffed, and stiff. Several tins sat on a shelf below the countertop and also small bottles filled with unidentifiable contents, not liquid. No other bottles stood out as being there for her use. She knew there would be a bucket hanging outside filled with water, which would be warm by now.

Moving with extreme care in order not to bump her arm, Nellie swung her legs around to rest her feet on the floor, but the bed was too high for her to do so. She slid off to stand up, and waited for the whirlies to settle down. Her headache no longer battered her skull. She almost felt good. It was such a relief to be alone that it took a while to wonder where her dog was. Probably off chasing squirrels or getting a drink from a rivulet or a creek. Where was she, other than in Alphonso's sheep camp?

It was only then that she realized what else was missing. Her camera pack! She remembered the sheriff handing it to Gwynn, who treated it nonchalantly. She remembered the sheriff walking ahead of the horse with the camera pack on his back. No other images came to mind. She turned back inside, hoping she had missed it. She hadn't opened the drawer underneath the bed. It wasn't easy to do with only one operable arm, but she managed to slide it out by pulling on one handle, then on the other. As before, it was jammed full of supplies and tools, even a rifle, which she pulled out, not knowing if it was loaded or even if it worked. Still, a gun would be handy to have if anyone other than Alphonso came around. No camera.

Would Charlie know what to do with the film in the camera back? He might open it and expose the whole roll, her grand experiment. Maybe Gwynn had left it outside, unprotected. She hurried down the steps to the fire-round. Nothing. She leaned over to peer under the wagon. Nothing except several wood boxes, none of which could hold her pack. She circled the wagon, hoping the camera hung from a hook or nail, and found the water bucket, the sheep crook, two more pots, rosemary drying upside down, an extra bridle, the kerosene lamp. No camera.

Without a livelihood, she could see herself descend into poverty. She would have to write her mother for rail money home, admit she had failed in the West, beg for her job back, live once again in the apartment with her mother, and, finally, lower herself to finding a husband to take care of her. Doom and gloom. Of course, she could marry there in the West, become a housewife for someone to cook and clean for and take care of children. She knew the sheriff was fond of her; she was fond of him. Or she had been.

Her arm began to hurt. She was working herself up over nothing. Charlie had taken the camera to keep it safe. Undoubtedly, it was safe. He was nothing if not competent. No need to borrow a whole new, disappointing life. She couldn't marry him. He didn't even approve of her working as a photographer, in spite of all the stories she'd told about other women photographers, about Julia Cameron and Imogene Cunningham.

Moonshine trotted into camp, as if he were coming in to check on her. He pushed his nose under her hand and she petted him, talking and moaning. A squirrel scolded from a nearby pocket of brush, and he was off, chasing and playing games with wood creatures, disappearing from sight, but she felt assured he wasn't wandering too far away.

She used the dipper to dampen the cloth on her arm and sat down near the fire pit and realized she was hungry. Surely, Alphonso had left her something to eat. She scavenged again in the sheep camp and found on the lower shelf another cloth wrapped around bread heavily slathered with butter and in which was a slab of mutton. Rarely had any food tasted so good.

While she ate, she mulled over the mystery of the hole in Wolfman Pitts's head. She had assumed Pearl killed the dreadful man, but Pearl had been halfway around the lake not too many minutes later. Nell thought she had recognized the gun as being her companion's, but there could have been more than one such gun. When Nell pulled the flashlight out of the woman's satchel, she had assumed the gun was gone, and then that she had been mistaken when she picked the weapon up off the ground. If Pearl didn't do it, then someone else was in the woods and the most likely someones were

Goodlight and his henchmen. Why would one of them shoot and then drop the gun, unless it was to place blame on either Pearl or Nellie?

She thought about following the sheep leavings and finding Alphonso, but realized she really was weak. Losing all the blood hadn't been good, even though she'd heard letting blood used to be the main treatment for illness, disease, and perhaps even wounds. Surely that theory was discredited now.

Instead, she climbed back into the wagon and lay down on the blankets, but grew chilly as the afternoon passed, so pulled the bedclothes over her. They were well used, but she didn't care. She had been poorly used. A menacing cloud filled the space beyond the doorway, turning the interior almost dark; an afternoon thunderstorm was approaching. She dozed, content to be lying still. Was her dog still chasing will o'the wisps in the woods? The first crack of thunder would send him in to crawl under the blankets with her.

Nellie wasn't certain what woke her up. She remembered falling asleep to the sound of distant rolling thunder, dreaming of Rip Van Winkle, and then wondering if years had passed her by while she wandered the wilderness. The crack of a horse's hoof on a rock? A *clunk* still echoed in the stillness, or was it just her imagination? She lay without moving, listening, and noticed, too, that Moonshine wasn't with her. A second *clunk,* a rolling rock, and then horses' hooves, more than one horse, so it wouldn't be Alphonso. Her own hackles stood straight up. Was it Dick Goodlight?

CHAPTER 15

Lulu's summer was one of the best ever. Tourists came and went. Outfitters stopped for supplies. The moonshiners had picked up a record order of sugar early on, paid cash, and hadn't bothered her since. She was happy until the rumors began to show up. Nellie Burns, the photographer, was missing. Wolfman Pitts and his dog were holding her for ransom. The cattlemen and sheepmen were at each other's throats. Domingo's death had sparked a range war, and it wouldn't end until there were more deaths, both animal and men. Lulu wasn't old enough to remember the last range war, but her father had told stories of lynchings, murders, and mayhem. Surely, it couldn't happen again in the twentieth century. There were lawmen and courts to handle fights over grazing allotments and water rights.

As if on cue, Sheriff Azgo turned up at

Galena Lodge. Lulu had a dozen questions for him, but as he drove in, so did three other automobiles, each carrying three men dressed in dark suits, white shirts, and ties, and wearing hats, a rarity of fancy clothing in the West. They had to be revenuers, Lulu guessed, probably up from Boise or Salt Lake City. Only federal officers would dress like they were going to a fancy party in July in the wilds of Idaho. Beside them, the sheriff appeared dusty and worn out. His expression was as grim as she'd ever seen.

Half an hour later, maybe longer, Gwynn drove his old truck up to the Lodge. Pieces of sagebrush were caught in the front grill and aspen leaves flew out of the truck bed, as if he had driven cross-country. The sheriff and the federal men stood out by the automobiles looking at a map spread on the hood of the sheriff's. When Gwynn stepped out into the open, the sheriff looked up. Gwynn nodded and climbed the porch to lower himself into a willow chair. He looked too old for words. Did either one know where Nell Burns was? Lulu couldn't help but worry for the young woman.

The sheriff strode into the store, checking out one of the shotguns handed to him by the federal agent. "Lulu, we need shells for shotguns, water, canteens, and whatever meat and bread and cheese you've got that we can take along." No chance to ask him questions.

"My icebox was raided this morning by a new group of tourists going on a campout, Sheriff. You can take what's left, but it won't be feeding all of you. My spare shells are up on a shelf in back. Help me reach 'em." She led him to the back of the store. Indeed, he could reach the shells using a footstool, and as he handed them down to her, she asked quietly, "Where's Nellie? I been hearing all sorts of stories. I know at least half of what I hear in the store is lie and the other half is exaggeration, but is the other half true? Is she all right?"

Sheriff Azgo didn't crack so much as a glimmer of a smile. Lulu thought he wasn't going to answer, when he stepped down and leaned close. "Nell Burns is not going to live to be thirty if she continues taking the chances she has been. For the moment, she is safe, but she has much to answer for. I will take care of that when we finish this . . . venture." He took the boxes and stepped back to the cash register. "Tote the bill up, Lulu. We're going back to the Basin, and you want to be paid now, I assume." His grim expression vanished for just a moment, but she might have just imagined a ghost of a smile. "Federal Marshall Keefe here will pay you." The sheriff motioned for one of the suited men to come to the counter. "In cash."

Only the sheriff wore boots; the other men wore regular shoes. Lulu figured they were going on a raid, probably Dick Goodlight's operation, which she knew was in the Basin somewhere. While the revenuers and the sheriff filled their autos with gasoline, she plumped down beside Gwynn, who leaned his forearms on his thighs and watched the activity. "My gawd, Gwynn, you look bushed. Where you been? Anything to do with Nell Burns?"

The face he turned to Lulu was creased with dirt, but faintly ashen under the deep leather-like tan. "I'm tired out, Lulu. I can't keep up with the sheriff or no one else these days. Women are changin' and men are dastardly. Sheriff swore me to secrecy, but I'm fit to burst. Got somethin' to wet an old man's whistle?"

Without a word, Lulu went back inside, fetched a bottle from under the counter, and poured two fingers, no four fingers, into a glass and brought it out to Gwynn. She cast an eye on the federal agents, but they weren't paying any attention. She could always claim it was cola. The whole Prohibition thing was a joke, as far as she was concerned and most everybody else in Idaho, but it was apparent these men took it seriously and intended to stop liquor operations. Might as well try to stop snow in winter and thunder and lightning in summer. She brought in a small stock of real liquor from Canada shipped down through Montana. The moonshine cooked up in the hills was dangerous stuff from what she'd heard. She didn't want any of her customers to go mad or blind. If her supply was a little iffy, so much the worse for those that needed it. She'd make money on selling good stuff, or none at all.

"All right, Gwynn. Talk."

"As near as we can figure out, Nellie took off with the moonshiners. Don't know if it was her idea or theirs, but knowin' how she likes to take pictures of gawd-all, the sheriff thinks maybe she followed them up Fourth of July Creek." He swallowed again and closed his eyes. "That's a secret, Lulu, where they're holed up. I know you won't say anythin' but be sure you don't."

"You know me better than that. I've kept secrets here for years, including some of yours." Lulu leaned her head back. She was tired too. "Go on."

"When we found Nell, she was with that

330

tart Pearl at the campout at Fourth of July Lake, frolicking about like she had no sense in her head. Told the sheriff she'd been kidnapped and Pearl rescued her and she couldn't leave Pearl. You know, she's the strumpet of that moonshiner, Goodlight."

"Some says she's married to Dick. I've seen her with Ned Tanner, too," Lulu said. "Tart might be just the right word for her. Looks pure as the driven snow with all that blond hair though."

Gwynn snorted and drank the rest of the brown liquid. "Any more?"

"Careful. You'll pass out if you drink much more in your condition." She took the glass and only added two fingers.

"Nell told the sheriff where the moonshine operation was, but she wouldn't come down with us. We found the still and the whole operation, just where she said. No one there, but it was clear they were comin' back. We headed down to Stanley where the sheriff placed a call to the government." He shook his head. "I tried to talk him out of it. Who cares if them crooks brew up some juice?"

Lulu's sentiments too.

"Just as we were heading out yesterday afternoon to meet these. . . ." He gestured to the group around the automobiles, at a loss for a name. "Hank somebody comes to Stanley with a dead body in his Model T. Wolfman Pitts. He says Nellie murdered him. Shot him in the head. He and Luke somebody else saw the whole thing. And what was the sheriff gonna do about it? He was off chasin' moonshiners when a cold, calculated murderer was on the loose up in the mountains."

Lulu whistled. "I imagine the sheriff didn't much like that kind of talk."

"You got that right. There was murder right there, lurkin' in Charlie's eyes. He told the barkeep to put the body on ice somewhere, made a couple telephone calls. Surprised you didn't see a big black auto comin' through here on its way to Stanley to get him. Pitts was a worse man than I've ever known, bar none. If Nellie murdered him, he musta needed it, is all I can say. Him and that half-wolf varmint of his."

Marshall Keefe stepped over to the porch. "Put the gas on a bill for us, Miss . . . I'll pay when we get back." He turned on his heel and gestured for the men to load up. Lulu followed him. "Marshall. I need cash. No credit here."

He ignored her, as did Charlie Azgo, who climbed into his own auto, started it up, and was pulling out when Gwynn half-stumbled down the stairs to chase him. "Charlie. I'm comin' with ya," he called. The sheriff ignored the old man, if he had heard him, and the procession pulled out onto the dirt road. Dust flew.

"Curse them," Lulu said. "Gwynn, get back to the porch." If she couldn't order the revenuers around, she could the sheep man. "You can't go anywhere. You're half-drunk and exhausted besides. I'll get you somethin' to eat and somethin' more to 'wet your whistle.' Now sit down." She headed in the door but stopped. "I got an envelope for the sheriff. Came from Twin Falls. Maybe you can deliver it to him."

While she cut a piece of ham and spread two slices of sourdough bread with butter and mustard, she pondered. Would Nell Burns kill a man? Yes, she supposed so, but only with good reason, was Lulu's opinion. Trouble was, reasons didn't always mean anything. She hadn't seen a big black automobile go by, but she'd been busier than a cow on skates the last day or two. Besides, more and more automobiles took the road past her lodge and up over the pass every day. It was high summer season. Not everyone stopped.

"So Nellie killed a man, or so this Hank-guy said," Lulu prompted when she returned and placed the sandwich in Gwynn's hands. "Eat this." Then, "How'd she do it?"

"Shot him is what Hank said. In the head. I saw the bullet hole. Clean as a whistle. Charlie checked him over some before we left the saloon. We drove all the way up that blasted Fourth of July Creek track, hiked up that mountain, and Charlie Azgo didn't say a blessed word the whole time. I never did see what my Lily saw in him. Tough bird is all I can say." He heaved a giant sigh and wiped his mouth with his hand, then drank again from the glass. This time Lulu had cut the liquor with water.

"We got to the camp just as they were breakin' it, headin' down themselves. Takin' the women to the saloon and the roadhouse. Some of the men was goin' huntin'. Charlie arrested Nell on the spot. You'd a thought she was a common criminal. Gave them dudes somethin' to see and talk about. I saw that tart. She kept her distance."

"What about Nell? What did she say?"

"She got her arm slashed, she says, by Wolfman Pitts. She said she shot him in self-defense. And she was bleedin' bad. I sewed it up when we got back to the road — had gear in my truck. We'd left it off on a side track when we headed down to Stanley earlier. Brave heart, she has. Hardly let a sound out."

Lulu felt proud of Nellie, as if they were somehow related. Shooting a man took guts and Lulu had no doubt he'd given her reason. But even more, she'd been brave when she didn't have to be, when Gwynn sewed her up. "Where was the sheriff by now? Standing by with handcuffs?"

"Nope. He took off. Told me to get Nellie to Alphonso's camp and leave her there, then meet him here. What about her arrest, I asks. He don't say a thing. Man went up in my estimation. He might make a good lawman after all."

After a few minutes of silence, Gwynn's head dropped onto his chest and Lulu realized he was sleeping. She prodded him awake and helped him to her apartment upstairs where he laid down on her bed and instantly was asleep again. His face softened in sleep, but he was getting too old to run around the way he'd been doing. What about his sheepherder who was killed, she wondered. Gwynn was one of the few ranchers who treated his workers like people, and she was sure the death of Domingo weighed on him. Now another man was dead, although, like the making of moonshine, who cared?

CHAPTER 16

The old rifle from the drawer stood against the end of the bed shelf where Nellie had placed it when she was searching for her camera. She began to climb off of the bed to see who was approaching outside, but when she heard voices, decided to wait and see what developed. In the meantime, she grabbed the gun and pulled it under the covers with her. The barrel was the same temperature as the air, warm. This was probably the same rifle — the Winchester — that killed Domingo, she thought, if Pearl told the truth.

"Camp's empty." The voice was familiar to Nellie, but she couldn't put a name to it yet. It wasn't Dick Goodlight, the one person she feared now that Wolfman Pitts was dead, but maybe he was the other rider.

A mumbled reply. The horses shifted and one of them moved closer to the wagon.

" 'Cause the door's open and the sheep

ain't here. Check inside if you don't believe me."

Nellie flattened herself as hard as she could, pulling a blanket over her head, hoping the bed just looked rumpled and unmade in the dim light. Through the blankets she could tell the inside of the wagon darkened as the light was blocked, briefly. She held her breath and hoped Moonshine would not choose to make an appearance then. The smell of sheep and man almost suffocated her in the heat, and the combination of dust and odor made her want to sneeze.

"Let's get outta here. The maggot's on his own allotment." A horse shifted again and the voice diminished, then grew louder, as if the rider had turned away and then back. "I don't want to leave the cattle for long. This storm'll spook 'em."

Ned Tanner, that's who was talking. The shadow at the door disappeared and Nellie peeked out from under the blankets, preparatory to getting up and disclosing her presence.

". . . told to destroy the camp, scatter the sheep to kingdom come . . ."

And that was Hank Fischer, whom she thought was an outfitter, not a cowboy. He was the one who identified her as a murderer to the sheriff.

"Since when did you always follow orders?" Ned guffawed, a disbelieving kind of noise. "We roughed him up before and he didn't leave, just moved and gone from the road. Now that blasted lawman thinks one of us killed the first one. We can say we didn't find the camp. I ain't goin' to jail for no one. Not even —"

"Hsst. Someone's comin'."

Nellie listened as hard as the two men outside. Sheep moved like sighs through long grass and sage, but the bell of the lead sheep could be heard for long distances if the wind were blowing just right. Unfortunately, the faint *ding ding ding* flowed right down into camp, followed shortly by the murmured bleating of a band of sheep on the move.

Moonshine must have heard the sounds too because he began barking from a distance behind the wagon and trotted out to a spot where Nellie could see him. Why he hadn't come out before, she didn't know, but she was both relieved and worried to have him appear. His presence would give away hers, and yet he was some protection for her and for Alphonso. So was the rifle.

". . . blasted dog. That cursed picture-taker is around someplace."

As quickly as she could with one half-useless arm, Nellie donned her boots, then stood in the doorway, the Winchester held low in her hands. She had no idea if it would shoot if she pulled the trigger or even if there was a bullet in it.

"I'm right here," she said. "Hello, Ned. Aren't you a little out of your territory? I'd think your cattle might need you shortly." She motioned with the rifle to the thick pewter clouds towering over them. "Here, Moonshine." He barked and trotted to the bottom of the steps, not crouched exactly, but wary.

Ned smiled, as if glad to see her. "Nell Burns. You do get around. What happened to you? You look like you been through the wringer, not that you ain't pretty as always." He winked at her. "Last time I saw you, you was headin' for bed at the roadhouse." He leaned forward on his horse, as if the two of them were alone in the world. "Them pictures turn out? I been lookin' forward to seein' if I look like a real Wild West cowboy."

His charm worked, and she smiled back. His mismatched eyes intrigued her once again. *Ding, ding, ding.* The sheep were moving closer. "I hope you're not planning to do what you said you didn't do before." She moved the Winchester closer to a horizontal level. "Rough up Alphonso, I mean." She faced the other man. "You, either. I didn't know you felt so strongly about me, Hank." He had the grace to duck his head. "You both better leave. I don't know a lot about guns, but I figure I could hit your horses if nothing else."

"My horse?" Ned's voice was as shocked as his face.

"Told you she was a witch. And she sure knows somethin' about guns. She shot a man up at the campout."

Shock turned to disbelief, and Ned snorted. "You been drinkin'?" He turned his horse toward the downhill side of camp.

"I took him down. Wolfman Pitts." Hank might have been bragging. Then a puzzle entered his expression. "Hey, I thought the sheriff was comin' back up to arrest you, picture-taker."

"Guess he forgot to do that," she said. Everyone in camp had seen her arrest, so she had to think that Hank and Ned hadn't run into the tourists or Luke and the other outfitters on their way down to Stanley.

The man's lip curled. "I heard you was his friend. Don't cozy up to this one, Tanner. She's taken."

"Just stopped to say 'howdy' to our friend, the maggot-herder." Ned tipped his cowboy hat. "Always nice to see a lady."

It was Nellie's turn to feel ashamed. If her face hadn't tanned so dark, he might have seen her blush. "Ned," she called as his horse began to walk away, "who killed Domingo?" She wanted to know if Pearl really did do it.

He reined in, and Nellie watched his face and Hank's. "Darned if I know. You know, Hank?"

The other man shrugged and continued on his way. Nellie didn't see guilty knowledge in either of them, but then Ned had lied to her before. He winked again, turned, and the two men on horses moved casually down the hill. When they were out of earshot and almost out of sight, Ned reined in to talk with Hank, behind him. Nell thought they were arguing, but couldn't be certain. Hank did most of the talking, as near as she could tell, and Ned listened, but before long, glanced toward the camp and walked his horse away, disappearing behind a ridge. Hank sat on his horse for a moment or two and then followed.

Not five minutes later, Alphonso rode into camp at a slow walk. The sheep's bleating indicated their presence a short distance up the hill from camp, beginning to bed down near the creek. The sheepherder waved to

Nellie. After he dismounted and grained and watered his horse, he came up to Nellie, who by then was sitting on a step, the rifle across her lap. She didn't trust the cowmen. He pointed to the Winchester.

"Two cowboys came in here. They were going to trash the camp again, maybe hurt you if you returned." She lifted the gun an inch or two. "This stopped them. I'm not certain they're gone for good."

He took the rifle from her and broke it open to show her it was empty. He laughed out loud, a cheerful grating sound, one that made Nellie smile along with him, and chuckling softly, he climbed back into the wagon, opened the supply drawer, and came out with a handful of bullets. He showed her how to load the gun, gave her another handful to put in her pants pocket.

"How do I shoot it?"

Alphonso's laugh was even louder. He pushed the lever down and up, lifted the Winchester to his shoulder, aimed it away from the sheep, showed how he would press the trigger with the index finger of his right hand, then shrugged. Easy, he might have said.

"I want to see if the cowboys really left. Can I take the gun with me?" Nellie held out her good arm and Alphonso placed it in her hand. "And the horse?"

The sheepherder pointed to her bandaged arm and shook his head.

"It's much better, Alphonso, thanks to you. I think I can ride all right. Probably they headed back to their cattle. That storm looks wicked. I'd just like to make sure. I'll be back in . . . half an hour, say." She wasn't sure how she would ride and hold the rifle but Alphonso took it from her again and placed it in a leather sheath attached to the saddle, then helped her mount.

"*Vaya con* . . . careful." Alphonso's face looked stern and dark.

I will, Nellie assured herself. This was foolish perhaps, but the cowboys had acted strangely as they moved away from camp. They wouldn't dare treat her the way they had treated both Domingo and Alphonso, so it made sense for her to check them out. She called for Moonshine, who followed her as she moved down the hill and then up a ridge. At the top, she stopped. Behind her, Alphonso had gone into the sheep camp and the whole area looked deserted, the same quiet scene that Ned and Hank had seen. Facing north, she saw no one, just a long slope filled with trees and shrubs, and in the few bare patches, sagebrush and flashes of Indian paintbrush, telling her the altitude was still high, along with white and yellow yarrow. Black clouds threatened heavy rain, and as she kneed the horse to go down, she felt dime-size drops of water begin to splash her face.

The air around her seemed to sizzle and she urged the horse down off the ridge as fast as possible. Permitting herself to be the highest point in the surrounding wild country was like begging to be hit by lightning. As she neared the first line of Alpine fir on what was probably a game path, a jagged brilliant spear cut the world in half, dazzling the sky. Within seconds, a tremendous crack of thunder assaulted her as if an explosive wind pushed against her. She felt the frailness of her being and cowered low in the saddle, still moving forward. She hoped trees offered some protection from the elements.

The horse was unused to Nellie and balked, then pranced sideways against the branches of a tree. Moonshine crawled on the ground, looking for cover. Another flash illuminated the forest, outlining each needle of each branch of each tree. Gunmetal-gray thunderheads towered over her, diminishing her as if she were an insect clinging to a pebble. The now simultaneous crash of air against air reverberated in the whole earth and drew a shriek from Nellie, a shy from the horse, and she tumbled off.

A clump of grass softened Nellie's landing and she scrambled to her knees, holding her arm, which was throbbing again. "Stupid!" she shouted at herself. The horse stood nearby and she approached it, wanting the rolled oilcloth tied onto the saddle, if nothing else. The raindrops spattered harder, catching in the branches, but also hitting her bare head. Just as she reached the horse, another flash of lightning turned the darkening afternoon into a bright tableau: horse rearing, dog cowering, man creeping. . . . Again, the thunder roared and the horse reared up and twisted around to trot away. Nellie fell backward, half-blind from the flash, half-stunned from the sound.

"For heaven's sake, Nell Burns. What are you doing out in this storm?" It was Ned, leading his horse through the forest. He helped her up, then pulled his oilcloth jacket off and placed it around her head and shoulders. Rain pelted down. Lightning flashed again, but this time, only half the sky was illuminated and the thunder rumbled from a distance, still loud, but not ear-splitting. He moved her and his horse deeper into the trees, sheltering them from what became a downpour.

"What are you doing here?" she managed to ask. "I thought you were going back to your cattle." She was thankful for the coat and pulled it around her, thinking briefly that she should share it, but making no move to do so.

"I was, but Hank had other things in mind." He turned toward the direction he had come from and sniffed the air, but stayed beside Nell. "The rain came just in time." He placed an arm around Nell's shoulder and said, "Let's get you back to camp."

Nell shrugged the arm away. "What do you mean? Where's Hank?"

"He better be hightailing it to the cattle, or his butt will really be in a wringer. Not that I care about them flea-bitten, stupid . . ." His face flushed red. What looked like a bruise on one cheek darkened as they stood propped against the trunk of a Douglas fir whose branches had fallen off from age or disease. The spreading upper branches acted like an umbrella, tattered but still providing cover. "Don't sound much like a cowboy now, do I?" He grinned. "Come on. Rain's letting up. I'll take you back. Looks like you got yourself a hurt arm and a sore butt besides. Want to ride my horse?"

"No, I think I'd just as soon walk. And I can manage alone." She looked around for Moonie and called him. At last, he slunk out from behind a large root-ball of a wind-blown tree. "You're the brave one. Poor Moonshine." She squatted and wrapped her arms around him. He was wetter than she was. She still felt shaky from the electrical storm and the possibility she could have been struck by lightning. The presence of Ned Tanner confused her and she wasn't sure if she could trust him. The dog seemed to accept him, so she stood up again. "You'll get all wet if you insist on leaving your coat around me."

"I'm used to it," he said, bitterness edging his voice. He stalked up the game path, the horse's bridle in his hand, looking awkward and bow-legged in his cowboy boots. He wasn't much taller than she, and off a horse, hardly imposing. If he had ever seemed dangerous, he didn't then. Nell noticed a gun tucked into his belt in back. She followed him on the side away from the horse, stepping as near as she could to study the revolver. This one was a different make from the one she'd picked up near Wolfman Pitts, and different from Pearl's gun, if she was remembering correctly in the first place. Most cow and sheepmen carried rifles to shoot coyotes and snakes and the occasional bear that threatened their charges, but few carried revolvers. Why did this cowboy?

The storm had moved north, and it was true, the rain lessened. Sun rays shone between the lingering clouds, lighting up the now wet sagebrush and bringing out the fresh smell of sage. Although the ground was wet, half an inch down, dust showed in the cowboy's footsteps. Nellie fell behind, then hurried to catch up again. "What did you mean that Hank had other things in mind?" she called to Ned. He continued to side-step through the brush; they were out of the trees now and picking their way to the ridge.

"He wanted to burn you out." He didn't stop to talk, just spoke to the air in front of him. When Nellie didn't say anything, he continued. "Not you, specifically. The sheep. Thought if he lit a fire in the trees back there, it would whip up the ridge and over and down. Never mind the whole mountain might be torched. Stupid . . ." His legs strode in longer steps. Then he did stop and turned to face her. "There's some mighty mean men in this world, Nell. I hope you don't get caught up with 'em.

"I rode ahead and when I realized he'd stopped, I rode back. He'd built a fire near one of them white deadheads that're all over the place. I kicked the fire apart and he jumped me. While we was wrestling around, one lick of fire got started uphill. I managed to trip the b— . . . oops . . . sorry, but there's no other word for someone like him . . . and was stomping it out when he hit me with his rifle, right across my cheek here. Lucky it didn't break. Then he ran, got on his horse, and took off. About then, the rain came." Ned began walking again.

"How'd you know I was following you?"

"I heard you scream." His laugh carried, and she stopped asking questions.

As they neared the sheep camp, Nell could smell the usual mutton stew cooking on the stove. The horse was tethered to the sheep camp itself, not usual, and was still saddled. It had known where home was, that was clear. "Alphonso," she called, not wanting to surprise him. "I'm here and I've got a cowboy with me." He appeared in the doorway, clad in hat, boots, oilcloth, and ready to mount his horse. "I fell off," she said, and gestured to the animal, "and he ran away. I'm sorry. I hope you didn't worry."

The stern expression did not leave Alphonso's face. His hand gripped the rifle, although it was pointed toward the ground.

Nellie noticed his finger was in the trigger guard. Clearly, he did not welcome the cowboy.

"This is Ned Tanner. I suspect you know him. I'm not vouching for him, but he stopped a fire that the other cowboy set. Or so he says." She glanced at Ned. He, too, carried a scowl, but looked battered and worn. "And I believe him."

Alphonso stepped back inside, then came out without the gun, but carrying a pot, and moved down the stairs. He pointed to Nellie's arm and motioned for her to unwrap it, which she did. With the touch of a butterfly, he lifted it upright so he could inspect the stitches and nodded his head. He emptied a few dried-up pieces of green from the pot and shook the green mess out of the cloth, and climbed up into the wagon again.

"What happened to your arm?" Ned reached to take hold of it, but Nellie wouldn't let him. The pain had grown intense after she fell off the horse, and she had ignored it with all the other action going on. On the walk back, she found a comfortable position for her arm, hooking her thumb into her belt. But now it pained her again.

"Wolfman Pitts sliced it with a knife." She didn't feel like going into any more explanation, and Ned seemed not to need one.

The sheepherder came out with another pot of spinach or whatever it was, and, once again, patted clumps of it on her upturned forearm, wrapped the cloth around it, securing it a little tighter with the kerchief from around his neck. It had worked before, so she let herself be ministered to. She touched Alphonso's arm. *"Gracias."* He gave her a quick, shy smile.

The three of them ate in companionable-enough silence around the firepit. The long evening was cut off by clouds and passing storms, this time some distance from them. Ned left the campfire once to ride to the top of the ridge and inspect the forest below, looking for signs of smoke, an indication that the fire might have continued under the surface. He reported he could see nothing. He couldn't speak Basque any more than could Nellie, and Nellie didn't feel inclined to talk much to Ned. She told Alphonso, and thus Ned, about the campout at Fourth of July Lake and the tourists, not mentioning how she happened to get there or anything about the fight with Pitts. When she mentioned Pearl's name, Ned looked up from rolling a cigarette and listened more closely, but then he seemed to shut down. After a while, he took a bedroll from his saddle and laid it out by the fire. Alphonso motioned for Nell to sleep inside again and she gratefully followed his order, taking Moonshine with her. She hoped she wouldn't wake to a dead sheepherder or a dead cowboy, but figured she could do nothing about either.

CHAPTER 17

Nellie awoke with the idea of getting Ned to take her back down to the moonshine camp, but without telling him where she was going and persuading him to leave her off and go away. She needed to search Pearl's tent and the other tents to see what kind of guns they had. She assumed that by now, Pearl had returned to the camp. But maybe she hadn't. Still, with Wolfman Pitts dead, Pearl was probably in no danger from the other men or from Goodlight. Until Nell satisfied herself that there weren't two guns of the same kind and make, she couldn't know if Pearl had shot Pitts. What Nellie would do with that information, she wasn't sure. Pearl had saved her life; did she owe Pearl the same duty?

Ned and Alphonso were not talking to each other, but neither were they scowling. Ned helped make coffee, stirred the fire, and waited on Nellie with a plate of potatoes

and fried sausage, the hot Basque kind —
chorizo. When the sheepherder once again
checked Nellie's arm and re-applied the
green stuff, Ned found a clean white hand-
kerchief in his saddlebag and offered it to
the cause. "It'll be ruined," she warned.
Moonshine stayed close by Nellie.

The cowboy shrugged. He rolled up his
sleeping blankets and saddled his horse.

"Ned, I need a ride back down. Would you
let me come along with you?"

Alphonso raised his head to look at Nellie
and then at Ned. "You stay *aqui*?" It came
out as a question, but Nellie wondered if he
meant it as an order, maybe instilled by
Gwynn before he left her there.

"I must get back, Alphonso. I need to find
my camera." She didn't mention that she
also wanted to straighten out the arrest for
murder. How she would do so depended on
what she found in the moonshine camp, she
hoped. "I'll be safe." After the peaceful
night, she didn't think the sheepherder was
worried about her safety, but she could
never be sure what he was thinking.

"Sure, I'll give you a hitch to wherever
you want to go." He didn't wink or leer, so
she was certain he had something else on
his mind. He turned to Alphonso. "I'll keep
an eye on her, if you're worried." They

stared at each other for a long minute and Ned added. "I owe that much to you, and to her." Alphonso nodded.

Nellie suspected that was as close to a confession of beating up the sheepherder that she would ever hear. Nell didn't have much to gather up, so Alphonso helped her swing up behind the cowboy without hurting her arm. He had given her a small leather bag filled with green leaves and motions to boil and reapply the poultice when the old one grew dry. He also motioned with two fingers cutting the thread that held the skin together and said, *"Dos, tres dias."* Nellie called Moonshine, who followed them out of camp.

As with Sheriff Azgo, Nell wondered what to do with her hands and came to the same conclusion. She would have to hold onto Ned, but she did so by gripping his sides at belt level. This was the second time she was this close to a man, and she found the experience unsettling but not unwelcome. What was unwelcome was the gun butt digging into her own waist. "Can you move that thing?" She poked at it.

The cowboy laughed and did as she asked, shoving the revolver into the front of his pants, as near as she could tell. After that, they moved along in amiable silence. The storm had left all the greenery refreshed, and even the sagebrush had a more intense color of gray-green. The evergreens and sage smelled brand new with the edge of kerosene that sage always carried. The track they followed had already dried out from the brief but heavy rain shower, but not enough for the horse to kick up dust into their faces. Not too long after they began the downhill trek, Ned rode back into the forest, dismounted, and searched around. A few black sticks marked where Hank must have tried to set the fire, but there was no sign of embers or smoke of any kind. Satisfied, he climbed awkwardly back into the saddle in front of Nell and they moved along again.

"Why did you stop him?" Nellie ventured. She crooked the thumb of her left hand into his belt and let her arm ride more comfortably than if she used her hand to hold onto him. When no answer came, she wondered if he had heard her or was ignoring her.

Ned stopped the horse again, motioned to keep quiet, and pointed down the hill and off to their right. A group of antelope grazed, their pronghorns distinct in the sunlight. Because the two of them on their horse were in the shade, the animals hadn't seen them. Moonie apparently didn't see or smell them, as he sat on his haunches, waiting for the horse to start up again. They watched for a few minutes and Ned clicked to the horse to move on. He began humming and soon Nell was singing the words along with him. "Home, home on the range . . ."

They moved down the mountain at a steady pace, sometimes trotting when the track became flatter and wider and by midmorning, they had met up with the Fourth of July Creek road, if it could be called a road. Certainly it was wider than the track they had followed, and to Nellie looked more well traveled than when she and Pearl had followed it by flanking it.

"Where was it you intended going?"

"To the moonshine camp. I have to find something."

The back of Ned's head moved from side to side. "You'll take me there, won't you? You can just drop me off and continue on your way. I can get back to the main road on my own." If no one is in the camp, she added to herself. Her plan, only half-formed, if that, seemed more hazardous as they neared the moonshine operation. Still, she must prove her own innocence by showing who killed Wolfman Pitts.

"I have a better idea. Why don't you and me just ride off into the sunset?"

Nell laughed. "Just like in the moving pictures? Or in Zane Grey?" What a romantic suggestion. She could almost wish he were serious. She squeezed him ever so lightly. "How gallant you are! But what would I do without my camera? And what would you do without your cattle? We'd both be out of our elements, wouldn't we?"

It was Ned's turn to laugh, but his didn't sound like he was entertained. "No more cattle for me. I quit when I stopped Hank from burning down the forest. I won't take orders from O'Donnell no more. I'll stop and get my gear and head on back to the Coast. Find me a job, a real job, 'stead of playing at cowboys and steers. This country's too dry for cattle anyhow. They're ruining the high country. Same with maggots . . . uh, sheep." He reined in the horse. "I'm serious, Nellie."

He turned his profile toward her with his brown eye on the side facing her. "You honor me, Ned, by asking." She touched his cheek with her fingers. He was so close, she could see where he had missed a small bunch of whiskers near his ear when he had shaved that morning. His smell of perspiration and shaving cream mixed pleasantly with the sage aroma where the horse stood. The flannel of his shirt felt soft against her arm and she could hardly resist placing her head on his shoulder and wrapping her arms around his strong body and saying, "Ride on." It would be so easy.

It was then a long whining sound grew in the distance. "What is it?" Nellie couldn't identify what she was hearing. Moonie barked, startling Nellie, and giving rise to guilt. She had completely forgotten about her dog, who had been ambling along with them.

"Automobiles. Let's get off the road. Someone's coming in a yank." He climbed down, helped Nellie down, and they led the horse and dog into a stand of trees. The whining stopped, ratcheting down rather than coming to an abrupt halt. "More than one, sounds like."

Nell studied their surroundings. She had ceased paying attention when Ned made his unexpected proposal. "Ned," she whispered. "I've got to get to the moonshine operation before anyone else does. Please help me." She began to walk hurriedly in the direction of the operation. She knew exactly where she was now.

"You can't go in there alone. Come on, we'll ride the horse. That'll be faster than anyone bushwhacking from the autos on the road. We can come up from the rear and see what's going on." He mounted and hoisted her up. "And what about your dog?"

"I don't know." Nellie was confounded. Moonie had given away her presence more than once. She couldn't let that happen at the illegal still. His presence or even his smell would cause their dogs to bark too. "Let's let him follow partway. Then I'll have to tie him to a tree." She had never done that before and hated the thought of it.

"Will he mind a direction to stay?"

"He has in the past." She remembered a risky situation in the winter when coyotes menaced the two of them. He had minded Rosy. Would her moondog follow her order? "But if there are dogs there, and there were last time I was in the camp . . ."

"You might be going into a buzzard's nest, you know."

Nellie had to decide. Ned furnished a short piece of thick twine. At her direction, he loosely coiled it around the dog's neck and then a small tree. "Stay Moonie. I'll be back." She looked at Ned. "And if I'm not, you can get him."

They moved quickly between trees and over hummocks, as if the horse were used to this activity. "Crazy woman," Ned muttered.

Less than five minutes later, Nellie could

see the tents of the camp. No one seemed to be around. She spied Pearl's tent and pointed it out to Ned. "That's where I need to go first. I can get in from the back, maybe." Once again, they dismounted. Ned dropped the reins of the bridle to the ground and he and Nell moved forward, keeping themselves behind trees or shrubs. Still, no one appeared outside. The camp looked much as it had when Nellie had been detained there. The fire was out, but the cooking pot hung over it. Small stacks of gear lay here and there, dusty and disordered. Bottles and tin cans still littered the grounds, still filthy with dog excrement and pieces of pipe. It was as if the last few days had never happened, that she had never left. The huge still by the creek reflected the only activity: a fire burned beneath the largest metal pot. Someone must be tending it and had moved away, perhaps to relieve himself, perhaps to get more firewood. As if in answer, the sound of an ax on a tree rang through the forest, breaking what had seemed a strange silence. On cue, the flap of one of the tents facing the fire opened and Dick Goodlight crawled out. "Pearl!"

Nell motioned for Ned to stop. If everyone was in camp, how could she explore Pearl's tent?

"Pearl! Get out here and whump up some breakfast. I'm hungry!"

As if she stood right in front of Ned and Nell, Pearl's voice rang out from her tent. "Fix your own breakfast, you lazy son of a . . ." The remainder of the epitaph was mumbled, and then Pearl appeared in the clearing as well. "Who was your servant this time last week? I been waited on for a few days, and I liked it."

The opportunity presented itself and Nell couldn't let it pass. "Stay here," she whispered in Ned's ear. "I'm going in the back of her tent." She kept her fingers crossed that Pearl had not refastened the stakes Nell had pulled when they escaped the moonshiners. As the young woman was not a diligent person, Nell felt she could rely on that assumption. She moved the skirt of the tent and it lifted easily.

Even the smells remained the same inside the canvas rigging: sun on dust, sachet, perspiration, and the musty tinge of wet boots drying. Nell glanced swiftly around the small space, looking for Pearl's carrying bag. Surely she brought it back with her. Rumpled sleeping bag, clothes tossed into a corner, dancing shoes dangling from the makeshift shelves by their ties — Pearl must have danced again the night before, hence

the late-morning awakening for the oc-
cupants of the camp. No bag. Failure.

The flap of the tent opened and Pearl
stepped in, hunched over to avoid hitting
the top of the opening. When she looked
up, there was Nell. Her mouth opened, and
Nell motioned with her finger to her lips.
"Shhh."

"What are you doing here?" Her voice was
low, but not a whisper. "I thought you'd be
in jail by now. I was planning on coming
down to see about you, soon as I got away
from Dick again."

Activity outside the tent raised the level of
sounds to cover her voice. Someone banged
on the pot, two men's voices talked, the
dogs barked, first one and then the other,
and then their barking coalesced into a
howl. Both women turned toward the noise.

Ned's voice came from outside the tent in
back. "Nell, get out of there. The revenuers
are coming." The back edge lifted. "Hurry!"

"Who's out there?" Pearl looked from the
front flap to the lifting edge in back.

"Ned Tanner. He brought me. How did
you get here? I thought you were with the
outfitters."

"Ned's right. Get outta here. Now!" Pearl
shoved Nellie to the back of the tent.

"I can't! I need to know where your gun is."

Pearl pushed at Nellie again, and Ned reached in to grab her arm. "Get out here. Now!" He pulled at Nell, then ducked down so his face could be seen. "You too, Pearl. Come out! I've got a horse in the woods and I'll get you both away from here."

Nell was out and scurrying for the woods. Ned still crouched by the end of the tent, entreating, when half a dozen men trotted into camp in dark suits, guns raised and pointed. In their midst was the only man dressed for the wilderness, Sheriff Azgo, and his pistol was in the holster around his waist. She was so surprised, she almost forgot to duck behind a tree, but did so before his face swung toward the tent where Ned and Pearl argued.

"Hands up!" the foremost suited man called. "We're federal marshals. You're all under arrest for illegal liquor manufacture." He motioned for three of his men to destroy the still. They did, forming a half circle in front of it. Two men raised axes and pounded on the copper pot, crushing it in as slurry mash poured out like oatmeal. The screech of metal hurt Nellie's ears. One man shot his rifle into barrels next to the still. Liquid spurted forth, draining in separate

364

streams from each hole. He levered the gun and shot again at ceramic containers. They blew into large chunks, again spilling moonshine in cascades of clear liquor. A man came dashing in from the forest. "Hey! What's goin' on?" Too late, he realized exactly what was going on.

Charlie Azgo stalked over to Pearl's tent, his pistol drawn. "Out of there," he ordered, lifting the flap. "And behind there," he called. "Come out in front. Hands up!"

Pearl stepped out, standing clear of the tent, and Ned had no choice but to climb to his feet and move around to the front. Nell waited to see if the sheriff had spotted her. He motioned for the woman and the cowboy to step to the center of the camp, and he followed them. The sheriff hadn't seen her. But now what was she to do? She couldn't let Ned be packed up with the moonshiners. He wasn't part of them, and it was her fault he was even near the operation. Then she realized that Dick Goodlight wasn't in sight. He must have gone back into his tent about the same time Pearl did, and unlike Pearl, hadn't argued with anyone loud enough to be heard. Sheriff Azgo walked toward the other tents. If Goodlight was in one of them, he might shoot first and flee out the back. She couldn't let that happen either.

CHAPTER 18

Nellie hurried to Ned's horse and, with difficulty, climbed on, her arm beginning to throb again. She urged him forward and almost galloped out of the trees, just as the sheriff leaned toward Dick's tent.

"Sheriff! I'll go quietly." She guided the horse to where he stood and slid off between him and the tent. "Those two talked me into giving myself up." She motioned to Ned and Pearl. "Ned brought me from the sheep camp to help Pearl escape." She was out of breath and in pain.

The sheriff stared at her as if she had lost all of her senses. So did Ned. Pearl hid a smile behind her hand and leaned down, letting a small pistol drop to the dirt. Nellie saw but could not hear a plop because of the chaos in camp. Pearl knocked it away with her foot and looked up directly at Nellie.

Nell glanced at Pearl and then at the gun.

It was the size of Pearl's hand and nothing like the gun Nell picked up beside Pitts's body. Nor like the gun Pearl had threatened Moonshine with. She felt the tent shake under her hand where she had steadied herself.

"Charlie —"

Dick Goodlight grabbed her from behind and then wrapped an arm around her middle and pulled himself out. He held a knife to Nell's neck.

"I'd as soon slit her throat as look at her, this cursed snoop. Move back."

The noise in camp cut off, except for the dogs.

"Get over here, Pearl. I need your help. Grab the horse."

Pearl hesitated as the sheriff moved back a couple steps. Then she did as ordered.

"Now follow me." Dick kept Nellie in tow. The stink of sour mash almost made her gag. She tried to stay on her feet, but he moved too fast and she couldn't keep up. He dragged her along the path leading to the road. His arm squeezed her chest and she struggled to free herself, ever mindful of the knife. Pearl took the horse's bridle and stepped along. If she sought help with motions or glances, Nell could not tell. The knife scraped the skin on her right arm under her sleeve. Dick's breath was deadly as she tried to get back on her feet. If only her arm were not so useless, she thought. They scrambled out of sight of the camp and onto the tree-lined path.

"Let her go!" Ned leaped out from behind a tree, lifted his revolver, and aimed it at Dick.

Dick swung Nell around so she faced Ned and stood between the two of them. She finally managed to get herself upright.

"What's going on here?" O'Donnell tramped down the path. "Ned, put down that gun. You, let that woman go. You boys think this is an old-timey Western?" Nell didn't see him shift, but a gun appeared in his hand.

And then Moonshine raced past Ned and leaped on Goodlight. A piece of twine trailed from the dog's neck, and his growl was as deep as a wild animal's. Dick began to fall, taking Nellie with him. She kicked her leg behind her, slamming into Dick's soft parts. "Owwwww." He dropped the knife and loosened his hold on her. Moonshine grabbed his arm and Nellie slipped away. As fast as she could, she rolled over, landing once on her bad arm. She groaned but scuttled to her feet to run to and behind the horse Pearl was leading. "Moonshine, come!"

Pearl grabbed Nellie's hand and pulled her close. "C'mon! To the trees." They began to scramble but Sheriff Azgo dashed around the bend toward them.

"Stop. Everyone stand still. Now."

Dick leaped toward O'Donnell, grabbed his gun, and fired at Ned. The huge boom stunned everyone. Ned fell sideways and his gun shot into the air. Dick leveled the gun he held to fire again as Ned rolled to his chest. Two guns fired simultaneously. This time, Dick fell backward and a red splotch appeared below his neck. Ned rolled again and pushed to his knees, one arm hanging and dripping blood.

At such close quarters, the noise almost deafened Nellie. Pearl ran to Ned, not Dick. "What have you done?" She swung her foot back to kick him, but stopped and turned, crying.

O'Donnell retrieved his gun from the ground and put it in his belt. He turned to the sheriff. "Now you know who was behind everything." He stepped over to Dick and shoved him with his foot. "The moonshine. Your sheepherder. Probably Pitts, too."

Nell and Moonie, Ned and the moonshiners, including Dick Goodlight, all returned to Galena Store, each in a separate auto with the revenuers and the sheriff. O'Donnell followed, at the sheriff's curt order, in his own automobile after taking the horse to the road and leaving it there to be picked up by a ranch hand. When they arrived, Gwynn was sitting on the porch with Lulu. He jumped up to greet Nell and put his arm around her. She sagged against him, knowing he would stand up for her. Moonshine would too, but he couldn't talk.

"Caught the whole shootin' match, I see," Gwynn said to Charlie. "You been waitin' for this." He handed the sheriff the envelope from Twin Falls.

Charlie nodded. "And then some," he added as O'Donnell's auto pulled in. It was sleek and black. The sheriff briefly glanced at the photos and shoved them back into the envelope.

"Lulu," the sheriff said, "can you ring up Ketchum and get a doc and the ambulance from Hailey up here? We have two shot-up men. Then we need a place to sit down: Nell Burns, Pearl, Ned Tanner, Gwynn, and O'Donnell. Goodlight is in no shape to sit. I have some photographs to show around. Can we use your back room?"

While Lulu did as asked, the sheriff talked

to Keefe and the revenuers. They left with Long John and Bob and a promise of Dick Goodlight if he survived.

Nell felt at home at Galena after her disorienting travels in the Stanley Basin. The store was neat and orderly, the back room quiet. She knew Charlie had found her photos under the bed in the river auto lodge near Stanley. Jacob Levine must have developed some of them and sent them back up. Now she owed him even more. He was like a guardian angel in the background of her life.

Sheriff Azgo ushered everyone into the back room and brought out the photographs. "These are photos by Miss Burns, taken at the sheep camp in the Basin. The first two are the camp. The next several are Domingo. I also have a report on Domingo's death from the coroner."

Nell studied her own work and remembered arriving at the camp and Gwynn's finding of Domingo. She thought about how she had been trying to distract herself from the dead sheepherder. There were the covered camp, the horse bridle, the tins of supplies, the saddle, the horse — a quiet scene with no person in it.

The sheriff was reading from the report. " 'The deceased died from trauma to his head and neck. Although there was a wound in his temple, this was not the cause of death. Blunt force to his head and a broken neck caused this man's death. The bullet wound occurred after his death.' "

Nellie glanced at Pearl, whose pale face turned even paler. She looked back at Nell. They both knew what this meant. The Boss killed Domingo, but who was the Boss? Nell knew in that moment that it was O'Donnell, but she was fairly certain Pearl would not tell. She had sat down next to him and touched him from time to time. He glanced at her but did not shake her off.

The sheriff pointed to the camp photo again. In the rocks above the camp, there was a figure, squatted down and apparently spying on the activities below. It looked like Wolfman to Nell, but she would have to enlarge that section to be sure. So, he had been spying on them and probably more than once. No wonder he wanted the photographs. Charlie brought out another photo, again of the sheep camp, but this time there was a rifle and a flute leaning against the wood base. Alphonso was in the photos, but nothing else had changed, so these were taken a little later. Between the time Gwynn and Alphonso buried Domingo and they all left to find the sheep, the Winchester and flute had been placed outside the camp. Either Pearl or one of the moonshiners had been tramping about the area and returned those items.

Although Nell waited for Pearl to say something, anything, about Domingo's murder, she did not. The sheriff seemed to wait, too. Finally, he said, "Domingo was dragged through the sage and rocks. Who did this?"

Nell cleared her throat. If looks could indeed kill, Pearl's stare at her would have done it then by some torturous method.

"Pearl fired the gun because Wolfman Pitts had loosed his wolfdog on Domingo. She was afraid the dog would kill him. She missed and the bullet hit Domingo. If he was already dead, as you say, then the man who dragged him behind a horse did this."

"And who was that?" the sheriff asked.

"I don't know. But Pearl does. It was the 'Boss.'"

Pearl looked at her hands. When she looked up, she said, "It is Ned Tanner."

"What? I never —" Ned was wounded but jumped up and rushed toward Pearl. "You liar. I had nothing to do with your torture of that m— Basque! I was out herding cattle."

Nell felt disappointment swarm over her.

Charlie stepped between Pearl and Ned. "Sit down, Tanner." He turned to Nell. "What do you know about this man?"

Nell didn't want to answer. "He helped me." Even O'Donnell hadn't accused Ned.

Gwynn spoke up. "He beat up Alphonso, turned the sheep camp upside down, wounded two sheep dogs and lassoed and killed my lead ewe. That's the kind of 'man' he is — he's a coward."

"I was just following orders — his." Ned pointed at O'Donnell. "And I quit so don't bother firing me. You owe me a month's wages."

O'Donnell snorted a short laugh. "You know how cowboys are, Sheriff. They're always up to some hijinks or another. They get bored poking cows and go off to cause some trouble."

"And I didn't shoot no sheep dogs," Ned said. He sat down. Nell wondered if she should comfort him.

Pearl glared again at Nell.

"Tanner here even suggested we torch the woods to scare off the sheep and the Basque," O'Donnell continued. "Of course, I put a stop to that."

"That's not true," Nell said. She knew she was on solid ground now. "Ned caught Hank, your cowboy, trying to set a fire and he stopped it and went back a couple of times to make sure it was out. I saw him."

Nell turned to Pearl. "Tell the truth."

Pearl turned her pearl ring round and round her finger. "I am." She shook her head and lowered her face.

"And the moonshine operation. You all referred to 'the Boss.' " Nell watched Pearl turn her ring. "It's Mr. O'Donnell, isn't it? I heard his voice the night I was kidnapped." She stood up and pointed outside. "And that was the car I was in."

"Hahahaha. You must have been drinking that 'shine yourself, Miss Burns." O'Donnell kept laughing, a strange sound from a face that looked stone dead. "I run a cattle ranch. I've got plenty to do and make a good living that way. I'm respected in my county — just ask anyone there. Why would I get involved in some shady moonshine operation? Hahahahaha." He ceased his laughter. "And you. You murdered Pitts. Who would believe you?" His flat gaze turned to Sheriff Azgo.

Lulu knocked on the door and then her head appeared. "The doc is here and so is the ambulance."

Gwynn stood up. "I'll get Goodlight loaded. What about Tanner?"

O'Donnell stood up, his arm around

376

Pearl. "We're leaving. You know where I live and Pearl works. You've heard our side of the story." They walked out in the general confusion.

Ned sat still, his head in his hands. The sheriff left to help Gwynn and the doctor. Nell didn't know what to do. She knew Ned was not the Boss. But she couldn't prove it or that O'Donnell was. They stayed in the room together, not talking. Moonshine lay sleeping next to Nell's chair. Her dog would not have accepted Ned so readily after the initial attack on the hillside, if the cowboy was mixed up with the moonshiners.

"All right, Tanner. Come out and let the doc bind up your arm. You can ride in the ambulance. I'll deal with you later." Sheriff Azgo stayed behind when Tanner left.

"How is your arm, Miss Burns?" He stopped in front of Nell.

"I thought we were on first-name terms, Sheriff. My arm is better, but I need to cut the stitches." She didn't look up at him, but just stared across at the gun in his belt. He was not a tall man, and he seemed now as cold as the gun metal.

"I talked again with Luke about Wolfman Pitts and your self-defense. I am not going to charge you. I needed to get you out of that wasp's nest you so blithely walked into, again and again."

"It all seemed reasonable at the time. I had few choices. And I didn't kidnap myself."

"I know you didn't. I will do what I can to jail O'Donnell." Charlie knelt beside her.

"I didn't kill Pitts," she said. "I think Pearl did it to save me. She'll say I did it." She shrugged.

"Either way, Pitts's death was self-defense." Charlie's face was strong in its brown-ness, but the smile he tried on faded with weariness. "Nell."

She leaned toward him. "Thank you, Charlie."

Chapter 19

Nell dashed into the boarding house. "Goldie! Mrs. Bock!" She carried mail in one hand and held the door for Moonshine with the other.

"Lands' sakes, girl. What's wrong?" Mrs. Bock came out of the kitchen, wiping her hands on a dish cloth.

"Look at these letters! They're from the tourists at the Stanley Basin campout. I mailed them photos a couple weeks ago. Every one of them has cash in it! I can't believe it!"

"Why not? Ain't that your business? Selling photos?" She dumped the cloth on an entry table and took two of the letters. "Now, isn't that nice. Thank you for the photos *and* all the excitement on their trip. Hmph." She returned the open letters. "Did you know that O'Donnell got off scot-free? Charlie tried to bring charges against him for murdering that Spanish man, but an-

other cattle man said he was at an associa-
tion meeting during the whole hullaballoo.
The local commissioners wouldn't even talk
to him about the moonshine operation."
She folded her arms over her chest. "Some
meeting. From what you told me, it must
have lasted a coupla weeks!"

"What's this one?" Mrs. Bock pointed to
a large manila envelope under Nellie's arm.

"Just a brochure from the railroad, I think.
They send them to me from time to time."
She pulled the top open. "See? An advertisement." A piece of paper fluttered to the
floor.

Goldie leaned down to retrieve it. "Some
advertisement, I'd say." Her whole face
turned up in smiles. "It's a check. Looks
pretty official to me."

Nellie reached for the check. "Oh, my."
She brought out the brochure. Her photographs of the Sawtooth Mountains, the
Salmon River, Pearl and Ned both, the tourist camp, and even the sheep camp were
splashed in black and white across the
pages. "Look Moonie! My photos and the
train will bring more people to Idaho!"

Footsteps clunked up the back stairs and
the door opened.

"Mrs. Bock, is Nell Burns here?" The
sheriff's voice called.

"I'm here," Nell called back and led Goldie into her own kitchen.

"I have your photos, Miss Burns, er . . . Nell. I thought you would want them back."

"We heard O'Donnell skipped, Sheriff." Goldie flapped her apron. "He's as slippery as a fish."

"If Nell's friend, Pearl, had helped, we might have snagged him," Charlie said. "She persuaded the revenuers that she was just an innocent bystander, but no one believed Tanner ran the moonshine operation. He's just a cowboy — and on his way back to Oregon."

"What about Dick Goodlight?"

"He's on his way to jail, probably not for very long."

"I wouldn't want to be Pearl when he shows up again," Nell said.

"Do you want coffee?" Goldie used a hot pad to lift the ever-present pot off the stove.

Nell had opened the pack of photos. "I don't want these," she said, handing over the pictures of Domingo. "I never knew him, but he played the flute for Pearl to dance to." She leafed through the rest. "Here's the sheep camp, Mrs. Bock."

Goldie took and studied the photo. "Hmph. Looks like close quarters to me. I think Alphonso is still there. Gwynn stopped by on his way up the other day."

The sheriff looked over her shoulder. "It is close but the outdoors is a green and stone world. The stars shine like diamond chips at night and when the full moon rises, it is like being in a wonderland."

"Yes, it is," Nell said, smiling at Charlie.

Goldie looked from one to the other. "Should I make myself scarce?"

Nell felt herself blush. Even the sheriff appeared off-kilter. "I came also to ask Miss Burns if she would help the sheriff's office with an assignment. Her photos helped solve the murder of Domingo. There are several other . . . circumstances where her photography skills would be useful."

When Nell opened her mouth, he added, "For pay, of course."

So far, the sheriff's "circumstances" had been murders of one kind or another. Even as she shuddered, she heard herself echo his words, "Of course."

ABOUT THE AUTHOR

Julie Weston grew up in Idaho and practiced law for many years in Seattle, Washington. Her debut fiction, *Moonshadows,* a Nellie Burns and Moonshine Mystery, was published in 2015 (Five Star Publishing) and was a finalist in the 2016 May Sarton Literary Award. Her memoir of place, *The Good Times Are All Gone Now: Life, Death and Rebirth in an Idaho Mining Town* (University of Oklahoma Press, 2009), received an honorable mention in the 2009 Idaho Book of the Year Awards. This book, *Basque Moon*, won the 2017 WILLA Literary Award in Historical Fiction from Women Writing the West. Her short stories and essays have been published in *IDAHO Magazine, The Threepenny Review, River Styx, Clackamas Review,* and other journals. Both an essay and a short story have been nominated for Pushcart Prizes. She and her husband,

Gerry Morrison, now live in central Idaho where they ski, write, photograph, and enjoy the outdoors. www.juliewweston.com.